The Barmouth Affairs

A heartwarming, nostalgic and atmospheric story of life,
love, and two women's search for happiness.
Based on true events.

Vanessa M. Tanner

To Jean,
Happy Reading.
Best wishes,
Vanessa.

1

First Edition, 2024.
Published by Winter & Drew Publishing Ltd.

ISBN: 9781739184988

Also available as an eBook.

CONTENTS

ACKNOWLEDGMENTS

For my husband for giving me the inspiration for this tale when he told me the story of Millie's Folly on our way to Barmouth some years ago.

Huge thanks to Christopher who patiently worked on the cover design and made the many changes. I think you'll agree, he has created something which brings to life the sense of place.

Thank you to beta reader, Mike Atkinson, for alerting me to the concept of head-hopping and for helping me sort it out in the story. To my friends who read the first draft and encouraged me to continue writing.

Also, gratitude and apologies in equal measure to the people of Barmouth for any liberties taken with your town. I've tried to be as accurate as possible but certain place names might not be entirely correct. 1974 was a long time ago!

CHAPTER 1

Isabella

It was raining hard and the road was slippery. Isabella held on tightly to the handlebars as she steered her battered moped carefully around each bend. Beneath her open-faced helmet, her goggles had steamed up and her vision was dramatically impaired. Her legs and back ached from sitting stiffly for the last two hours. Her heart ached with the pain of unfaithfulness.

"Bloody man!" she said aloud to the wind. "Bloody, bloody man!" The words flew around her like big, fat bluebottles with nowhere to land.

Through the mist of her lenses, she could see another bend down the hill and to the left over a bridge ahead. She gently touched the brakes. Nothing happened; the tyres had no traction on the tarmac. She tried again with an added sense of urgency. Still no response. She tried once more. This time the back wheel locked. Isabella fought to keep the moped upright as it slid from side to side. The bend was fast approaching. She yanked the handlebars round to the left, trying to keep herself on the road. Instead, her moped skidded across the road to the right. Again, she tried to pull it to the left to straighten up. No response. In what felt like slow motion, Isabella's bike slid into the wall of the little bridge where the engine cut out. Perfectly parked.

An old man up on the hill with his dog witnessed Isabella being thrown into the air and somersaulting over the parapet. With a thump, she landed in a pile of sticks and leaves. She rolled a few times and came to a stop face up in the fallen leaves.

Alongside her, a fast-flowing, engorged stream continued its journey down towards the estuary.

Silence and stillness settled. The forest closed around her protectively.

---0---

A black and white sheepdog sniffed around Isabella's body, barked twice, and dashed back to its master. He ran around the legs of his owner with his tail wagging, encouraging him to follow him back.

"Well done, Dewi. Have you found someone?"

Somewhere in the background, Isabella could hear this faint muffled sound. The dog walker approached the bedraggled heap on the ground. Dewi walked quickly around the body as his owner knelt down in the mud, one knee at a time, and peered carefully at a woman's placid and serene face. He waved a gnarly hand in front of the goggles covering her eyes. Nothing. He held a shaky hand in front of her nose and mouth. Shallow breaths left a slight warmth on his mottled skin. He laid his head carefully against her chest. There was definitely a faint movement, up and down.

"Hey, lady." He touched her shoulder lightly. "You're just a slip of a thing, it's a wonder you didn't snap on the way down." He shook his head then touched her shoulder again; still no response. "Hey lady, wake up." Still nothing. He stroked his wet dog sitting next to him. "What are we gonna do now, Dewi?"

Suddenly, her eyes shot open and she breathed in sharply. "Where am I?" she whispered.

Isabella took in the man's brown and wrinkled face—kind, dark brown eyes framed by grey, bushy eyebrows. As he stood up, with a slight stoop, he took off his hat to reveal a full head of curly, white hair. She smiled weakly at him.

"It's okay, lady. I was up on the hill and saw you come off your bike. Called the ambulance afore we come down to find you. What's your name, now?" His lilting accent was reassuring.

"I'm Isabella." She tried to sit up. "Why can't I move?"

"You've had an accident, Isabella. What d'you remember?"

"I was on my moped. The road was wet, there was a bend. I tried to brake, but I lost control." She tried to lift her shoulders. "Why can't I move?"

"You're gonna be all right. I'm Owen. This here's my dog, Dewi. He's the one what found you. I'm gonna leave him with you and go up to the road to show them where to come. Dewi'll be right here next to you. He's a good dog." He turned to his dog. "You look after this lady now, Dewi, I'll be ten minutes."

Through her goggles, Isabella's hazel eyes followed Owen as he looked up at the bridge then back at her. Despite his obvious age, he started to scramble agilely up the bank through the soggy undergrowth and dripping amber leaves, grabbing at the spindly trunks of silver birch and sycamore trees providing an autumnal shelter for the woman on the ground below. He looked back, she acknowledged him with her eyes.

"Not long now, lady. Just got to get to the road up here," he called.

"Thank you." Her voice sounded feeble to her own ears.

Isabella tried to move her body. She closed her eyes, clenched her stomach tried to pull herself upright. No movement.

The black and white dog lay down on the ground next to her, as though to protect her from further danger, keeping her warm with his own body.

"Right, Dewi..." She addressed his big brown eyes staring into hers. "Let's start with my fingers." Her hands were encased in thick, sheepskin gloves. She willed her fingers to move. Maybe there was a slight bending at the knuckles. "Okay, now my toes." She tried moving her toes inside her leather boots. Again, a barely perceptible movement. She tried to move her head from left to right—nothing. A leaden box on her shoulders.

"Oh, Dewi." The dog looked at her and licked her exposed cheek, "What am I going to do?" Her eyes filled with tears as the dog nudged her arm. "I'm no use to man nor beast if I can't even move my own body."

Suddenly, Dewi pricked up his ears and a low growling started in his throat. There was movement above them. People were making their way tentatively down the embankment. One of them called out, "You all right down there, Isabella love?" She recognised Owen's soft Welsh tone.

"Yeah, still here." *My voice is so weedy*, she thought, *but at least it works.*

"Be with you in a minute. Hold on."

Owen appeared standing over her. Two men in dark green uniforms were slightly behind him. "They got here right quick, so they did."

"D'you mind if I take a look at you? It's Isabella, isn't it?" asked the first ambulanceman. Their soft melodic tones made her feel safer already.

"Hmm. Yes."

He knelt down in the mulchy leaves and flashed a torch in her hazel eyes. "I need to feel your legs and back; check for broken bones now. Is that okay?"

She tried to nod. "Yes, that's fine."

He ran his hands along her left leg, pressing his thumbs on her thigh, then her knees, then her shin. He repeated the operation on her right leg.

"Well, there's nothing broken there. I'm going to remove your helmet, then put my hands under your body and feel your back and neck now." Carefully, he wiggled the helmet off, unfurling her wavy, auburn hair, redder than the dying leaves of autumn. Then he ran his hands from the base of her neck down her spine then up again and felt around the back of her neck and throat.

"Nothing obviously broken, Isabella. It's a miracle really; you fell a long way. And you still can't feel anything?"

"No, nothing, and I can't move, not even my head."

"We'll get you to hospital as fast as possible. They'll be able to do more tests. Don't worry."

"What about my husband?"

"Who's your husband?" asked Owen.

"Jim Cartwright. Lives in the cottage up the hill from Bontddu."

"I think I've seen him about. I'll get my one of my sons, Bryn or Dai, to go up and tell him what's happened. They can collect your moped too. I've got the keys here in my pocket."

Isabella watched the ambulancemen carefully unroll a canvas sheet, pull out two poles and slot them together, then another two and slide them down the sides of the canvas sheet to create a stretcher.

"We're gonna get you up the hill and into the ambulance, Isabella," explained the second man, his words slow and deliberate.

I'm not a bloody brainless invalid, Isabella thought, as she tried once again to move into a seated position and an involuntary groan escaped. *Actually, maybe I am.*

"Are you all right? Does anything hurt?" said the first man.

"Nothing hurts. I can't feel anything."

The two medical men glanced at each other, faces solemn. They laid the stretcher on the ground next to her. "Can you take my goggles off me please? I want to see you."

The first one got down on the ground, gently lifted her head and unpeeled the strap. He laid her goggles on the ground next to her and looked at her face. She looked back at him, eyes bright and questioning, a myriad of freckles covering her pale nose and cheeks.

9

"We're going to slide you onto here, love," said the other ambulance man.

He knelt down in the leaves next to her, on the opposite side to the first medical man, who slid his hands under her shoulders and hips on one side, while his colleague did the same on his side. *Could she feel a tingle?*

"Right, we're ready. One, two, three... and slide," said the first as he very slowly inched her body over; the other man wriggled the stretcher under her until she was safely in place. The canvas smelt damp and musty; she inhaled through her mouth and focussed on the tree canopy.

"Try not to move, love," said the second man. They were now at either end of the stretcher holding the handles.

"How on Earth are you two going to get me up that slope?" Isabella asked.

"Just you wait."

Owen looked up to the bridge as he shouted, "Dai, Bryn, are you two ready up there?"

"Yep, do you need us now?" A disembodied voice floated downwards towards them.

"Yep, we're ready to go."

Isabella could see two more young men sliding down through the trees. *They've all come to help me. Better than my bloody cheating husband,* she thought as her eyes again filled with tears.

CHAPTER 2

Jim

Jim watched Bryn climb back into his brother's van leaving him alone with his guilt looming large in the kitchen. He slumped onto one of the chairs. He smacked his head with his hand and breathed out. *What have I done? I was such an idiot. My poor Bella, I didn't even think about her when I looked at Susan. I'm such a stupid, stupid man. Now look what's happened. I need to get to her now.*

He jumped up and pulled on his boots and coat. On his way to Dolgellau Hospital, his thoughts returned to how he and Susan had got together. She was round the house all the time, Bella's best friend since school days. He'd never thought of her as anything but his wife's friend.

Until that one fateful evening.

He'd been working at the big house in town, decorating the sitting room. They'd wanted it done for their Christmas party. He'd wanted to be sure he did a good job so they'd recommend him to their friends and family. They could be a good source of work, that rich lot. He'd stayed late every night that week making sure every inch of the room was perfect and he had finally finished that day. Certain they would ask him to do more work, he'd come home excited to talk to Bella about the prospects of more work.

They had plans, the two of them, now the children were grown. Freddie had joined the Navy and Irene was with a man called Gerald and working at the cinema in town. Jim wanted to sell up and move to Wales permanently—that was his dream. He just needed to persuade his wife. He was content with the cottage but it wasn't much. He didn't want his wife to have no running water, no electricity nor phone, nor to use an outside privy. No, he wanted a bigger, nicer place, closer to Barmouth, with all the modern amenities. A new life, away from the city and his memories of the war.

But that evening in December, back in West Bromwich, Bella wasn't there when he got home. It wasn't unusual, she often worked overtime. He had a wash and got changed. She still wasn't home so he sat down in the kitchen with the paper and a glass of water, hungry. When Susan knocked at the door, he was relieved: a woman in the house and someone to talk to.

"Hello Susan love, come in." Susan walked into the hall, took off her coat, hung it on the peg and bustled into the sitting room.

"No Bella?"

"No, must be working late."

"Well, let's get the kettle on and wait for her, shall we?" Susan smiled, put her hands on Jim's waist and moved him out of her way. He liked the feel of her hands on him. She opened the door and stepped into the kitchen. He followed behind like an obedient puppy.

Jim sat down in one of chairs and watched as Susan swiftly filled the kettle and pulled two cups, two saucers and a tea pot from a cupboard. She placed them carefully on the small, orange melamine table and turned to look at him. He studied her face closely.

Not bad for a woman in her fifties. Not as good my Bella, mind, but nice blue eyes and a pretty smile, he thought as she poured the boiling water onto the tea leaves and pulled the cosy over the pot. She got a bottle of milk from the fridge and the sugar bowl from the cupboard, then sat down on the chair opposite him. She waited for a moment then poured two cups.

"Here you go, dear. You must be parched. Busy day at work and come home to an empty house."

"Thanks Susan."

For a moment or two they said nothing, both contemplating the steam rising from their cups. Then he poured some hot tea into the saucer.

"What are you doing?"

"It's too hot. Put it in me saucer and it cools faster."

"Well, that's new one on me. Enjoy." She laughed.

He looked at her face again. *She looks good when she laughs and she don't have many wrinkles.* Susan looked away, a faint blush rising. Jim saw it too.

"What are you having for dinner, Jim?"

"I dunno. Bella does it. She's right late now, though."

"Let me have a look in your fridge, love. I might be able to rustle something up."

She opened the door and bent over to look inside. Jim watched her closely. He'd never noticed how round and shapely her backside was before. She turned around with the leftovers of a ham hock on one of his mother's old plates.

"Will this do you, love?"

"Yes, looks perfect, Susan."

"I'll boil up some spuds and veg to go with it in no time."

"Ta. I'm starving now." He smiled. She flushed again. She placed the ham hock on the side then peeled the potatoes and chopped the cabbage slowly. Her back to him the whole time.

"Why d'you never marry, Susan?"

She turned sharply. "Oh, Jim. You must know the answer to that. I had a fella before the war, but he died like so many young men. Happened to me and lots of us young women. Bella was the lucky one, she found you. You weren't sent to the front. Don't get me wrong, you did an amazing thing, being a fireman and all that. Pulling all those people out of burning buildings. Must've had a huge effect on you." She poked the potatoes in the pan. "But you're still here to tell the tale, Jim. My Stan was in Singapore, and we all know what happened there. Bloody Japanese."

13

"Sorry, wrong thing to say, Susan. Thoughtless of me. Sorry."

"It's okay. It's been thirty years, I've got used to it now. I've seen your two grow; they're like my kids too. You must be proud. Freddie in the Navy, and Irene working now too."

"Can't take no credit for my two. It's down to Bella: she did all the work. Talking of her, where the hell is she?"

"That bloody boss of hers. Takes the mickey he really does."

"Um yeah."

Jim was beginning to think he was glad Bella wasn't there. He was beginning to think maybe Susan would like a bit of male company. He was beginning to contemplate how he could make Susan's life a bit more exciting. The kitchen was filling with steam and all he could focus on was Susan's beautiful, tall frame and bouncy blonde hair as she lifted the lid of the pans.

"Almost there, love," she said as she sat down again.

"Great, I'm ravenous." He leant across the table and placed one hand over hers. "Susan."

She snatched her hand it away. "Stop it, Jim. Bella is my best friend. Don't you know that's rule number one?"

"She'd never know, Susan. And besides, I bet it's years since you held a man in your arms."

"Jim, not here, not in my best friend's kitchen." She jumped up and went over to the cooker.

"Think about it, Susan." He detected a chrysalis of hope. She hadn't entirely refused his advances.

"Dinner's ready. No more talk about it."

Susan opened the cupboard, got out three plates and plonked them down on the table with a crash. She went to the drawers, pulled the top one open with a bang, and threw three sets of cutlery on the table.

"Go and get another chair. Bella will be back any minute, I'm sure."

Right on cue, they heard a key in the lock. The front door swung open and Isabella's voice called out.

"I'm home, love. Sorry I'm so late."

"Best not talk about this, Jim," whispered Susan.

---0---

Jim shook his head to dislodge the memory. He'd been a fool and he knew it. Now his Bella was paralysed and he carried the guilt deep in his chest.

Isabella was sedated when he arrived at the hospital. He stood next to her bed, studying her pale face, devoid of makeup. Even her freckles had faded. He slumped in a chair and held her small hand against his face then caressed her fingers and turned her narrow, gold wedding ring with his own rough calloused hands.

"I love you, Bella. You've always been the one. I'm so sorry." There was no response. His head dropped forward.

"I'm sure she knows you're here, love," said a nurse who stopped at the end of the bed to look at the chart hanging there. "She won't wake up for a while."

"If you think that's the best. I've got her bag here. What shall I do with it?"

"You can put her things in the locker there." She pointed to the side of the bed.

Jim methodically unpacked Bella's things, placing her sponge bag on the top shelf, folding her knickers and nightie and putting them on the bottom shelf in the locker. He then put her book and her reading glasses on the top.

"I'll be off then, dear," Jim said. "I'll come back tomorrow."

"Cheerio lovey. The Doctor'll do his rounds later. You can phone the ward sister later to find out how she is if you like."

Jim drove slowly through the grey, dolerite stone of Dolgellau and out onto the road towards Penmaenpool where the majestic George III hotel guarded the toll bridge. Once across the bridge, he was almost home. With a sigh, he remembered there was nothing to eat in the cottage so he drove past Bontddu and down towards Barmouth. As he came round the mountain, the sea ahead of him was silver with foamy tips on the waves; the horizon a sliver of light below grey clouds. Drizzle was falling and his windscreen wipers squealed across the glass, leaving a smear. His head was now full of how they might manage if Bella was damaged forever.

He drove past the harbour and onto Barmouth's High Street. Engulfed by his own personal demons, he didn't see the two little girls with the black dog as they stepped out on the zebra crossing.

The dog's wagging tail jerked him back to consciousness just in time. He slammed on the brakes, screeching to a halt as the angry father waved his fist. Jim held up his hand in apology. The little girls skipped and laughed across the road oblivious to the danger.

With the sudden stop, the car had stalled. He turned the key in the ignition; the engine spluttered and whirred. He tried again, and again. No joy. He climbed out of the car and, with one foot in and one foot out, tried to push it to the side of the road and out of the way, car drivers beeping at him.

"Need a hand, mate?" He turned to see Dai coming out of his garage. He'd not noticed this morning when he'd come up to the cottage to tell him about Bella, but now he could see Dai was lean and muscular beneath his overalls and his thick, dark curls poked out from beneath his woollen hat. There was a hard look about his face; knocks visible in his chin and nose, deep blue eyes sharp and watchful.

"Bloody car won't start."

"You've probably flooded the engine. We can just push it into the forecourt, it's not far. I'll get you on the road in no time."

"Can I help?"

Jim turned to see the father. His two daughters and the dog waited on the pavement.

"Sorry about that before, I were a bit distracted."

"It's fine, no harm done." He turned to the girls. "I'm going to help this man push the car to the garage. Just walk with us; keep Charlie tightly on the lead."

Dai and the father took their positions at the back of the car while Jim leaned in and grasped the wheel. "Right, you steer, Jim, and we can push..."

"Tony."

"Right, Tony, let's do it."

CHAPTER 3

Barbara

Barbara's eyes flicked open. She looked around the dim room, faint shards of light creeping through the curtains and the patter of rain just about audible against the panes of glass. An insistent ringing forced her to sit up straight in bed. *What time is it?*

She leaned over to look at the alarm clock on the bedside table, trying not to disturb her sleeping, snoring bedfellow. *0645, not so early then. At least I've slept through the night.*

As she jumped out of bed, the lump on the other side rolled over and groaned. She looked at his dark-haired head as she pulled her navy-blue dress over her head and attached her white collar. Every time she put on her uniform, a ball of pride welled in her heart. Her qualifications were hard won and worth every moment of the training.

From the room down the hall, the sound of giggling was followed by a shout. She headed towards the familiar sound of her seven and nine-year-old sons.

"Get off it, Daniel!"

"It's mine though, you nicked it!"

The boys were sitting on the floor in their pyjamas, a book and Lego model between them.

"Morning my gorgeous boys," she said leaning down to kiss the tops of their heads. "So, who has nicked what?"

"He took my book," said Daniel, taking it from his brother's hands.

"I was just looking at the pictures." George looked her up and down suspiciously. "Are you going to work?"

"Well noticed, love. I certainly am. Daddy's here though. Why don't you go and wake him up?"

They leapt up and darted towards the door, pushing each other and their mother out of the away in their haste, all thoughts of the 'stolen' book forgotten.

"Race you!" shouted Daniel, the oldest boy.

She started down the stairs as her boisterous pair tumbled their way across the landing to the main bedroom. She heard a thump, a whoop and a groan as the boys landed on their father.

As she put on the kettle, she heard playful shrieks, followed by heavy steps clonking along the hallway, then a door squeaking open. The sounds of morning drifted down from the bathroom; there were footsteps on the stairs, then her husband Dai appeared in the kitchen.

"What's on your agenda today?" he asked. She stiffened as he kissed her on the cheek.

"You remember that woman who came off her moped at the bridge?"

"Yeah, Bryn went up to Bontddu to tell her husband. I fixed his car."

"Well, she's come out of hospital. No broken bones but she's paralysed. Doctors can't work out why. Anyway, she's my first appointment, then I'll go into the surgery and find out who else I'm seeing."

"She's in that shack up the mountain? In her condition?"

"Yep, up a lane just outside of Bontddu with her husband. You know that old chap who comes into town sometimes with a purple and grey Hillman Minx."

"Yeah, course I know him. Didn't I just say that?" Dai scowled.

"Yeah, you did, sorry."

"His name's Jim, from the Midlands somewhere, got a Brummy accent anyway. Sorted his car out at the garage the other day. Stalled when he nearly knocked those English girls over."

"Really? You didn't mention it."

"Must've forgotten. Do you need a lift?"

"No, it's fine. Owen's coming to pick me up. He knows Jim now, and where his cottage is. I'll walk down and meet him on the sea front. Anyway, you need to take the boys to school."

"I know that, for goodness' sake. No need to keep reminding me."

In the hallway, Barbara pulled on her cloak, smoothed her brunette hair into a neat bun and straightened her starched white cap in the mirror on the wall.

"I'm off now, you two!" she called up the stairs. Two little faces appeared at the top and she blew a kiss.

"Bye, Mummy," they said in unison and returned the kisses.

With a deep breath, she walked out of the door carrying her medical bag. Dai would get the boys ready for school: he was certainly used to it now. He'd been taking them to the school two mornings a week since she'd started her new job as District Nurse in September. He wasn't happy about it.

Owen, her father-in-law, drove Barbara out of Barmouth in his little mustard Mini to the tinny tones of The Stylistics singing *You Make me Feel Brand New*. The tide was out so a number of little fishing boats were leaning precariously in the muddy Mawddach estuary. A two-carriage train clattered across the wooden railway bridge towards the toll house, Fairbourne, and beyond. They passed a row of tall houses backing onto the forest then over the stone bridge crossing the stream. In the village of Bontddu, they turned off the main road and climbed up a hill for half a mile then took a sharp right turn and onto a muddy, stony track. *How's this woman going to manage out here?* Barbara thought. *It's miles from anywhere.*

"That was quite an accident she had, wasn't it?"

"Yeah. She was unlucky: the weather was bad and her brakes jammed. But at least the road was empty. Weird the way the moped ended up, parked right up against the bridge wall."

"Yeah, I suppose it was. Lucky you're an early riser and saw it happen. She could've died of hyperthermia in the woods for any length of time."

"Yeah, I s'pose it was lucky I saw it happen. I saved her life. Not every day you can say that," said Owen as they pulled up outside a mottled grey stone, single storey building with a battered, wooden door. There were small, leaded windows either side of the door, while the slate roof reached low over them. A stumpy chimney stood against the lightening sky. The rain had cleared and the sun was trying to come out. "I'll just wait here for you Babs, love."

"Thank you, Owen." He parked his Mini next to Jim's Hillman Minx, turned the engine off, and opened his door. He let Dewi out of the back and watched his daughter-in-law's back as she walked up to the front door. He noticed a slight hunch to her shoulders: she wasn't the confident, happy, young woman Dai brought home ten years previously. He wondered what had happened.

Before Barbara could even knock on the wooden door of the cottage, it was flung open. She was greeted by a tall, slim man with a mess of salt and pepper hair sticking up every which way. He had a slightly grizzled and dishevelled look about him. She guessed he was in his fifties.

"You the nurse?" He had a strong Midlands accent.

"Yes, I'm Nurse Jackson. I've come over from Barmouth. What's your name?"

"Jim."

"And your wife? I understand she had an accident."

"That she did. Came off her moped. Hit the bridge on the bend coming into the village. Been in hospital a week; doctor said there's nothing wrong so they sent her home."

"Can I come in and see her please?"

Jim moved his tall frame out the doorway so Barbara could enter the cottage. He stooped as he placed his foot on a worn, stone step. Barbara followed him into the kitchen and glanced around the dark room. Under the window was a Belfast sink which had a pink stripy curtain on a wire underneath and a water pump over the top. A small table was next to it with a dinner plate and a mug drying on a tea towel. On the far wall was a dark oak Welsh dresser with a collection of old, chipped crockery on the shelves. A wooden table and two rickety chairs dominated the centre of the room and in the corner was a wooden rocking chair, an orange cushion on the seat. It was a basic room and in need of a good clean. She spied a kettle on the range.

"Maybe you could put the kettle on for a cuppa, Jim? I'll go and see your wife, shall I? What's her name?"

"Isabella. In sitting room through there." He indicated with a nod of his head. "She's on settee. Can't move much." He moved towards the kettle and carried it to the water pump.

"Don't you worry, Jim. I'll check her over and we can go from there."

Barbara stooped through a low doorway into the sitting room. It was also dark—the heavy, green curtains shut fast. She could just make out a small, slight woman propped up on cushions on the settee, a cream, woollen blanket with blue stripes around the edges over her knees. She pulled the curtains open to let in some light, then turned to the woman.

"I'm awake. I can still hear, so I know you're Nurse Jackson." Isabella's eyes followed Barbara as she walked towards the settee.

"Morning, Isabella. Yes, I am Nurse Jackson, but just call me Babs."

"Okay, Babs."

"So how are you feeling? Jim tells me you can't move. Is that right?"

"Yes, nothing works. I still can't move my arms or legs properly." She sighed and continued, "You're not from round here either, are you?"

"No, I'm actually from Glasgow. What about you? Where are you from?"

"West Bromwich."

"Oh right. So this is your..." She looked around, "um, holiday home?"

"My husband's idea. He wanted a place to escape to."

"You can certainly do that up here." Barbara took a step closer to her patient and added, "so you came all the way from West Bromwich on your moped?"

"Yes, I did, it was a stupid thing to do now I think about it. I was nearly here but I was so tired and it was raining really hard. That bend came up suddenly and I just lost control. Thank goodness that man with the dog found me. What's his name?"

"Owen Roberts. He phoned the ambulance from the phone box on the main road. You had a really nasty fall over that bridge. It's a rotten bend, that one."

"Well, I owe him one for saving me. Though I'm not sure I wanted saving if I'm going to end up like this."

"Try not to think like that. Let's focus on getting you better now, shall we? Do you mind if I have a look at your notes?"

"There's a folder here." Isabella nodded towards the side table. Barbara picked it up and flicked through the papers.

"Can you feel anything in any part of your body now?"

"I can sort of wiggle my toes and fingers. And I can move my head from side to side."

"So that's a bit of progress. You couldn't move at all before, could you?"

"No, I was completely immobile when it first happened. They were good to me in the hospital; tried to make me move every day."

"Do you mind if I have a look at you now?"

24

"Carry on, can't feel much anyway."

Barbara untied the bow at the neck of her dark blue nurse's cloak, swished it across her shoulders and hung it on the chair by the window. Then she took a small medical torch from her leather bag.

"I'm going to have a look in your eyes, Isabella. Is that okay?"

"Mm, fine. Whatever you need to do."

She leaned forward and shone the light into each of Isabella's eyes in turn. She noticed her lovely skin, soft and clear, almost translucent, with a smattering of freckles and only a few wrinkles. She put the torch back then knelt on the threadbare rug and gently peeled back the blanket. Isabella was still wearing her coat and boots, dressed as she was when she was discharged from hospital. Babs pulled up the sleeves of her coat and blouse then placed her fingers on Isabella's slim wrist for a pulse. She nodded.

"Well, you'll be pleased to hear you're still alive, Isabella," she joked.

"Ha, not sure that's such a good thing." Isabella sighed heavily. Her eyes filled with tears and she turned her head carefully to the back of the settee to hide the sob rising from deep in her heart.

"Oh come now, we'll soon get you back on your feet." Babs stroked the back of Isabella's hand.

"Why did he do it? Why did he have to ruin everything?"

"What do you mean? Who?"

"Jim. He's being going around with my best friend. That's why I was coming here. To get him back." Her sobs were growing now and her chest heaved with the effort.

A slight flush appeared on Barbara's cheeks and she involuntarily felt the pocket of her uniform where a letter was stowed. *I can't wait to see you again and run my hands over your smooth skin.* She pushed away those hurtful words, blinked

25

away her own pain and lifted her patient's right hand. She looked up to see Jim standing in the doorway with two mugs of tea. She shook her head. He silently turned and went back to the kitchen.

"Oh love, what a shock for you. No wonder you're in a state now. Come on, let's find out what's going on with this body of yours. Do you mind if I open your coat so I can have a listen to your chest?"

"Of course," Isabella snivelled and wiped her nose on the back of the settee. The nurse took out a stethoscope from her bag, warmed it, then placed it on Isabella's chest, listening to her heartbeat.

"Your heart may be broken, love, but it's still beating well. I'm going to feel your arms and legs now."

Barbara rubbed her hands together to warm them up, then felt each delicate limb up and down, pressing and pushing, trying to get a reaction. There was nothing. She removed the boots as she reached Isabella's little feet. She frowned.

"The doctor in the hospital couldn't find anything obviously wrong but I'll check you over again now. I'm going to lift your left arm and I want you to try and hold it up."

"Okay, I'll try."

"Okay *now*. Look, it's up, can you see?" Barbara released the arm. It flopped down heavily into Isabella's lap.

"What's wrong with me?" She sighed heavily.

"I think the shock of the accident's caused your body to seize up. It's not an uncommon reaction to shock: people either fight, flee, or freeze when something traumatic happens. It's the body's way of protecting itself. When this numbness wears off, you're going to have a bruise and a painful right leg where you took the impact against the bridge. But other than that, there's nothing obviously wrong with you."

"Except my bloody husband."

"Yes, that might take some time. But for now, the best thing is to get you into bed with a nice cup of tea."

"I'm so sorry. I don't want to be a bother."

"It's fine. It's my job." She turned and called to Jim. He reappeared, still holding the mugs of tea, his head hanging.

"Right, Jim, we need to move your wife. Put those cups down and come over here. You can carry her into the bedroom. You're a big strong man."

Jim grunted slightly as he bent his knees in front of the settee. Effortlessly, he lifted his wife in his arms and carried her to the next room where he placed her carefully on the mattress. Barbara followed with the mugs of tea. He took them from her and put them down on the bedside table. He turned and left the room, his head still lowered.

"You okay, love? Where's your nightie?"

"It's in my bag," Isabella sniffed.

Jim returned holding up a canvas overnight bag and a small floral sponge bag. "Brought these back from the hospital for you, Bella."

As he left the bedroom again, Barbara pulled out a pink brushed cotton nightie and a dressing gown.

"I'm going to get you into these, then we can a have a cuppa and proper chat."

Isabella nodded. "I can't believe he did it. We were so happy together. We had a good life—the children had grown and got good jobs. Why did he have to go and spoil it all?" She stared up at the ceiling, studying each black spot, inhaling deeply and exhaling completely.

"It must be so hard for you, love. He's broken a rule that should never be broken." Babs sighed. "Tell, me when did the affair start?"

Barbara sat down on the end of the bed and pushed away her own thoughts of infidelity. Instead, she focussed on her patient sitting upright, her auburn hair with a few strands of grey flowing against the pillow, her hazel eyes full of sadness, while slight purple smudges underneath hinted at sleepless nights. She couldn't believe anyone would want to hurt this woman. Unbidden, feelings of betrayal broke over her: how could someone hurt another so much? Shoving her thoughts to one side, she held the mug of tea to Isabella's mouth and tipped gently. She put that mug down on a small, dark wooden bedside table and picked up the other to take a big gulp.

"Well, I think it was a while ago. Irene, our daughter, saw them together at the cinema holding hands. He, Jim, the cheating rotter, told her to say nothing to me. Well, she's only nineteen and that was too big a burden to carry for very long so she told him she was going to tell me. The coward didn't want to face the music so he left home and came here. We've had this cottage for a while, you see, so he had an escape."

"What a horrible situation. So, you decided to follow him here and that's when you had the accident?"

"When I found out, I waited a day for the dust to settle and make sure Irene would be okay on her own at home."

"Must have been difficult for her, telling you about her own father's affair." Barbara's stomach turned over. "So, then what happened?"

"I told my boss I was taking a few days off—he wasn't happy; makes me work all the hours God sends—and packed a bag for a day or two. But I couldn't sleep so I got up really early and started out before it was light. And you know the rest."

"Poor you. A broken heart and now this..." Barbara smiled at her patient and stroked the back of her small hand with its green veins and faint age spots. There were remnants of pink nail varnish in the creases of the nail bed.

"Doesn't feel like it all happened a week ago."

"No, I don't suppose it does. You've been on sedatives for a week so they'll make you feel a bit groggy. Did the doctor give you a prescription for more when he discharged you?"

"Yes, I think Jim picked them up. He came every day. Don't know why, bloody cheating man."

"You're clearly in a bad place right now, both emotionally and physically. I think the one has affected the other. But you're moving your toes and fingers now so it looks like things are slowly getting back to normal. I'll come in tomorrow to check on you."

"Thank you. Might take a bit longer for my heart to heal, and for me to forgive Jim."

"Yes, I'm sure, but for now I want you to rest. It'll help your body heal. Take one of your sedatives. I know it's hard, but just try to relax."

Barbara went back into the kitchen for the small, brown bottle of magic. Standing by the bed, she tipped a round white tablet into the lid and held it up to Isabella's mouth, then picked up the tea and held it up to her lips as Isabella swallowed hard.

"When you're awake, there are some exercises you must do. First, move your fingers for me now."

Isabella squeezed up her face and made fists with her hands. "Look at that, they're already moving more than before! How long before I can move my body? I feel so useless like this."

"You're not useless, you're unwell. There's a big difference. When you wake up, keep doing that and the same with your toes. Do you need the loo before I go?"

"Oh yes, I do."

"Well let's sort that, then I'll be off, and you can sleep."

Afterwards, Isabella's chin dropped, the medication kicking in quickly. Barbara turned and left the bedroom to make her way to the front door.

"So, Jim, I've given Isabella a mild sedative so she should sleep for a few hours. Keep checking on her and make sure she has drink of water or tea when she wakes up."

"Yes, Nurse." His head was still hanging, his chin almost on his chest, and his greying hair flopped forward.

"And Jim..."

"Yes, Nurse?" He lifted his head slightly, his blue eyes full of sadness and remorse.

"You and she need to have a talk." Even as she said the words, Barbara knew they applied to her, too.

"I know. I was an idiot."

"Well, it happens. But she's with you now and that's a good sign, surely?"

"I suppose it is."

"Right, I'm off. By the way, there's a bed pan by the door you need to deal with." Barbara laughed as she stepped up and out of the door.

CHAPTER 4

Dai

"Come on, you two. Why aren't you ready? Put your shoes and coats on now. Where's your satchel? Is it PE day?" Dai hurried his children along, impatient to be out of the door and in his garage workshop.

"Not for me, Daddy. Don't you know anything? PE's on Monday and Wednesday. Today's Friday," said Daniel, standing straight. He was already wearing his Clarks school shoes; his duffle coat done up neatly. He was a serious boy, tall for his age, with gangly limbs.

"Mine's today. Mummy puts my bag at the end of my bed," added George.

"Well run up and get it then."

"It's here," laughed George, waving his canvas drawstring bag from behind his back.

"Stop mucking about. We'll never get out of the house." Dai stood with the fingers of one hand wrapped tightly around the back door handle, the other fist thrust deep in the pocket of his black Harrington jacket.

The boys finally ready, the small group left the house for the walk to school. George jumped and ran down the path to the sea front.

"Can we walk the beach way, Daddy, please?" asked Daniel.

"Yep, it's the quickest way, isn't it?"

At the school gate, Dai gave each son a cursory kiss before they ran into the playground to join their classmates. There was Tony, that English chap, also dropping off his children: two girls who looked the same age as George and Daniel. The older one headed straight for a small circle of girls who stepped back to let her in. The younger one stood slightly away from the second-year class. Dai looked at the youngsters, wondering how long it would take for them to be accepted. He knew exactly how close-knit this community was, the women especially. He watched as one of the group finally spoke to the little one. He then turned to speak to her father.

"Morning, Tony. How are you this fine morning?"

"Oh fine, thanks Dai. Worry a bit about my two. I hope they'll be all right. I'm not sure we should've brought them here. We just wanted a better life."

"Takes a while sometimes. People round here don't like change or strangers."

"I suppose we'll just have to be patient then." He sighed then looked down at his dog which gave a low growl and pulled on the lead. "Oh, all right, Charlie, we're going. You like it here, don't you boy? You can have a proper run on the beach on the way back."

"I'm walking that way too. Need to get the van and get myself into work."

"Oh yes, the garage. See you've managed to work out childcare between you."

"Yes, Babs drops them off twice a week, my Da does two days and I do Fridays. It's after school that's tricky. I have to take a late lunch, drop them with a neighbour then go back to the garage. Babs gets home around four thirty and picks them up."

"It's a juggling act when you both work, isn't it?"

"Yeah. I wish Babs was like the other mums and stayed at home, but she insists on working. Says it's good for her, keeps her brain ticking over."

"My wife is exactly the same. But at least she got a job: I'm still looking. I've got an interview today actually." Tony picked up a stick and threw it down towards the water. Charlie bounded after it.

32

"Well, I need to go this way now. Cheerio, Tony. And good luck with the interview."

"Bye for now then, Dai."

Dai paused briefly to look up and down the familiar, deserted beach. In the summer, the wide sandy expanse was peppered with colourful towels and stripey windbreaks. The town thronged with sunburnt tourists eating ice-creams, buying red Welsh dragons and swilling beer. The visitors were smiling and happy, enjoying their holidays. The locals smiling and happy to be making a profit, especially from the English.

That year, they'd taken a week off in July and spent a few lazy days soaking up the relaxed atmosphere with the boys on the beach, before he'd been needed elsewhere. He grinned at his memory of the summer, a slight twinge in his groin at the thought of bikini tan lines and salty skin. The boys were busy with their friends and Babs was preoccupied with her new job. She'd hardly noticed her husband or his long absences.

Driving from their house near the school and through the town, he noticed how different Barmouth was now summer was over. Everyone was a bit taut and edgy in the winter months. Lucky he and Babs had year-round jobs. Bit of security for the family. He pulled his Transit van into the garage and climbed out.

"Morning, Bryn!" he called out to a pair of feet poking out from under a Ford Zephyr.

"All right, Dai. Mind if I don't get up?"

"You carry on down there. I'm going to check what we've got on today."

Dai headed into the office and pulled on a pair of oil-stained khaki overalls, then picked up a clipboard and looked at the jobs on the worksheet. There were few small repairs and two MOTs. Not a bad day at the office.

At three o'clock, Dai waited outside the school gates, stamping his feet and checking the classroom doors repeatedly.

He looked around to see Tony arrive with his soppy dog, Charlie. He was the only other man at the school gates, surrounded by a gaggle of mothers switching between Welsh and English. He sauntered over, smiling at a few of the women who tilted their heads coquettishly at him. He lapped up their attention, then turned to Tony.

"You'll right, Tony?"

"Yep, fine."

"You don't sound great, mate. How was that interview?"

"Not great really."

"Shame, what happened?"

The answer was interrupted by a sudden clanging bell indicating the end of the school day. Charlie wagged his tail excitedly. Each classroom door opened to disgorge a swarm of children heading towards their respective mothers, and the two fathers. The older of Tony's daughters stood by the door and beckoned him over. Dai spotted Daniel saying goodbye to his friends and striding towards him.

"Where's George?"

"Dunno. Still in the classroom?"

"Well go and get him. I need to get back to work."

The other children dispersed with their mothers as Daniel headed back towards the main door. Impatiently, Dai followed him. As he entered the warren of high ceilings and long corridors, the smell of sweaty children combined with polished floors and the last wafts of school dinners hit him in the face. He breathed in, the smell bringing with it memories of times tables and ox-bow lakes. He looked down a dark, dimly lit corridor to see George, dragging a trolley behind him. He peered closely: what looked like a cage was on the back.

"What the hell is that?"

"It's the class rabbit. It's my turn to have it for the weekend."

"Oh what? For goodness' sake. When was this arranged?"

"Mummy signed up and it's my turn now." George's eyes filled up as he looked up at his father's black visage.

"It happens every year, Dad. We take it in turns. We did it when I was in that class too. Remember?" Daniel implored.

Dai turned around, shaking his head and muttering under his breath. Beyond his son with the rabbit cage on a trolley, he caught sight of Tony's face, hard and judgemental.

"Oh, all right then. We'll have to take the blooming thing home. You've got all the food and stuff, I suppose?"

"Yes, Daddy. Everything's here."

"Come on then, let's go. You got everything else you need now? Coat, bag, PE kit?"

Dai glanced at Tony, who had reached the school office. The school secretary was bending over a small child sitting on a chair with tear streaks on her cheeks. He watched, intrigued by the proceedings.

"Daddy!" The little girl with blonde pigtails burst into tears and a snot bubble appeared from her left nostril. She got up and threw her arms around her father's legs. The other girl held Charlie's lead, both watching the scene.

"What's happened, love?" Dai heard Tony say. He felt like an intruder on the events unfolding but could not help himself from listening.

"Take the rabbit and wait outside you two," he whispered sharply and pretended to do up a lace on his left boot.

"She had an accident," said the secretary glaring at Charlie. "We've lent her some spare knickers." She thrust a bag at him. "And get that dog out of the school building."

"Clare, take Charlie outside." His daughter pulled the dog towards the door and Tony turned back to the secretary, "What do you mean, an accident?" asked Tony, stroking his daughter's hair. "It's all right, love. I'm here now, you can stop crying."

"I'll let her tell you, Mr Saddler. Goodbye." The girl sobbed out loud again.

"Come on you two, let's get home. Shall I give you a piggyback, Cathy?"

"Yes please, Daddy." Tony bent down and the girl clambered aboard. "I'm sorry," she whispered into her father's ear.

Dai turned away, only slightly ashamed of eavesdropping. He walked swiftly down the corridor and out into the playground where Daniel and George were waiting with the rabbit. He saw Charlie growling at the bars and his sons shooing the dog while Clare tried to pull him away. The rabbit stood firm, staring the dog in the eyes, ears up. Charlie cowered and withdrew.

"Seems your dog is afraid of the killer rabbit!" Dai laughed.

"Oh dear. Looks like our Charlie is a bit of a softy," Tony said as he appeared with Cathy on his back.

"Can I get down now please?"

Tony lowered her down and the four children ran on ahead, pulling the trolley between them, Cathy's ordeal now forgotten as she skipped over the cracks in the pavement, half-laughing.

"You heading home now? What happened in there?"

"I'm not sure of the details, Cathy wasn't keen on telling me. I'll find out later, I'm sure."

Clare ran up to them. "I know what happened, Daddy."

"Do you? Tell me then."

"All the kids were laughing at her in the playground at afternoon break, calling her 'pee pee pants'. I heard one of them say that Mrs Llewellyn wouldn't let her go to the toilet unless she asked in Welsh."

"She what?"

"She's really horrible, Daddy. She wants everyone to speak Welsh all the time. Poor Cathy didn't know how so she made her stand there for ages."

"Really? That's cruel."

"That Mrs Llewellyn has always been a bit of a dragon," explained Dai.

"Well, she couldn't hold it anymore and she wet herself."

"Bloody teacher, I'll have a right go at her on Monday," Tony fumed. He pursed his lips and strode down the street as his children stumbled along behind, satchels bashing their legs and Charlie pulling Clare's left arm out of its socket. Dai strode to keep up.

"It must be hard for you lot, being outsiders and all."

"Well, it's a challenge. The girls are taking it in their stride. Well, they were until today." Tony was upright and angry.

"Least you've got the weekend to get over it."

"Yes." Tony went quiet, lost in his thoughts.

"Right, well. This is us. See you again."

"Cheerio Dai. Have a good weekend." Then to his girls, "Shall we stop at Woolworth's for some pick 'n' mix?"

"Yes please!" the girls shouted in unison

Dai opened the gate wide to accommodate two sons and the rabbit trolley, then turned to watch the English family disappear down the road.

---0---

Dai pulled up at the garage once again. The boys were with the neighbour from number six until Babs got home. Only an hour or so to cover, but it was always awkward. He didn't like it: why couldn't Babs stay at home and look after the children like all the other mothers? The money was good though, two incomes were definitely better than struggling by on just his wages. Meant they could afford the nice things and the odd holiday. And his work van, her wages had helped buy that, and it was a really good runner. Plus, it was jolly useful with a few blankets in the back in the summer. He grinned at the memory. He just needed to get Babs through her driving test then they could buy a better car too.

At just past five o'clock, Dai wiped his oily hands on his khaki overalls. He packed away his spanners, pushed the jack into the corner and called out to his partner and brother who was at that moment positioned under a Morris Minor.

"Time to go Bryn. POETS day and all that."

"That doesn't apply to us. It's my turn to be here tomorrow morning." Bryn dragged himself out from under the car, stood up straight and rubbed his lower back. "Give us a minute, just need to tighten these nuts," he added, as he bent over to inspect the wheel.

"Get a move on, Bryn."

Bryn replaced the ratchet and took the few steps to the corner sink. He rubbed Swarfega into his hands and rinsed them under the tap. "What you up to this weekend, Dai?"

"Out to the pub tonight, something with Babs and the kids tomorrow. We're having dinner with Da on Sunday after the rugby. You?"

"Much the same, but not the Babs and kids bit, obviously."

"Have a good one then."

Together, they walked out. Bryn slapped his younger brother on the back and walked off down the road. Dai locked the white double doors on the front of the workshop and climbed into his orange Transit.

When he walked into the kitchen, Barbara was busy at the sink, a pile of potatoes and carrots waiting their turn on the stainless-steel draining board. He admired her pert bottom and thanked his lucky stars he'd been discreet in the summer.

"Hi, Babs love."

"Hi, Dai. Good day?" She didn't turn around; she peeled faster.

"Same old, same old, really. Nothing exciting. Yours?" He was drawn towards her, watching the muscles of her back

38

twitching as her hands deftly moved over the potatoes. He wanted to put his arms around her waist and feel her breasts under her green jumper.

"All right. Saw Mrs Cartwright up at Bontddu. You're right about that cottage. It really is a shack; no inside toilet or proper running water. It'll be freezing in winter too."

He took a step closer to her. She didn't turn around, her attention on the potatoes. He spoke his words into her left ear as he slid his arm around her waist. "She all right though? Getting better? Her legs wouldn't move when we picked her up."

He felt her body tense and her shoulders straighten. His breath was close, each exhalation falling directly onto her cheek. He could just see the tiny hairs standing on end like icicles.

"She'll recover, I think. More to the point though, her husband's a cheating scoundrel." She pushed his hands off her waist and turned to him, the peeler pointing at his face.

"Whoa, Babs! Careful with that thing. You'll do someone an injury." He half-laughed, held up his hands and backed away.

"Go and see to the boys, I need to get dinner ready. Suppose you're up the Pendragon tonight?"

"Yeah, arranged to see the lads."

"I'll stay in and watch the telly, like every Friday since we had the kids, then."

"Not this again, Babs. You're like a stuck record."

"Oh, just leave me to get on with this will you?"

Dai turned and headed towards the sound of boys laughing in the next room. At the door, he glanced back to see his wife's shoulders drooping and her brunette curls falling around her face.

CHAPTER 5

Owen

Owen thrust his hands into the pockets of his overcoat and pulled his woollen hat over his ears. "Come on, Dewi, it's getting a bit nippy now and it's time for a cuppa." He was walking in the hills above the town, his feet crunching in the fallen twigs and leaves. The bracken was turning too, yellow and brown creeping from the edges of each frond. He hoped that this time he wouldn't need to rescue any women lying in the undergrowth. That was odd, riding her moped from the other side of Birmingham in the middle of the night. It was over a week ago now and he wondered how she was doing; if she could move her arms and legs yet. And if she'd sorted things out with her husband. He'd heard a few stories about the man living in a shack whispered about the town, but he gave little heed to those old fish wives.

He followed the path back towards to Barmouth. Autumn had definitely set in and he was glad of his hat. It wouldn't be long before all the trees were bare and the wind whipped around Cardigan Bay. No tourists came to the town then. It was quiet, like it had been when he was a lad. He preferred the summer; he liked chatting to people from all over Britain and beyond. One time in July, he'd even met some German folks as he walked along the beach with Dewi. Plus, he welcomed the trade they brought to this old town. During the winter, all the local business owners grudgingly looked forward to the summer and the ringing of their tills.

He heard the distant sound of children's screeching and he thought about his grandsons. George had told him about the youngest girl of the new English couple up the hill, that she'd

41

had a tough time at the school. Maybe he could help her—teach her a few words, get that Mrs Llewellyn off her back. Yes, that's what he'd do. He changed direction and headed towards their house on the cliffside. He climbed the paths up two sets of slate steps, rounded the corner and pushed open the gate to Pen Y Craig, a three-storey house built into the rock. There were hundreds of interlinking footpaths leading to all the houses on the hillside; his own house was one of them. As a child he'd run around them hiding and jumping out on his friends. Bryn and Dai had been the same and he reckoned children would be doing that for ever.

As he walked up the slate steps, he spoke aloud to Dewi, trotting alongside him. "Wonder if Bryn'll settle down and have a couple of children like Dai. He's so good with his nephews, better than their own da. It'd be nice for him to have some little ones of his own. What do you think eh, Dewi?"

Dewi looked up, almost nodding in agreement. Owen continued as they made their way up the hill. He stopped to take a breath. "Thirty-five isn't too old, is it? He gets a lot of interest from the local lasses, but he don't seem that bothered. Not since Elaine ten years ago—he took ages to get over her. His mam would be right disappointed, if she was still around. What're we gonna do about him, Dewi?"

They'd reached the house now and, with his hand still on the gate, he looked down at his faithful friend. "If he leaves it too late, he'll be too old to be starting a family, won't he?" Owen breathed out heavily then took a few steps to the back door. He removed his hat and knocked on the glass. A large black Labrador barked loudly and, spying Dewi, jumped out of its bed in the corner the kitchen and ran hard towards the door, banging into the glass. It barked again, moving its head quizzically from side to side.

From inside, he heard a girl's raised voice, "Be quiet, Charlie!" and saw the slight figure of the older girl, still in school uniform, coming towards the door. She slid her fingers under the dog's collar, holding it tightly, but Charlie was desperate to get to the dog on the other side of the door. Dewi put his nose against the glass, also interested in this potential friend or foe. The girl opened the door and poked her head out. Charlie pushed his way around her legs and ran outside, immediately sniffing around Dewi.

"Charlie, come back! Sorry, Mister. What's your dog called?"

"He's Dewi."

"And who are you?"

"Owen Roberts. Are your mam or da in?"

"Mum's at work. She's a nurse." The girl smiled. "Dad's been working all night so he's having a little nap."

"Oh, right. I'll come back up another time then. And what's your name?"

"Clare." She put her hand out to shake Owen's.

"Nice to meet you, Clare. Tell your mam and dad I came round."

"Who is it, love?" A sandy-haired man appeared in the kitchen, yawning and stretching. His towelling dressing gown was open to reveal checked pyjamas. On his feet were sheepskin slippers.

"Daddy, this is Mister Roberts and his dog's called Dewi." His daughter sat down on the floor with the two dogs, who had now made friends.

"Sorry about the state of me, Mr Roberts, I started working nights at Shrewsbury Hospital a few days ago and I'm still getting used to it. I was just having a rest before I go in again later. Do you want to come in? I'll put the kettle on. I could kill a cuppa myself." He took the kettle to the sink, filled it, then took it back and plugged it in.

"Only if it's no trouble, don't want to disturb you..."

"Tony, I'm Tony. I'm just going to nip upstairs and put some clothes on. Won't be a sec." He disappeared through the door and the sound of footsteps stomping up the stairs followed shortly after.

"So, Clare, you've got a sister, haven't you?"

"Yes, Cathy. She's upstairs playing with her Sindy dolls. She might come down with Daddy now though."

"Ah, okay." He watched the girl throw a stuffed duck across the kitchen floor for the two dogs to follow. "You like dogs then?"

"Yes, Charlie is my best friend. I like Dewi too. How old is he?"

"He's ten; quite an old fella now. He's my best friend, too."

Tony reappeared in the kitchen now fully clothed. The little one, Cathy, followed behind, sucking her thumb. The kettle clicked off. He took a teapot down from a shelf above the sink and two mugs from the hooks.

"Milk and sugar, Mr Roberts? Do you two want a drink?"

"Call me Owen. That 'mister' thing's a bit formal, isn't it? Milk and one sugar please."

"Can I have an orange squash please, Daddy?" said Clare.

"Yep, here you go. Cathy?"

"I'm fine thanks, Daddy."

"So, what can I do for you, Owen?" said Tony sitting down at the kitchen table.

"I heard about poor Cathy and old Mrs Llewellyn. She's always been a tough one, even when my Dai was in her class, and that was oh, twenty-five years ago. So, I thought I might be able to help. I speak Welsh like, seeing as I was brought up here, and I wondered if your Cathy—" He looked at the tearful eyes of the small girl sipping her drink across the table, "—would like some help learning a few Welsh words."

"She's horrible!" sniffed Cathy, the memory still painfully clear in her mind. "And all the others in the class pick on me now. They call me 'pee pee pants'. And she won't let me speak in class unless I can do it in Welsh. I hate school."

"Poor little mite. That was well harsh of her." Owen shook his head with his lips pursed. "I don't know why she's still teaching. She must be way beyond retirement age. Maybe they're hoping she'll go of her own accord soon."

"Cathy, would you like to learn some Welsh? That'd help you in class, wouldn't it?" Tony looked over encouragingly at his daughter.

"Not sure, it sounds hard. Like they're all shouting at each other."

"I can help you, Cathy." Owen smiled and looked over at the other daughter. "And you too, Clare, if you want."

"Cathy, I'll learn with you. It'll be fun and you can show that Mrs Llewellyn!"

"I'll do it if Clare does too. Thank you, Mister Owen."

"Just Owen's fine. I can start now if you like, a few words each day; build up slowly. I've no rush to get home. That okay with you Tony?"

"That's so kind, Owen. Finish your tea first, though. Fancy a biscuit anyone?"

Tony went to the cupboard and pulled out a packet of custard creams which he tipped onto a plate. As he placed it on the table, a set of little fingers reached towards them and carefully took two. Cathy slid down onto the floor and from under the table the two dogs leaned towards her with their tongues lolling. Cathy held out her hands, a biscuit in each and both dogs excitedly pushed their noses to sniff the treat. Charlie carefully took one and rapidly wolfed it down. Dewi looked up at his master, who nodded at him. Then he gently took it from Cathy's hand and slowly chewed it, one eye on Charlie.

"Any idea why she's like that? It's not normal for a primary school teacher to be so hard on the little ones," said Tony, as he ruffled Cathy's hair and wiped a few crumbs from around her mouth with a handkerchief.

"Well, she lost both her sons in the war. They were only young like, maybe only even sixteen or so. She took that very hard—no surprise there. They were no more than kids themselves. What a waste! And then her husband came back and he was damaged, like most of them were. Very difficult to live with by all accounts. He died a few years back. I reckon she's been suffering a long time."

"That must've been hard for her. But she could be a bit nicer to Cathy: she's only seven and it's not her fault."

"Ah, but you're English and she blames the English for sending our Welsh boys to the front."

"I see. It's beginning to make sense. I almost feel a bit sorry for her." Tony paused. "But my daughter comes first."

The outside kitchen door swung open, bringing in a cold draught and a tall slim woman in a dark blue nurse's cloak and navy-blue leather gloves.

"Hello everyone, this looks cosy." She pulled her gloves off and rubbed her hands together then kissed the heads of her daughters and her husband in turn. "Nice to see you here. It's Owen, isn't it? Babs told me you found that lady who came off her moped."

"Yep, that's so. Sorry, I don't know your name."

"Oh sorry, we've not been introduced, have we? I'm Hazel. Any tea left in that pot, love?"

"Yes dear, I only made it a five minutes ago. Good day?" He stood up and got another mug out.

"Yeah, not bad. I'm just going to get changed."

Owen looked around at the family, casting his mind back fondly to when his own children were little. These girls were so well-behaved and polite, they'd be a joy to teach. He smiled over at Cathy.

"Right, you two. We'll start with the most important phrase."

"What's that?" said Cathy getting up from the floor and onto a kitchen chair.

"Can I go to the toilet." Owen grinned. Cathy forced a half-smile, Clare gently thumped her sister's arm.

"So how do you say it in Welsh?" Tony laughed as he set Hazel's mug on the table.

"Ga i fynd i ty bach? Can you say that after me?"

---0---

Bryn was sitting at the end of the kitchen table, shovelling in the last of his stew and dumplings, the favourite of his father's short repertoire of meals. He picked up a piece of bread and wiped it around his bowl.

"I'm glad you like it, Bryn."

"Sorry, Da. I was starving, I forgot my sandwiches. Left them in the fridge, so I did."

"They'll be all right for tomorrow then. Busy day at the garage?"

"We had that old Morris Minor and Lloyd's lorry to fix. You know, the ones that came in last week and we were waiting for the parts? Oh, and an old English couple stopped by just before closing time, asking for directions to their daughter's house."

"Oh right, that'll be the couple moved into Pen Y Craig on the hill. They've come to help out a bit while her husband's working away."

"Is he? What's he doing?"

"Couldn't get a job locally. Tried at Harlech hospital but they didn't want a man, particularly not an English man. Goes all the way to Shrewsbury now, working nights."

"What does he do?"

"Specialist nurse of some sort; works in an operating theatre. I think that's what he said anyway."

"A nurse, that's an odd job for a bloke. Anyhow, how d'you know so much about them, Da?"

"I went up there today. Heard about Mrs Llewellyn and that little girl."

"Oh, she's a right witch, she is. Still have nightmares about her. What were you doing round there then?"

"I decided to help the little ones learn some Welsh. Give the younger one, Cathy, a bit of a leg up in the classroom, like."

"That's a nice thing to do for strangers. Don't know what other folk round here'll say though."

"Sod them. If I want to help people, I'll do it. Besides, they're lovely young kids, really polite and the older one loves dogs. He leaned back in his chair. "Wish you'd find yourself a nice girl and settle down; give your old man some more grand kiddies, girls maybe. Dai's got the boys."

"You're like a stuck record, Da!" Bryn laughed.

"No choosing another married one this time. Near broke up a happy marriage with your flirting you did. Lucky I warned her off you."

"That was nothing serious and you know it. She just took my meaning all wrong. Why would I choose someone married anyhow? Nothing but trouble." He laid his cutlery in his bowl with a clang.

"I just wish you'd find yourself a nice young lady to settle down with."

"I'll do it when I'm good and ready, Da, so just stop your worrying!"

CHAPTER 6

Isabella

Isabella rolled onto her front, swung her knees onto the floor next to the bed and pushed her body straight. She bit her bottom lip and straightened first her undamaged left leg then tried her right. A small squeal escaped her pursed mouth and she laid her head on the mattress. The sound alerted Jim. He stepped purposefully from the kitchen and stood in the doorway of the bedroom.

"What you doing, Bella? Didn't that nurse tell you stay in bed until she'd been? And the doctor too."

"I'm fed up with staring at the ceiling and these horrible damp patches. I need to get outside in the fresh air." She turned her head to see her husband hovering, the top of his hair skimming the doorjamb. "You could at least give me hand."

He took a step closer into the small room and leaned forward to put his hands under her armpits. Then with the minimum of effort, he lifted her into a standing position and turned her round to face him, keeping his hands on her for a moment longer than necessary. He had hardly touched his wife since he'd lifted her onto the bed a week ago and he had almost forgotten how slight and light she was. They were facing each other now. He could feel her breath and smell her hair. She shuffled backwards, supporting herself on the bedframe. Jim took a step away and cleared his throat. Isabella broke the silence.

"Nurse Babs wasn't wrong. My leg is killing me and the bruise on my thigh is the size of Australia."

"Well, least you got the feeling back, love." They stood still, looking at each other. Jim's guilt and Isabella's resentment forming an invisible barrier between them.

"I need to get dressed." She pointed to a chair in the corner. "My dress and cardy are over there."

Jim sidled over and helped her sit on the bed. Then he picked up her clothes and placed them on the bed next to her.

"Now turn around." Jim faced the wall as Isabella slipped her nightie off and pulled her dress over her head and her cardigan around her shoulders. Her underwear would have to wait; her knickers were clean on yesterday. Babs had given her a bed bath.

"You ready, love?"

"Yes, you can turn round and help me again now. I'd like to go outside." He lifted her gently up from the bed. She winced as she put the weight on her right leg and sat down again with a long sigh.

"Hold on, love. I've got a walking stick somewhere. That old one of my da's."

He left her for a moment as she dropped her chin to her chest and took a few deep breaths. He re-appeared a moment later with a curved-handled wooden stick.

"Let's see how you get on with this, shall we?"

He held it steady as she put her hand on it and pushed down to lift herself up. Jim held her free arm and together they made slow progress across the bare wooden floor of the bedroom.

"Mind the step, love."

Then they stepped into the sitting room. Isabella looked around the room. The curtains were still drawn but she could make out the pillow and blanket on the settee and a pile of dirty clothes on the floor.

"Mind the carpet, it's crumpled."

"That's the least of it, Jim. It's a blooming mess. You need to have a clear-up in here."

"Well, I've been running around with meals and the like."

"It doesn't take a moment to open some curtains and pick up your clothes."

"I suppose not. Let's get you into the kitchen."

As one, they made their way with tiny steps past the front door and into the kitchen. Jim stopped at the table. Isabella held the edge tightly and had a look around. There were dirty plates piled up in the Belfast sink and stained teacups waited on the table. The stove was covered with bits of burnt potato and brown gravy was spilt down the side. The blackened saucepan and lid sat defiantly on the top along with an eggy frying pan. There was a collection of dirty tea towels in a heap on the floor by the Welsh dresser.

"Oh my goodness! What happened in here?" Isabella sank into one the wooden chairs, leant her stick next to her and found a clear space on the table to place her hands.

Jim dropped his head. "I ain't so good at housework. It's all right when it's just meself. I wash up as I go along. But we've had all sorts of people coming in and I've had to cook and clean for you too. It's been a bit much."

"I can see that. It's a miracle you haven't killed me off with all the germs!"

"Sorry, love."

"Let's start with a cuppa. If you could wash a couple of mugs that is."

Sitting at the table surrounded by her husband's mess and a steaming cup of tea in front her, Isabella felt a pang of sympathy. He'd had to work hard that week, and he wasn't used to housework.

"We'll get this sorted, Jim."

"I hope so, Bella." A slight glimmer of hope ignited in his eyes as he spoke again. "I'm sorry..."

The misunderstanding hung heavily between them as she shook her head and gave her cursory instructions. "Put the kettle on and get the sink filled with some hot water."

Her words cut through his apology. She wasn't ready for that conversation quite yet. She took in his slumped posture and dejected face as he realised her meaning. He stood up slowly and obediently, picked up the kettle and filled it with water from the pump by sink. "You might as well fill that pan too: you're going to need a lot of hot water to clean this lot."

While Isabella directed from her chair, Jim scrubbed and scoured every item of crockery, pan and utensil in the kitchen then placed them neatly in the dresser and cupboard. He collected up the dirty washing from the sitting room—the sheets and Isabella's nightie from the bedroom—and put them with the tea towels in a bag ready to take to the launderette in Barmouth. He opened the curtains, took the carpets outside and gave them a good beating. He swept the kitchen floor, wiped the surfaces in all three rooms, then opened the windows to air the cottage. Exhaling loudly, he sat down across the table and looked hopefully at the smiling face of Isabella.

"That's better Jim. I've never seen you do so much in the house."

"Never appreciated how much you do, love. To make the house nice, I mean."

"Yes, I do and I always have. And now I've got a job where I work all hours. It was harder when the kiddies were younger, mind. Things have been a bit easier now Freddie's gone and Irene's working." Her face crumpled slightly, then she pulled herself upright again. "Can you take me outside, please?"

"'Course love." He supported her under her arms as she put her weight on both legs and took her stick. "Come on, up you get."

They made slow progress across the kitchen. Jim leaned her against the wall as he pulled open the front door and helped her over the threshold. She breathed in the autumn air deeply and looked down across the valley. With her free arm, she pulled her cardigan closer with a shiver.

"I didn't realise how many sheep there were up here, Jim. Or how few people. There's not a house for miles."

"There's a little house up the hill from us a bit. Couple of retired teachers from London come up in the holidays. I helped them with a few bits this summer. They might be here again for half term. That must be soon."

There was the distant sound of a chugging engine. "Is that someone coming up the track now?"

Jim looked at his watch. "It's about time for the nurse."

"She'll be surprised to see me up, I bet. Why don't you go and put the kettle on? I'll wait here." She leaned against the door frame and watched as the Mini slowly appeared on the dirt track. *It must be almost impossible to get a car up here in the winter or when it rains*, she thought. *We won't be able to stay here much longer.*

The driver pulled up next to the cottage and Nurse Barbara stepped out of the passenger door. Owen Roberts rolled down his window and called out. Dewi's head was hanging out of the front window, his tongue lolling.

"Morning, Mrs Isabella. Just realised I dunno your surname, like. Good to see you up and about, mind."

"It's Cartwright, but Isabella is just fine. Thank you for bringing Babs."

"And what exactly do you think you're doing standing up like that, Isabella? Your leg is nowhere near healed." The nurse strode towards her patient, swinging her leather bag. As usual, she was wearing her dark blue cloak over her starched uniform and as she walked, Isabella caught glimpses of the red lining.

"I was fed up lying all day in bed like a lazy invalid. Jim helped me up and I made him clean up the cottage. He's in the kitchen now making tea."

"Well come on, let's get you back inside so I can have a look at you."

"Hang on, Babs." She turned to Owen. "There's a bag of washing for the launderette. Would you mind dropping it off? Jim'll give you the money."

"No problem." He jumped out of the car. "I can give you a hand getting back inside too."

He picked up her stick and supported her elbow. With Owen on her left and Jim on her right, Isabella shuffled back inside the house, through the sitting room, to the bedroom, Barbara leading. She ushered Owen and Jim out then shut the door behind them.

"What on earth made you think you could walk around? You've only been home a week and you're hardly able to balance." Barbara shook her head and restrained herself from wagging her forefinger at her patient.

"I couldn't lie there just thinking about all that happened and seeing Jim looking so worried every time he brought me a tray of food. I just needed to do something. Anyway, it wasn't so hard."

"I suppose the exercise will make you stronger. Does it hurt much now you've got the sensation back?"

"It's agony when I first wake up."

"That's probably because the tablets from the night before have worn off."

"But once I move a bit and take another one, it's manageable. That's why I wanted to get up. Start to be a normal again."

"So, let's have a look at the bruising. Can you lie on your left—that's good. I'm just going to lift your dress and have a look at your hip."

"It's huge, isn't it?"

"You did hit a wall at speed, Isabella. It's hardly surprising is it? And yes, it's very big, and as expected, has spread around your hip and down your leg. It's the right colour though, bright purple with a hint of yellow at the edges."

"You make me sound like a rotten plum!"

"Yes, it is a bit like that. I'm just going to press it. This might hurt a bit."

"Ouch, that's painful. How long before it goes down?"

"Well, bruising happens because you damage blood vessels in the tissue underneath your skin. Usually, a bruise will heal in two weeks or so, but yours is bigger than most so I think it'll take longer. Maybe three weeks. It'll change colour and shrink as your body heals. Some people use arnica cream to speed up the process. I've got a tube here: you can try it, but the bruise will eventually go away on its own."

"I'll try anything. It's really ugly." She looked down at it. "Reminds me of the damage Jim has done to us." She sighed.

Isabella looked up to see Barbara's face tense and her mouth pinch as she busied herself with her bag. *What's happened in her life? What is she hiding?*

"There's not much more I can do for you today. Just take it steady, don't rush yourself or you'll end up falling over. I've brought a few more books and I found a crossword puzzle book for you, too. They're in the car. Is there anything else you want from town?" Despite her professional manner, Isabella could see a cloud in her nurse's eyes, and her words and her mouth seemed to be disconnected.

"I need to post a few letters and I'd like to choose my own meals. I'm a bit fed up of mince and potatoes—that's all Jim can manage. Any chance I can go into town?"

"Why don't you get used to moving around here first? Maybe in a day or two, Jim can drive you down. That track is really bumpy, so you might need to sit on a cushion."

"Thank you, Babs. And you take care, won't you?"

"What do you mean?" Barbara stood upright and looked her in the eye.

"I can tell you've got something you're worried about. You can't keep it hidden forever."

"Thank you for that piece of wisdom, Isabella. I'll bear it in mind." She dropped her gaze then picked up her bag and cloak, taking the short step to the door.

"Are you leaving me in here? I'd rather be in the sitting room please."

"Of course, sorry." She opened the door, "Jim can you come and help Isabella to the settee?" She turned back to Isabella. "I'll nip out and get those books."

Barbara hurried out of the bedroom, through the sitting room, and out of the front door. She leant on the side of the Mini and took a couple of deep breaths. In through her nose, out through her mouth. *How does she know? Who else knows?*

"You all right, Babs? Look like you've had a shock."

"Oh, I'm fine, Owen. Can you take this bag in for Isabella? Then we can head back into town. Would you mind dropping me at the surgery please; I'll do the rest of my rounds on my bike."

She looked back into the house through the sitting room window. Isabella was on the settee, propped up with cushions, looking at the selection of books from the library. Jim walked in with a cup of tea and placed it carefully on the table. She looked up and gave a little wave and a knowing smile. Barbara looked away and climbed into the passenger seat, desperate to get away from this cottage before the secret was spilled.

CHAPTER 7

Jim

Jim pulled the stiff door of the telephone box with his head hung low. The conversation was not going to be an easy one. He pulled a pile of tuppences out of his jacket pocket and placed them on the shelf. He slowly dialled the familiar number of home and balanced a two pence piece in the slot. He heard the ringing and imagined Irene dashing down the stairs to the sitting room.

"West Bromwich 7274," a telephone voice breathed heavily, followed by a series of pips. Jim shoved the coin hard.

"Hello love, it's Dad."

"Dad, thank goodness." His daughter's tone pierced his conscience all the way down the telephone cables from his other home. "Where's Mum? She left days ago and I've heard nothing," she added,

"Don't worry, Irene. She's fine now."

"What d'you mean now?"

Jim took a deep breath. "She had a little accident."

"What d'you mean an accident?" Her voice sounded strangulated.

"Look, don't panic. Everything's all right." He paused as thought about his next words. "She came off her moped and hurt her leg. She was in hospital for a while but now she's at the cottage."

"Came off her moped! How? Why didn't you tell me before?" The accusation filled the small space.

"I wanted to wait till she was a bit better, didn't want you to fret."

"Poor Mum. She must've been so scared."

"You know your mum, she's a fighter. She's already up and about." Jim leaned against the glass in the phone box as the stress of the last week dissipated and his own relief washed over him. "Anyhow, I'm looking after her."

"You? Looking after Mum? That's something I never thought I'd hear." Irene's pitch returned to a more normal level and he thought he detected a hint of amusement in her tone.

"Needs must, and I'm not doing a bad job of it." The pips sounded and Jim shoved another coin in the slot. There was silence at the end of the line. Jim could hear his daughter take a deep breath.

"You know I had to tell Mum, don't you?"

Jim stiffened. "Yes love," he said quietly. "And I'm so sorry I put you in such an awkward situation. That weren't right of me."

"No Dad, it wasn't." Irene inhaled sharply. "Poor Mum doesn't deserve that—and with Susan for crying out loud. That wasn't fair. She's lost you and her best friend. What were you thinking Dad?" Her words tumbled out, each one pricking Jim like a thorn.

"I weren't thinking. I were selfish. Anyway, it's over now." He hung his head, glad nobody could see his guilt and remorse.

"I should blooming well hope so," his daughter remonstrated.

"Sorry, love. I really am. Shouldn't have put you through that."

"No you shouldn't have." She paused and the silence was palpable. Finally she continued quickly, "What's going to happen now? Is Mum staying with you? What are we going to do with the house here? Where am I going to live?"

"Slow down, Irene. We ain't going to make you homeless. We ain't decided fully what's best, for all of us. Your mum's still really angry with me, obviously. Let's just wait and see." Jim struggled to answer all her questions.

"When's she coming home, Da?"

"Mum ain't decided what she's doing yet, and anyhow, she's still too sore to travel all that way."

"Well, can I come to you this weekend? I'm not working," she almost pleaded and Jim's heart ached.

He spoke slowly, "You could come here; it's a bit basic, mind." He paused. "But it might actually be easier to wait for her to get better. There's hardly space for us two."

"Maybe you're right. But when do you think she can come home? I miss her and I don't like staying in the house on my own." Irene sniffed, then added, "Gerald stayed a few times. Don't worry, he was on the settee in the sitting room."

"I trust you, love." Jim paused, choosing his words with care. "Look," he said, "your mum's written a letter so you should get it in a day or two." Irene was silent, so he continued, "Why don't you wait for that and decide what to do then?" The pips started again.

"You got any more money Dad?" Irene's voice sounded urgent so he hurriedly pushed another coin in.

"It's all right, love, I'm still here. Tell me what you've been up to. It's nice to hear your voice." He leaned his head against the glass as he listened to his daughter chattering in his earpiece.

"...and a letter arrived from Freddie. It's got a foreign stamp on it."

"That'll please your mum. He usually only sends a postcard whenever his ship's in port." The pips went yet again.

"Bye, Dad. Ring me to tell me when Mum's coming home."

"I will. You take care, won't you? I'll call again soon." The line went dead. Jim replaced the receiver, gathered up his spare coins and put them in his pocket. He leant heavily on the door and stepped outside into the chilly air. Pulling his coat around him, he walked slowly back to his car, his head hanging low. At least that conversation was over. Now he just needed to fix his marriage.

CHAPTER 8

Barbara

Barbara came out of the surgery with her itinerary. She leant over to unlock her bicycle which was chained up against the railing. Not that anyone would steal it: Barmouth was so much safer than Glasgow. She placed her bag in the front basket, positioned her legs either side of the frame, lifted the back of her cloak and sat on the saddle.

Her next stop was old Mrs Jenkins at the Gatehouse. A big, black cloud sat ominously just ahead of her and she hoped the rain would hold off for a while, at least until safely inside. Barbara pushed away thoughts of Isabella's words and the letter in her pocket as she huffed and puffed up the hill.

She wiped her sweaty face and pulled the butler doorbell hard, just as the first fat raindrops landed with a splash on the porch above her. The bell reverberated and echoed down the corridor, followed shortly by the tapping of a wooden walking stick and the shrill tones of her next patient.

"I wonder who that is, Cerberus my love. Nurse Jackson is due so maybe it's her?"

The heavy wooden front door was pulled wide. A little black poodle yapped and ran excitedly around her legs. A stooped older woman with a number of colourful shawls around her shoulders appeared in the doorway, leaning on her stick. She moved over to let Barbara inside.

"Morning, Mrs Jenkins. Hello, Cerberus."

"Come on, Cerby. Let Nurse in now."

They made their slow way down the long corridor into a vibrant sitting room which ran the width of the house. The bright room was full of pots containing verdant rubber plants, spider plants and ferns. Tall glass patio doors opened onto the garden, showing the remnants of beautiful floral displays and an immaculately manicured lawn. The lower branches of the taller trees dipped down onto roses, echinacea and geraniums, with the rain dripping from the last remaining yellowing leaves. Down the side of the house was a Victorian greenhouse where the last few tomatoes, red bell peppers and other Mediterranean vegetables were growing. It was coming out of this greenhouse that Mrs Jenkins had slipped and cut her leg on a broken terracotta pot.

"So, Mrs Jenkins. How are you today? How's the leg?"

"It's still painful. And the wound is seeping a bit. The dressing looks a bit messy."

"Let me have a look, then. Sit here and put your foot up on this chair." Barbara knelt down and lifted the bottom hem of the heavy woollen skirt. "Are you feeling the cold, Mrs Jenkins? The weather has definitely changed this week."

"Yes, I am. I really dislike the winter months. Might see if I can go to the South of France again, once the bloody leg has healed."

Barbara unpacked her medical bag onto a small side table, then peeled off the old dressing with a pair of tweezers and dropped it into a metal pan next to her. "Oh, that doesn't look too good. Have you been taking the antibiotics the doctor prescribed?"

"I missed a day or two; they made my stomach upset. Couldn't, you know..." She lowered her voice. "...use the lavatory."

"Mrs Jenkins, that's why this cut isn't healing. You need to finish the course or the infection will come back. You'll have to start again now. I'll have a word with the doctor and this time, finish them all. All-Bran might help in the other department."

"I'm sorry to be so awkward, dear."

"It's fine. Right, I'm going to clean this up and put on a fresh dressing then I need to phone the doctor. Hopefully he'll get the prescription sorted so I can pick it up and drop it back later. Do you want me to get you some All-Bran while I'm at it?"

"Yes please, dear. Oh, and can you pass me that catalogue on the side table?"

"Right, here you go. Can I use the phone after you?"

Mrs Jenkins flipped deftly through the pages and stopped at the ladies' underwear section. Barbara stood up and walked across the large room to a door at the end which led into the kitchen where she could wash her hands and dispose of the soiled dressing. When she returned, Mrs Jenkins was on the phone.

"Oh hello, this is Mrs Gwendoline Jenkins from The Gatehouse, Dolgellau Road, Barmouth. I have an account with you. Yes, I'm a regular customer. I'd like two combinations." There was a pause, then, "Yes, that's right. Size fourteen. For delivery as soon as possible. Thank you so much." She replaced the receiver then turned to Barbara. "Great service; never use anyone else."

As she repacked her nurse's bag, Barbara hesitated then asked, "What's a combination?"

"It's an all-in-one undergarment. So comfortable—never worn anything else. Can't get on with this new-fangled two-piece malarkey. Harrods have always stocked them."

"Ah, okay." She shook her head almost imperceptibly, then asked, "Can I phone for your prescription now?"

"Yes of course, dear." She pushed the phone over. Barbara dialled the number while Mrs Jenkins perused other items in her catalogue. Barbara explained the situation to the person on the other end of the line then replaced the receiver with a click.

"All done."

"So, when will I see you next?"

"I'll pop in later with your new course of Penicillin and come back tomorrow to change your dressing. You really need to be more careful when you're gardening, Mrs Jenkins. You don't want any more injuries like this one."

"I know, dear. It was rather unfortunate that Cerberus got under my feet just at the wrong moment."

"Don't get up, I'll let myself out. Cheerio, Cerberus." The old dog under her chair moaned softly in his sleep. "See you later, Mrs Jenkins." Barbara shut the door behind her.

---0---

In the tiny, windowless staffroom at the surgery, Barbara was sitting at the table with Hazel, the new English nurse. They had thirty minutes' lunch break and unusually they were taking it together. She took a bite of her egg sandwich as Hazel unwrapped her Scotch egg. There were two cups of steaming tea in front of them.

"I've never heard of combinations. Have you, Hazel?"

"Yeah, I think my grandmother used to wear them but eventually gave up on them because they're so difficult to get on when you get older. You have to put your legs in then sort of roll them up from your bum over your tummy and lift your boobs in before putting the straps over your shoulder."

"What a lot of hassle; sounds like getting into a swimming costume."

"Well yes, a bit like that but tighter. Holds everything in."

"Like a girdle or a corset then?"

"Sort of. I'm amazed you can still get them, even from Harrods." Hazel took a sip of tea. "I'm surprised Mrs Jenkins can manage up there in that huge house on her own!"

"She's a tough old bird that one. Talking about going to the South of France for the winter. Wouldn't that be nice?"

"Oh yes. A bit of sun on your face would be fantastic."

"Better than cycling around in the wind and rain here for sure."

"Yeah, definitely."

Barbara chewed thoughtfully, then said, "I heard about your Cathy. What an old bag that Mrs Llewellyn is!"

"I know, it broke my heart. Poor Cathy was devastated; didn't want to go back to school. She thought all the others would pick on her."

"Oh, poor lass."

"Good of your father-in-law to offer to teach her Welsh though."

"Yeah, Owen's got a heart of gold. Always helping someone or other. Takes me to the places I can't get to on my bike and all sorts. Shame his son didn't inherit any of his kindness." Barbara dropped her head and touched the pocket of her uniform.

"Are you all right, Babs? Has something happened?"

She glared, her eyes heavy, then words tumbled out in a torrent of anger and disappointment. "My fucking husband has been playing around with some bimbo. She wrote to him! The bloody gall of it! Wrote a fucking love letter to my fucking husband at the garage. That means he must've taken her there. Oh God! What an utter arse!" She thrust her hand into her pocket and pulled out the pink envelope with hearts drawn in red ink on the outside and slammed it on the table.

"Oh God, I'm sorry, Babs. What are you going to do?" Hazel handed her a handkerchief with purple flowers embroidered around the edges.

"I don't know, Hazel. I've been carrying this around for over a week now. You're the first person I've told." Barbara sniffed and blew her nose. "I'm sorry to spill all this on you, I hardly know you."

"It's fine, it's often easier to tell someone you don't know well. Like you're trying out the words and see how they land."

"That's certainly true, isn't it?" Barbara picked up her cup. "It was Isabella. She noticed something was up—told me I had a secret that needed telling. She must be a witch!" Barbara laughed, the sound cracking rather than tinkling.

"She can probably just recognise hurt, Babs, having been through it herself, that's all." Hazel reached across the table and stroked her colleague's hand. "Look, you need to talk to your husband. It'll be tough, but it has to be done. But you'll need support. Have you got any family around here?"

Barbara shook her head. "My mum and dad are still in Glasgow."

"Do you think they'd come and stay for a bit?"

"I suppose I could ask them. They've not been to stay for a while. It'll be a help with the boys, too. Dai is getting fed up with taking them to school."

"Well, that's a plan. You always need a plan. The worst thing about big conversations is starting them and the next part is following through with your decisions. When you get home, phone your mum and dad, get them to come and stay as soon as possible. Once she's here, you can talk to Dai."

"You're so sensible, Hazel. Thank you. I really need a good friend at the moment. I've been here ten years and I only really socialise with the mothers from school on the odd occasion. That's why I decided to start working again."

"Well, I'm in the same boat on the friends front, so let's stick together, shall we?"

"Thanks, I needed this chat." Barbara looked up at the clock. "Shit, we need to get back to work!"

They leapt up, straightened their uniforms, pushed their hair into their caps, and fixed smiles on their faces.

"Right, let's do it!" Hazel said, linking arms as the two nurses walked out together into the surgery.

CHAPTER 9

Dai

Dai opened the back door and stepped into the cold, throwing his bag over his shoulder. Walking down the stone pathway and turning right onto the main road, he saw faint glimmering lights through the curtains in the other houses built on the cliff. Cosy families tucked up with their loved ones. He wondered why he had never been contented with family life; why he had wrecked his own marriage with the temptation of younger skin and a pert bottom. It began to drizzle, so he put his head down and walked along the abandoned road towards the Pendragon Arms.

He pushed the door open. Immediately, a fuggy wave of stale beer and cigarettes washed over him. He walked through the narrow doorway and made his way across the floor to the bar. A group of young men were playing darts down one side of the bar; he recognised one of them as his brother. He went over to the bar.

"You'll right, Bryn?"

"Yeah fine, Dai. What're you doing here on a Tuesday?"

"Long story mate but seems I've been chucked out. She's got her mum and dad down from Glasgow for the week."

"What the... What've you done now?"

"Let me get a drink and I'll tell you about it." Dai turned to face the attractive young barmaid. "I'll have a pint of your finest ale please, love."

"Banks do you?" smiled the barmaid, her dark eyes moody and suggestive.

"Yes please, love."

"Here you go, love." She handed him a thick dark pint with just the hint of a head. Her fingers deliberately touched his as she turned the label on the glass to the front. He smiled at her.

"Come and sit over here with us, Dai. We're in the middle of a game. My turn next."

Bryn led him round to a rectangular table. Three pints of beer and a few empty packs of crisps and nuts stood on it.

"You'll right, Dai?" asked one of the men.

"Yeah fine. You, mate?"

Dai sat on a stool and watched as his brother hit an eighteen, then a double twenty and finally a six. Bryn thumped one hand into another and walked over to sit opposite him.

"That was my last turn. So, Dai. What's occurred?"

"She found a bloody letter, didn't she? I had a little encounter over the summer, one of them women who came on the trip from Birmingham. We were right discreet while it was going on. I took her off in the van, with a few blankets in the back."

"What are you like, Dai?" Bryn shook his head and took a sip of beer.

"It was just a bit of fun. She didn't know I was married, and Babs never suspected a thing. Then the stupid woman goes all soppy and sends me a letter, to the garage. Well, Babs pops in one day last week and finds the pink envelope with love hearts drawn all over it, and my name on the front and well, course she gets all uppity."

"You idiot, Dai! Why can't you just be happy with what you've got? Babs is lovely—she doesn't deserve this. And your kids, poor old Danny and George. They'll be broken-hearted."

"I'm just not cut out to be a married man. Not like you. You should've been the one to get married, not me."

"That might well be, but you're the one in a mess now, aren't you? What's Da gonna say? He'll be so upset. Why can't you just keep your dick in your underpants? All these people you've hurt for the sake of a quick shag. What is wrong with you?"

"Don't get your knickers in a twist, Bryn. This is my problem, not yours. I'll deal with it, all right?"

"So where are you staying tonight? And after that? No room at Da's anymore. Our bunk beds are long gone. That room's mine." He exhaled and shook his head, his exasperation clearly visible.

"Don't you think you need to consider moving out? You're older than me and still living at home."

"Don't twist it and start on me, Dai." Bryn took a gulp of his beer and turned to watch as the last of his team members took his turn. There was a cheer and round of applause as they won the match.

"Looks like you've won. Doing well in the league?"

"Yeah, we've won four in a row now."

"So will you tell Da for me? Surprised he's not in here tonight."

"Absolutely not, Dai. You can do that yourself. And he's gone up to that English couple to teach the little one some Welsh. Guess he stayed for dinner."

"That's nice, getting himself invited for dinner."

"He doesn't do it for a free dinner, Dai. He does it 'cos he's a good man. Likes to help out where it's needed."

"I suppose." Dai drained his glass, turned towards the blonde-haired barmaid and nodded.

She brought another pint over and placed it carefully on the round mat. "Here you go, love." Her breast brushed his shoulder lightly and a smile whispered across her pink lips. She collected the empties and swayed back to the bar.

"Seriously Dai? Already?" Bryn sighed and shook his head.

"What? Can't help it if women like me, can I?"

"I'm off. See you at the garage tomorrow." Bryn shrugged on his old donkey jacket and pulled a red woollen hat over his

69

ears. "And you need to tell Da before he finds out from someone else. You know what it's like around here."

"Yeah, I'll tell him tomorrow."

Dai stood up, picked up his bag, and headed over to sit on the bar stool where the barmaid was still smiling. She leaned forward and he caught a glimpse of her black lacy bra, heavy breasts resting on the bar. He imagined holding them in his hands, feeling her nipples between his fingers. He leaned forward, holding his palms upwards, and smiled as his groin clenched.

"So, Dai, what you doing in here on your own on this cold, windy night?" she asked.

"I need a room for a few nights, Bethan. Had a bit of a to-do with the missus. Giving us some space."

"Deary me, that's unfortunate. Hold on. I'll get a key." She disappeared out through the back of the bar. He noticed her very rounded behind, just like a ripe peach encased in a tight pair of jeans. She was definitely wiggling it for his benefit. He smiled at the thought then stood up, downed the remainder of his pint, picked up his bag, and walked round the back of the bar where the smiling Bethan was expecting him.

"Shall I show you to your room?" she invited.

"That would be perfect, thank you..."

He followed her up the stairs and along the corridor. Her long blonde ponytail swished from side to side, mesmerising him. She stopped at a door halfway along on the left, bent over, then slid the key into the lock. The door swung open and he pushed her inside, kicking the door closed behind him with his foot. He dropped his bag and pushed her against the wall. Their mouths met and hands fumbled at each other's bodies.

Bethan pulled herself away. "Oh God, I have to get back to the bar," she panted. "We'll finish this later." With that, she pulled her blouse straight, hoicked her breasts into her bra, wiped her mouth and pulled her ponytail back into position. "I'll leave you here to get yourself sorted." She looked down and smiled at his crotch where a small tent had been erected.

Dai watched her leave and shut the door behind her. He'd definitely have a bit of that later. Bethan had always been available, and more importantly, married, so not likely to blab about their occasional encounters. He plonked down on the lumpy double bed and looked around the room. It was acceptable: a wooden wardrobe with one door, a small chipboard chest of drawers, a sink in the corner. The toilet must be down the corridor—not ideal, but if he played his cards right, he wouldn't be here long.

The curtains were pulled halfway across a sash window. He stood up and walked over to look out. It was dark but he could see the yard below full of beer barrels and a battered old Ford Escort—that must be Bethan's, well, her husband's actually. He'd replaced the alternator just that week. Beyond that was the outline of the railway station where holiday makers arrived full of expectation, and where Trisha had arrived that summer. Foolish woman, what was she thinking writing to him? Farther out, the reflection of the pale moonlight on the sea was just visible. The inconstant moon, that was exactly what he was: inconstant and changing.

Alone in this room, his thoughts turned to Babs and how they had met. He'd been on a stag do with some mates in Glasgow. Goodness knows why they'd chosen that city. They'd been out in the pubs during the day and later at the club, he spotted a tall, brunette woman with sultry eyes and a way about her which transfixed him. She told him she was doing her nursing training, in her final year, then the world would be her oyster. A few Babychams later and she was under him in his hotel room, panting and moaning. He grinned at the thought. Shame the passion didn't last long. Trapped by her pregnancy and shamed by her nagging letters, he had to do something. Da hadn't helped once he'd found out about it, insisting Dai invite her to

71

Barmouth. Then he had to marry her, Da said. It was 'the right thing to do'. Once they were married, and especially after George was born, she was stuck with him, and him with her. Didn't matter what he did, they had no way out. Well, that's what he'd thought until this particular transgression. The letter gave her all the evidence she needed and she'd undoubtedly use that against him. Then he changed his mindset.

I'll win her over and be back at home in no time. She'll forgive me. She'll have to; she's got nowhere to go.

His thoughts were interrupted by a knock on the door. He grinned and opened it. Bethan stood squarely in front of him. The top three buttons of her blouse were undone, and her big amber eyes were blazing. Without saying a word, she planted her forearm across his chest, and leaning forwards, marched into the room, propelling him backwards. She kicked the door shut behind her.

Dai had no option but to go where he was pushed. He stumbled against the bed and fell across it on his back. She jumped up astride him, sitting heavily on his upper thighs and leaning forward to grind her hips into his groin. His cock sprang to attention in his trousers and he pushed back against her. "Argh," he growled, "where have you been, my Bethan?"

Her eyes widened. "Trying..." Her breasts rose in front of his face as she heaved in a breath. "...to pretend you don't matter to me anymore."

He reached up, flicked her remaining blouse buttons undone with practised ease. He stretched around her back and in one single-handed movement, unclasped her bra. As her breasts swung free, he caught them, caressing and tickling each erect nipple with his tongue. Meanwhile he ran his fingers lightly down her sides to grasp her shapely backside and pull her tightly against his swelling erection. As she arched her back, he glanced up to see her head tilt back and her eyes close. He smiled to himself. He hadn't forgotten how to press her buttons.

Bethan fell on him hungrily, then rearranged herself in order to pull at his belt and drag his jeans off over his hips. She panted and licked her lips as she sat upright to undo her own. Dai flipped her on to her back and she wriggled free of the denim, now lying with her legs apart; her rounded, nakedness waiting for him.

"Oh bliss!" he said, burying himself inside her body.

CHAPTER 10

Shirley

"I never trusted Dai. Didn't like the way he made our Babs come and live here and not the other way round. She'd have been so much better off at home, closer to us."

"So you've been telling me for the last ten years, Shirley love."

"Yes, but I was right, wasn't I, Douglas? See what's happened now? I knew he was a bad one."

"Well, we just need to support her and the lads now."

"She's going to need all the help and support she can get. It's not easy bringing up kids on your own, especially when you work."

"Don't you tell her she needs to stop. It's what keeps her going."

Barbara's parents had just dropped their grandsons off at school and were walking into the town along the beach. It was a clear crisp morning. The tide was out so the water was a good hundred yards out. The weak sun reflected off the distant sea and the light sand of the wide beach. A few dogwalkers were strolling in the damp sand, leaving momentary footprints as they stepped round the scrabbling crabs and mounds of seaweed, some desiccated, some still slimy with seawater.

In the distance, they could see an old man walking with a black and white dog. As they got closer, Douglas recognised the stoop, the woollen hat and the coat. He waved and beckoned the other man over.

"Who's that you're waving at?"

"It's Owen, Babs's father-in-law."

"Oh right, so it is. Didn't recognise him without my glasses. What's his dog called, again?"

"Dewi. And here he is." Douglas rubbed the top of Dewi's head as the dog appeared beside them. "Hello boy, you're a lovely fella, aren't you?" Dewi looked up then ran off to chase a group of seagulls.

Owen approached. "Morning to you both. Grand morning it is, too. Just dropped the lads off, have you like?"

"Yes, our Babs was out early to see that Mrs Jenkins in the big house, then she's going up to Mrs Cartwright, you know the one who came off her motorbike? That's an odd story, isn't it?"

"Yes, it is like. Me and Dewi found her in the woods. Lucky I was walking there that morning. Don't usually go that way."

"Poor woman. Babs said she's up and about though, bossing her husband around!"

"Nothing new there then!" Douglas laughed. Shirley shot him a stare. He raised his eyebrows and said, "What? I'm only stating a fact, men do what women tell them to do."

"True enough," added Owen. "Miss my wife though like. You probably remember she passed a few years back. The house feels right empty without her around. Even with Bryn still at home, but he's often out of an evening." He looked wistfully towards the little bridge crossing the estuary in the distance. The three parents continued along the beach, admiring the glorious view and clement weather. Shirley finally broached the subject hanging heavily between them.

"Owen. Please come and see the boys soon, they need both their grandads at the moment. Especially as their dad isn't so keen on coming to the house while we're there."

"That's hardly any big surprise. I should apologise for my son, Dai. He's not made me proud with this latest escapade of his."

"No, I can't imagine he has. But it's not going to be easy for any of them. They'll just have to find a way to work it out."

76

"That they will. Anyroad, how long you two here for? Good of you to come all this way."

"That's what me and her mum are here for," said Douglas. "Plus, we love to spend time with the grandkids. Shame the circumstances aren't brighter."

"We're happy to support Babs for as long as she needs us. But please, come round whenever you want and bring Bryn. In fact, why don't you come for dinner tonight?"

"I'd love to but tonight I'm up at the English couple's house. Teaching the little girls some Welsh."

"Oh yes, George told us about her and the mean teacher. Good of you to help out, Owen. Babs always said that it was hard getting accepted in this town at first. They must really appreciate your help, don't you think, Douglas?"

"What? Yeah. Good of you, Owen."

"She's a tough one, that Mrs Llewellyn. Been teaching at the school for years, since just after the war, after she lost her own boys, I reckon. She must be in her seventies. I heard say that this is her last year, and she'd retire, like."

"Blimey, that is a long time. Lost her sons, you say? That must've been so hard. I can't imagine what it's like to lose a child, let alone both of them." Shirley sighed heavily. "We need to be a bit more understanding, I suppose."

"Sounds like that Mrs Llewellyn's had a tough life," Douglas added.

"She were my Bryn and Dai's teacher. Tough, even all them years ago. Husband died a few years back. School's her life. Don't care to think what she'll do each day without it."

"I feel sorry for her. Hope she finds something to fill her days when she leaves. I know what it's like when you first retire, looking around for hobbies to fill the days. Waiting for your children to invite you stay. We'd be here all the time if Babs would let us, wouldn't we, Douglas?"

"Yes dear. But they have their own lives now; Babs has a sister and a brother. They're all married with kids. It's a shame Babs moved away. The boys have four cousins around the same age."

"Oh right. Big family like, that's nice." Owen nodded.

"Well let's do dinner tomorrow instead then and let Bryn know he's welcome to come and see his nephews too," said Shirley quickly.

"We'll definitely be there and thank you, Shirley. Best to show the boys that they're loved. This really isn't a good situation." Owen shook his head sadly and threw a ball he'd just found in his pocket. Dewi raced after it, brought it back, and dropped it with a thud in the sand. He picked it up and shook off a glob of spittle as his dog tried to grab it from his hand. They reached the bottom of the steps up to the road. Owen looked out across the water. "Tide's on the turn now, it'll be right up to these steps shortly."

"We'd better get off the beach then!" said Douglas, as the three of them climbed up the steep, concrete steps, the dog weaving between them.

Owen leaned on his stick and looked up towards the mountain sitting protectively around his small seaside town. "I love this place. Lived here all my life; only leave if I have to."

"I can see why. It's beautiful in a rugged sort of way. Better than living in the big city. Glasgow gets busier by the year, doesn't it, Douglas?"

"What?"

"I said Glasgow's getting too busy, so many people and the traffic."

"Yes, but Glasgow's my home though. Can't imagine living anywhere else."

"I'm not asking you to, love. Just agreeing with Owen that's it's nice here. Quiet; a pleasant change from the noise and pollution of a city."

Together they walked past the amusement arcade and over the railway tracks at the level crossing, heading up past the shoe and toy shops. At the junction with the high street, Shirley and Douglas needed to turn right. Owen would head up the path that led to his house on the hill.

"Well, Owen, it's good to talk to you again and remember, dinner tomorrow night, around six. The boys will love to have us all together."

"Cheerio, Douglas, Shirley." Owen walked slowly up the road with Dewi following obediently at his heel.

Shirley turned to her husband. "We need to pick up some things for Babs. She needs all the help she can get at the moment. What do you fancy for dinner?"

CHAPTER 11

Isabella

Isabella was sitting at the kitchen table, methodically chopping carrots in preparation for a chicken pie. An unopened letter lay on the table, urging her to deal with it. The handwriting was familiar and the postmark brought reminders of a job, a home and a daughter. She'd ignored the envelope since Owen had dropped it off with the washing. A rhythmic thud of axe on wood drifted from outside the door as Jim chopped logs for the stove and fire. She carefully slid the carrots from the chopping board into a pan and started on the onion. The first incision made her eyes water. She sniffed hard and slumped in her chair. She pulled herself up straight and continued to slice, each stroke of the knife peeling away another layer of her self-conviction. *Why did Susan do it? I've lost my best friend and my husband.* As she slid the onion into the pan, the sound of an engine reached her, followed by the slamming of a door then voices.

"Hello, Jim. How are you today?"

"I'm fine, thank you, Nurse Jackson."

"I presume Isabella is home."

"Yes, in kitchen. You all right, Owen?"

"Yeah, thanks, Jim. You been chopping a bit of wood there?"

"For the winter. Gets bloody cold up 'ere."

"Right, you are there."

There was a knock and she heard Nurse Barbara. "Can I come in, Isabella?"

"Door's open."

Barbara's tall, slim figure appeared in the doorway, wrapped in her navy-blue woollen cloak. Isabella watched her closely as she tucked a strand of hair into the bun under a starched, white cap and gently bit her bottom lip, smudging the perfectly applied lipstick. As Barbara walked into the room, she unclipped the cloak and swished it off with a flash of red and folded it over the back of the other chair. She placed a bag of books on the end of the table.

"Hello, Isabella. Brought you some more library books. There's another crossword magazine in there too."

"Thank you, Babs. I've finished the last lot."

"How are you feeling today?"

"Better. My body works again and as you can see…" she indicated the carrots and onions now in the pan, "…I'm back to normal in the kitchen department."

"Well, I just need to have a look at that bruise. Can you make it to the bedroom to lie down?"

Isabella held tightly onto the side of the table and pushed herself up into a standing position. A walking stick clattered from the back of the chair to the floor.

"Let me get that." Barbara bent over, picked up the stick and held it in place. Isabella put out one hand and placed it on the curved handle then tentatively pulled herself into position.

"You're making great progress. You could hardly stand upright last time I saw you. Can you walk on your own?"

Isabella lifted each foot and took slow, definite steps forward, "Yes, I can. I'm a bit clunky but I can walk with the stick fine."

In the bedroom, Isabella heaved herself onto the bed and turned onto her left side. Barbara rubbed her hands together to warm them up, then lifted the edge of Isabella's dress.

"That's so much better. The arnica has helped but even so I'm really surprised how quickly it's healed. Have you had a look?"

"Yes, I have. It's not pretty, is it? All yellow and green. How long before it's gone completely?"

"I'd say another few weeks. Sadly, as you get older, these things take longer."

"Humph. Getting older's not for the faint-hearted, is it?"

"But you've got the experience and the memories." Barbara bit her lip as Isabella tensed. She pulled Isabella's dress back down briskly. "How's the pain?"

"In my leg? Bearable. In my heart, less so." She paused as she sat up again and reached for the stick. "She sent me a letter, you know."

"You mean the other woman?"

"Yes, Susan." Isabella stressed the name with pursed lips.

"So, what did it say?"

"Don't know. Haven't opened it. Don't want a lot of old excuses."

"It might be worth reading. Understanding the reasons might make you a bit more forgiving."

"Like you, you mean?"

"What do you mean, Isabella?"

"Gossip drifts about in a small place like this: you never know who'll hear it. Especially about us interlopers. Jim picks up bits when he's out and about town."

"What have you heard?" Barbara whispered.

"That your husband's moved out. They say he's behaved badly. I know what that's like, Babs. How it can break a heart into a thousand pieces."

Barbara breathed in sharply through her nose, then exhaled loudly. "You're right. Each day is like walking through treacle, but I've still got a job to do, so let's get you back to the kitchen and I'll be off. I don't think you need to see me again. The leg is healing nicely. You don't need any more painkillers and you're almost back to normal."

"Thank you for all you've done, Babs. It's been good to have a woman to talk to, even if it's only a couple times a week." They made their way slowly to the kitchen and Isabella hobbled to the wooden chair, leaning her stick against the table. Barbara went to the sink and pumped some water to wash her hands.

"It's my job. But I enjoy this part of it the most. Getting to know new, interesting people like you. I'm just so sorry about the circumstances. These men have a lot to answer for. We're simply their playthings. We're interesting for a while, then they chuck us aside when a new toy comes along."

"Very true, and it rips you in half being betrayed by people you love and trust." Isabella plonked herself in a chair and let out an extended sigh. "They can't all be like that. There must be some good ones out there." She looked out of the window at Jim and Owen chatting amiably. "Your father-in-law, for one. He's always doing someone a favour. That kindness is deep in his heart; strong like the mountains, he is."

"Yeah, Owen is a good man. And he's helping out with the boys so much now Dai's moved out. And his other son, Bryn, they're both being so kind."

Isabella looked up sharply. "Single men circle like piranhas once they hear of a hurt woman."

"I'm sure Bryn's a good man—got more of his dad's genes than my rotten husband has. I definitely found the wrong brother. Bryn's such a sweetheart. Gets on with my mam and dad too." Isabella studied Barbara's face as it lightened and her voice lifted.

"That may well be, but tread carefully."

Defiance, authority, and confidence seeped out of Barbara one at a time and her head dropped. "You're right. I'm just so hurt that any attention from a man makes me feel better."

"I'm sure it does, but this is your husband's brother you're talking about. That won't end well."

"I know. You're absolutely right. I need to..." Barbara's chin sank to her chest and her shoulders rounded, "...stop it before it starts, I suppose."

"Yes, you probably do. Now say it like you mean it."

Barbara sighed and picked up her bag while Isabella looked at the books on the table.

"I've not read this one," Isabella said, to break the awkward silence. She picked up a book and turned it over to read the back cover, then flicked through the pages. "I'll start it after dinner."

"Sounds like a good way to spend your evening."

"I'd rather be out dancing, but well, you know."

Barbara looked at her watch and shifted from one foot to the other. "Are you going to read that letter then?" She nodded to the envelope just visible under the bag of books on the kitchen table.

"I need to have a glass of something strong before I do that."

"Well, now you've finished your painkillers, that's allowed. Just be careful on your pins afterwards."

"I will. Now you do what I said, Babs, and don't go doing anything silly with Bryn or you'll be the one accused of cheating. I know what people in small communities can be like, they love to blame the woman."

"Thank you, Isabella, I'll remember that." Barbara picked up her cloak and the previous week's library books, opened the door and stepped outside into the weak sunshine.

The tones of her husband's voice saying goodbye to Owen and Babs drifted in as Isabella picked up the letter. She turned it over methodically before sliding it into her pocket. She would look at it later.

In the meantime, she needed to get this pie baked. She put the bag of books on the floor, stood up and made her way to the dresser. She pulled out a mixing bowl followed by a battered old McDougall's flour tin from the cupboard, then swung round to put them on the table. She clonked her way to the Belfast, pulled back the pink and white striped curtain to take the butter and lard from the slate underneath, then once more swung round to place it on the table. She looked around the room, opening the drawers of the dresser, looking for a rolling pin. *Where would he put it? Has he even got one up here? I doubt it, I'll just use an old bottle*. Keeping busy kept her mind away from the contents of the letter. Once that was opened, the words would be free as birds ready to nest in her heart and mind.

She heard a whoosh as the axe firmly embedded in a log, then all sound of chopping ceased. Jim pushed open the front door and wiped his feet. She noticed that touch; he was trying so hard to please her, now. She smiled thinly as she expertly measured out the flour, then cut the butter and lard into cubes.

"Y'all right, love?" he asked, as he stooped to get through the open doorway and made his way to the sink to wash his hands.

"Yes dear. Just making a chicken pie for dinner. Doing the pastry now. Have you got a rolling pin up here?"

"A rolling pin? Why would I need one of those?" He chuckled as he lifted the pump handle for some water. "I can make you one, if you like."

"No, it's fine, I need it now. I'll just use an old bottle. Can you find me one and give it a quick wash?"

Jim wiped his hands dry and bent down to look underneath the sink. He pulled out a brown bottle and washed it carefully in the bowl, wiped it dry and placed it on the table in front of his wife. "This do you?"

"Thank you, dear. Can you put the kettle on? I'm gasping for a cuppa. Oh, and light the stove for this pie, please." Isabella kneaded the pastry into a ball and tipped it out onto the floured surface using the beer bottle to roll it flat. "Oh no, I've just realised you haven't got a pie dish have you!" Tears filled Isabella's eyes as she looked up at her husband.

"I dunno, love. Not summat I use." He looked away, tears were outside his capability. He sat down heavily in a kitchen chair.

Isabella had watched his every move so often throughout their years of marriage, but only now, sitting in that chair in that

86

kitchen, did she realise she knew so little about him. She wondered how this man whom she knew so well had changed so much given the option of a different pair of knickers. Her frustration and anger flew out of her mouth like dirty dishwater.

"What am I going to do? I've made the pastry now. What a waste! You're a waste. This is all your fault, you stupid man." Isabella sobbed and rested her head on the table in front of her, making indents in the pastry with her hands.

Jim stood up, then swayed backwards and forwards, deciding eventually to step towards his wife. He stood next to her and placed his hand on her back. "It's okay, love, I can go into Woollies in town and get you one."

"Oh, you stupid idiot! It's not about the pie dish. It's about us. I just want to go back to normal. Go back home as if nothing ever happened." She lifted her head slightly from the table and looked up at his side. From under her arm, his chin was just visible. Tiny bits of sawdust were attached to the bristles.

Jim quickly pulled his hand away from her back, noticing the flour in her hair. "We can go back if you want. You're all better now. We can close up the cottage, get in the car and drive home. Together." He touched her hand, picking a bit of pastry from her ring finger.

"It'll never be right though, Jim." She moved her hand away. "Everyone knows what you did. I'm not ready for you and me to be together, not at home, not in our house. Maybe I never will be."

"Whatever you think is best, Bella. I'll do whatever. Just want us to be together." He sighed loudly.

"Just go and get me a pie dish, Jim."

CHAPTER 12

Jim

Jim climbed into his purple and grey Hillman Minx. This definitely was not his first choice but it was all they had at the garage back in Bromwich. He put his foot hard on the clutch and negotiated it into reverse, then glanced behind him to see the rear window was misted up. He got out, leaned into the back seat and wiped it clear with a long sigh. Climbing back into the driver's seat, he turned the car around with a crunch on the stones. With another grinding push it was in first gear and he moved slowly away down the mud track onto the main road and into Barmouth. His sighs were deep and heavy, bursting out every time he hit a pothole or drove over a hump. He thought of his wife's tears and her loaded words boring into him like midge bites.

What have I done? Irene thinks I'm an idiot, Bella hates me. At least our Freddie don't know anything—not yet, at least. And Susan, well Susan, least said soonest mended on that front. What a complete pillock I've been!

He passed Nurse Jackson on her bike coming out of Mrs Jenkins' drive and gave a little toot. She wobbled a bit, straightened up holding her handlebars tightly, and smiled. *She's a lovely looking woman. Shame that husband of hers is such a cheating bastard. Just like me.*

Luckily, there was a space outside Woollies, so he pulled in neatly and climbed out of the car, nearly bumping into an older gentleman with grey hair poking out from under a flat cap.

"Sorry about that," the old man said. "I didn't see you there." A Scottish accent.

"My fault, wasn't looking," Jim replied. He looked the man up and down. "You're not from round these parts, are you?"

"No, just here for a while with my wife, visiting my daughter and grandsons. You sound like you're a Midlander."

"West Bromwich. Got a holiday cottage up in Bontddu."

"Don't know the names of places round here, but are you the one whose wife came off her moped?"

"That's right." Jim took a step closer to the entrance of Woolworth's. "I need to get off."

"Nice to meet you."

"Bye."

Jim hurried through the shop doors, turning briefly to see the man staring at him quizzically. *Bloody hell, does everyone know?*

Jim shook his head to dislodge the thought, then looked around at the unfamiliar setting. Shopping wasn't his strong suit. Until he moved here on his own, Bella usually did it all, presenting him new socks and underpants just as his were going home; a new shirt for a presentation evening at the club; even her own birthday presents. He bought the card and wrapped what she bought but that was all.

He walked uncomfortably up and down the aisles hoping to find what he needed. He passed the pick 'n' mix surrounded by children with their paper bags grabbing and snatching at metal tongs and spoons. Then past the mothers picking up the children's clothes with the Ladybird logo on the racks. He was a man out of place here. At the end of the aisle was a woman in a uniform.

"Excuse me. Where's the pie dishes?"

"What my lovely? Pie dish for cooking like?"

"Yeah, that's right."

"You going to cook pie, are you?" She laughed.

"No, it's for my wife."

"She's gonna love you for that. They're down the next aisle with all the cooking stuff."

"Ta."

He walked briskly to the place indicated. There was too wide a selection. He picked up a round glass dish with fluted edges and pursed his lips thoughtfully. *Too fragile.* He put it back on the shelf. He picked up a rectangular, white metal tray with blue edging, wondering if it would be the right size. He ran his hand across the middle, thinking he could eat that much pie. Just as the decision was made, his eye was caught by a brown circular dish. They had one like that at home. He exchanged it quickly and headed to the till with a smile. Bella would be pleased.

With his proud purchase in his possession, Jim clambered back into his car and turned around to go back home. As he waited at the junction by the harbour, he watched a couple walking under the railway bridge, having what appeared to be a heated discussion. Suddenly, the man stopped, turned and took the woman's face in both hands. With a flash of blonde locks, she also turned and he kissed her full on the mouth. Jim saw the back of a dark-haired head and black Harrington jacket. He smiled knowingly.

There was a beep from behind. He quickly put the car into gear and drove away, shaking the thought of infidelity from his mind. How was he going to fix his own marriage? Bella seemed to suggest it couldn't be fixed. The questions buzzed like flies around the interior of the car and he tried to bat them away. Bumping back up the track, he hoped Bella had recovered from her earlier outburst. It was very unlike her. She was usually independent, calm and unemotional. He liked that about her. This was a very different Bella, one he would have to get used to all over again.

"Y'all right, love? I'm back. I got the pie dish," he called from the front door as he wiped his feet. There was no response. "Bella?"

He looked in the kitchen, put the pie dish on the table which was now clear of the earlier baking debris. He turned to go the other way into the sitting room, stooping as he went. Bella was lying face up on the settee with her head on the orange cushion from the rocking chair in the kitchen. The old cream blanket—now clean and fresh after its trip to the launderette—was over her. His first thought was Owen. He was good to them, seeing as he hardly knew them, taking their dirty washing, bringing the Nurse, and their post, up from the town. He looked again at Bella: her arm was dangling towards the floor. On the old rug was an envelope, the stamp and an address facing upwards. His eyes were drawn to another more ominous piece of paper in her small hand.

"Bella?"

"I've had a letter from that Susan. Very enlightening. You'd better get me a stiff drink."

Jim blanched, then stiffened his back ready for the inevitable onslaught. He'd hoped he'd got away with the worst of it. His resolve faltered as he looked at down his small, vulnerable wife. Shame worked its way from the soles of his feet up through his body, finally reaching his face where it blossomed in big red patches on his cheeks.

"Well, go on then," Bella said. "A big whisky should do it." She stared at him impassively. He felt her eyes willing him away.

He crept out of her line of vision and returned a few moments later with two mugs containing the caramel-coloured liquid. He handed one to Bella who sat up and took a glug, screwing up her face as she swallowed. He put the other on the windowsill and returned to the kitchen for a chair. He sat on it heavily, swilling the whisky around in his mug. Seconds clicked past, and neither of them spoke. Jim gave in first.

"So, what did she say?"

"It was going on more than six months, Jim. Started before Christmas she says. Here, I'll read you a bit: *It had only just started, so obviously me and Jim tried to keep it from you at Christmas dinner. The kids and your mum and dad were there.*"

Bella looked up at Jim's face; he was looking down into his drink. She continued reading from the letter, her voice gradually rising in pitch and tone. *"I tried to stop so many times, honest I did Bella. I never wanted it to start but once it did, it was like I was addicted, I couldn't stop."* Bella exhaled loudly and shook her head. "Oh and here's the best bit, Jim. *All those years but I've been so lonely, watching you and Jim so settled and happy, I just wanted a bit of what you had.* Anything to say to that, Jim?"

A silence settled on the room. Neither spoke. Bella took a glug from her drink and Jim continued to stare into his. Finally, he spoke, barely more than a mumble.

"I thought it were best if I didn't tell you. Thought it might hurt more." He took a sip from his mug.

"Well, look at you, not wanting to hurt me more. The truth might have helped. I thought it was a one off, you and she going to the pictures while I was working late. But no, you've been having it off with my best friend for more than six sodding months. You're a bastard, Jim."

She downed the remainder of her whisky, inspected the mug carefully, then launched it inexpertly across the room at him. It landed a good foot short and rolled onto its side, balancing on the handle. She then turned her back to him leaning on her good hip and buried her head in the cushion.

Jim stood up, walked over the settee and picked up the letter from the floor where Bella had dropped it. He read it to himself.

Please forgive me Bella. You're my best friend. We've known each other since we started at the same school, do you remember? We were two little girls in pig tails and short dresses.

He could hear sniffles coming from the cushion and remorse overwhelmed him. "What are we going to do, Bella?"

"Just sod off. If you want to do something useful, get me another drink." Her voice was muffled.

"What about the pie?"

She sat up again, her face red and swollen, her eyes puffy. She really didn't look like his Bella. "Oh, for crying out loud, Jim, do you really think I give a monkey's about a pie? Just get me a drink."

"You need to take it steady, love. You're not used to this stuff and it's only five o'clock."

"Oh, so now you care about me, do you? I just want to go home, Jim. I'm going to drink your whisky tonight and tomorrow you're going to drive me home. What you do then is your own business. Now, just get me that drink."

Jim retrieved the mug and walked into the kitchen with his head drooped. His stomach was full of lead as he opened the bread bin and took out the remainder of a loaf, placed it on the board with a knife. Tears pricked behind his eyes as he opened the curtain under the sink and took a lump of cheese. On a plate on the dresser, there were two overripe tomatoes. His mouth was dry as he added those to the board on the table with the cheese. His heart was weighed down as he got two plates and two knives from the dresser. Carrying his guilt and remorse, he walked back into the sitting room.

"We're gonna have a spot of dinner, soak up that whisky."

"Why do you care?"

"Bella, I've been a bastard, as you put it, but I still love you and care for you."

Her face crumpled again, but she held out her hands, "Help me up."

Bella watched as Jim devoured four thick slices of the wholemeal loaf, both tomatoes and most of the cheese. He watched as she chewed slowly, as if the food were corrugated cardboard in her mouth. Except for the sound of jaws moving and teeth grinding, there was silence. Suddenly, Bella drew in a breath and exhaled it with the words, "Anyway, how did she know where to send her bloody letter?"

"Bella, don't get yourself worked up."

"Don't speak to me like a child Jim. How did she know?"

He exhaled heavily. "Before you got here, I wrote to her to tell her that I wanted to break it off. She knows about this cottage and must've seen the postmark. She only needed to send it to the post office in Barmouth and everyone knows we're up here. That's probably how Owen knew to bring it."

"So, you led her to us, Jim. I never want to see her again. And I'm beginning to think I never want to see you again."

"Bella don't make any rash decisions, love."

"Like I said before, just take me home tomorrow. I miss Irene, and my own bed, and an inside toilet. I want to forget about all this. And stop calling me love."

"I'll do that, l—sorry nearly said it again. Habit of a lifetime." He cleared his throat and added, "What about that pie? You started it. What shall I do with it now?"

"Oh, for goodness sake! You and your stomach. The veg is all chopped and in that pan on the stove. I was going to add the chicken pieces, cook it up and put it all in the pie crust. You can just cook it up and have a stew. Give the pastry to the birds."

"Where's the chicken?"

"What chicken?"

"The chicken for the pie?"

"Isn't it in the cold store?"

"No love—sorry. Wasn't there when I got the cheese out."

"Didn't you get some when you got the carrots and onion?"

"Er, no."

"Well, we aren't having chicken pie if there's no chicken, are we?" Isabella harrumphed and slumped in her chair. "Give me another whisky, I need to get through this evening somehow."

Jim stood up and took the plates to the sink. He returned with a cloth and wiped up the breadcrumbs, returning the board to the dresser. His movements were slow and deliberate, and Isabella watched each one carefully.

Jim turned to see her observing him. He also wondered how he had changed so much, whether Susan was just the beginning, a catalyst for new life. A better way of living. In a sudden wave, he wondered if Bella was actually all he wanted, or had she become just a habit? He poured the whisky and plonked the two glasses on the table.

"How's your leg? Wanna sit in the other room? Or in the nice chair?" He nodded to the rocking chair, now devoid of its orange cushion.

"It's fine." She lifted the mug to her lips. "A few of these and I won't feel a thing."

Sensing a slight thawing of her icy attitude, he decided to air his plan for the future. "Bella, how about I take you back home tomorrow and I come back here?"

"What are you going to do here on your own? You haven't got any money. We've used all our savings, what with me not working at the moment, and you only doing odd jobs. That's not going keep you going. Not that I want you home. I'm still too angry." She sat upright as if to prove her point.

"Stop talking for just one moment, will you? Just hear me out. So, you're on sick leave and getting some money in to cover our bills at home. We haven't even touched our savings. I've been keeping an eye on things so don't you worry. Once you're fit, you can go back to your old job."

"If he'll have me. You know what he's like. He'll have replaced me already."

"Well, if that's the case, then it's his loss. Anyway, I've been keeping my ear to the ground and I hear there's a few people in

96

town who need my line of expertise. That woman in the big house, Mrs Jenkins, is it? Don't get why she's got a Welsh name but talks like the Queen."

"Jim, that's not relevant. So, you think you might move your business to here? What'll you do with your customers at home?"

"Sell that business. It's got to be worth something: I've got about a hundred customers."

"Will someone even buy it?" Bella's voice drifted as she appeared to losing interest.

"Yes, they will. And with that money, I can buy us a better place here."

"Why would I want to move here? All my family and friends are in West Bromwich. Friends, not Susan." The alcohol was taking effect and Isabella was beginning to slur.

"What I'm trying to say is that I'm not coming back to West Bromwich. There's nothing for me there. I want a new life. Are you with me or not?"

Isabella sprung back into life as she snapped, "Somehow, this has become all about you hasn't it, Jim?" Her eyes flashed and she continued. "Let's sleep with the wife's friend and use it as an opportunity for a new life."

"I obviously can't talk to you about this now. But just you mind, it's my plan and I'm doing it. With or without you, Bella."

CHAPTER 13

Dai

Dai let himself in. He could hear the clanging of pans from the kitchen and children's laughter from along the corridor. Normal family noises. He smiled and pushed open the door of the sitting room and took a step inside, narrowly avoiding a pile of plastic bricks. There were two piles of bricks and two projects in varying stages of construction. A book lay open next to one of them.

"Hello, you two."

"Daddy!" George threw his arms around his father's legs and held them tightly. "Are you going to work late tonight?"

"No. I've got a night off." He peeled George's arms away and sat down on the settee, observing his sons playing on the floor.

"You've worked a lot this week haven't you, Daddy?" said Daniel earnestly. "You must be really tired."

"You're right, Danny. I'm definitely a bit tired but I'm looking forward to spending the evening with you two and Mummy. Anyway, what are you making here?"

"My one's a bridge," answered George.

"Mine's a crane," added Daniel.

"Well, they're looking good, boys. You'll make great engineers."

"What's an engineer?" asked George, his thumb balanced on the edge his mouth.

"Take your thumb out of your mouth, George. An engineer is someone who builds stuff, just like you're doing." The clanging from the kitchen got louder and a mild expletive escaped. "Sounds like Nanny's cooking dinner."

"Yes, she is. Grandpa's in there with her. Mummy's still at work," Daniel explained.

Dai stood up. "Right you are then. I'm going talk to Nanny now."

When he walked into the kitchen, Douglas was sitting reading the paper. Shirley was opposite her husband at the kitchen table preparing vegetables to go with dinner. They both looked up.

"I didn't hear you come in, Dai. Are we expecting you?"

"No Shirley, I thought I'd surprise my sons. No problem with that, is there?"

"No problem, Dai," added Douglas.

The smell of homecooked food wafted invitingly around the room. Dai sat down and put his hand on Shirley's. She stopped slicing and quickly pulled her hand away.

"Thank you both so much for being here this week. It's been a great help for Babs, I'm sure she really appreciates it."

"Well, we didn't have much option did we, Dai?" said Douglas, "Babs can't manage on her own."

"She's not on her own, I'm here. Anyway, I'm sure you love spending time with Danny and George."

"Hmm. How's that going to work out, Dai? We can't stay forever so you'll need a routine for the boys." Shirley chopped the broccoli slightly more vigorously, dumping the diced pieces into the saucepan.

"I'm sure we'll patch it up. We always do. Won't be long till I'm back home again." A smile crept over his face and he nodded as he looked around the room.

"I see." Shirley got up and filled the pan at the kitchen sink, then put it on a ring at the back of the cooker. She opened the kitchen door and called, "Dinner's in ten minutes you two."

Two replies of, "Okay, Nanny!" drifted back from the sitting room. There was a clunk as the front door opened then slammed shut.

"Sounds like Babs is home," said Douglas. "You'd better leave, Dai."

The kitchen door swung open. Barbara's figure appeared in the doorway.

"What the...?"

"Hello love, thought I'd come and surprise the boys, maybe stay for dinner?"

Barbara's eyes flicked from her mother to her father and back to husband. She walked slowly into the room, kissed her father on the head, then stepped tentatively around her husband's chair over to the sink to kiss her mother on the cheek.

"I really don't think so, Dai."

"Well technically, love, this is my house, remember? It's in my name."

"Whatever, Dai. Please just leave."

Douglas stood up. "I'll see you out Dai."

"No, you won't, Douglas. I've come to have dinner with my children, so if you'll excuse me..." He left the room abruptly, pulling the door behind him. He leant against a wall in the hallway, from where he could hear his wife's voice.

"Oh God! What's he doing here?" A chair was scraped on the lino, and he heard Barbara exhale as she sat down heavily.

"Right. First thing, go upstairs and get changed then come down here and we'll have a proper meal together. We'll deal with Dai later, once the boys are in bed," Shirley's voice instructed.

"Yes, love, you do that. It'll be okay—we're here to support you." That was Douglas.

Barbara went out of the kitchen to find Dai leaning against the doorframe to the sitting room. "What are you doing, Dai?"

"I'd think that was obvious, don't you? I just wonder how your da is going to deal with me."

Barbara let out a small gasp and ran up the stairs. Dai grinned and let himself into the sitting room where the boys were watching television. He shuffled himself between them on the settee, and George slid over to make more space.

As the credits for *Blue Peter* finished, they heard Shirley's voice. "Dinner's ready. Come and wash your hands!"

The two little boys rushed into the kitchen followed by their smiling father who pulled out a chair and settled himself into it. He watched as Douglas laid the cutlery and mats on the table. At the sink, his sons were jostling to get to the soap and water. Daniel finished first and jumped up onto a chair next to his father. George followed and his eyes widened.

"He's got my mat!" he shouted.

"Which one is yours, George? I didn't know you had a special one," said Douglas.

"The Rolls Royce."

"It's not yours, George. We take it in turns. You had it yesterday, so it's mine today," explained Daniel.

"But it's my favourite!" sobbed George, climbing up into a chair next to his grandfather.

"Don't be a baby and just have another one," snapped Dai. "No need to cry over everything. You're not a girl."

"Why don't you all sit down and I'll serve up?" said Shirley.

Shirley pulled a huge dish of shepherd's pie out of the oven and carried it carefully to the table. She returned to the oven, drained the boiling water from the saucepan into a gravy boat, stirring quickly to avoid lumps, then tipped the broccoli into a serving dish with a lid. She put both down onto the table.

"We need to wait for Mummy," said Daniel.

"Well, I'm right here," said Barbara as she entered the kitchen.

A small gasp escaped Dai's lips. Her brunette waves free from her work bun were now cascading over her shoulders. Her tight, blue, bellbottom jeans fitted where they touched and her red, ribbed, rollneck pullover accentuated her breasts. Thoughts of his hands on her hips, flicking his tongue over her nipples, flooded into his head. His groin ached. He wanted her; he wanted her right now. He missed her and would do anything to get her back. She walked to table, kissed the top of sons' heads and sat down.

"Oh good, we can all have tea together," said Daniel.

"I know it's been ages, hasn't it? I've missed it too," said Dai smiling. "It's not much fun having tea on your own in the hotel."

"Why are you having dinner in a hotel?" asked Daniel, his head on one side. The adults carried on, ignoring his question.

"In, die, tri, pedwar, pimp," George counted in Welsh. "We haven't got enough chairs, only five. We need another for Nanny to sit down."

"There's a stool in the bedroom, I'll go up and get it," said Dai, side-stepping his son's question. "Babs, come with me." He grabbed her hand and pulled her out of the kitchen.

In the hall, she shook herself free of him. "Get off, Dai, and why are you even here? You're not welcome. And you're confusing the boys."

He pushed her against the door of the under-stairs cupboard, held her hands above her head and shoved his tongue roughly into her mouth. He gyrated his hips against hers. Barbara's eyebrows shot up to her hairline as she tried to extricate herself from his unwelcome embrace.

"God, I've missed you Babs," he breathed heavily.

"Get off, Dai! You're totally out of order!" she hissed, bashing her elbow on the wall as she wriggled free from his grasp.

"You two all right out there?" came Douglas's voice as the door swung open.

"Yeah, we're fine, I'm just getting that stool," said Dai, letting go of Barbara and running up the stairs.

103

She turned and went back into the kitchen, shaking her head and smoothing her hair. Sheila looked at her daughter, her eyes seemingly speaking to her, full of love and encouragement.

"Right, I'll sit between you two," said Dai returning to the kitchen, making a space to place the stool with a son either side of him. "This looks fantastic Shirley: a wonderful home and a cooked meal with the family. Such a treat." He looked at each person at the table in turn and smiled broadly.

After Dai had bathed and put the boys to bed, he stood in the kitchen holding a beer and looked around at the order and cleanliness. Barbara, Shirley and Douglas were at the table with furrowed brows and slitted eyes, watching and waiting for his next move, cups of tea going cold in front of them.

"Don't you need to be getting on?" asked Douglas.

"Well, funny you should ask that Douglas. I don't really think it's me that should be getting on with it being my house and my town and my sons we're talking about. How about Babs here moves out and sees what it's like?"

"Dai, you can't really mean that. I look after the boys, I cook their meals, wash their clothes, clean the house. You can't even manage to take them to and from school a few times a week. How would you manage to run the house and your garage on your own with two little ones? It's a ridiculous suggestion!"

"You don't know I can't do it, I'm perfectly capable, just you see." He took a deep gulp of his beer and put the glass down heavily on the worktop. "I'll give you a few days to make arrangements then I'm moving back in, with or without you." He walked towards the door.

"You can't do this, Dai. The boys need their mother," said Shirley, leaning across the table to rub the back of Barbara's hand.

"Dai, please, this will never work. The boys need me."

"You've got till the end of the week Babs, then I'm coming home." He left the kitchen and they heard the sound of him pulling his coat from the hook. The front door slammed behind him.

CHAPTER 14

Barbara

"What am I going to do, Mum? Dad?"

"The first thing is to find out if he can do this. Make an appointment with a solicitor tomorrow as a matter of urgency," said Douglas. "I'll come with you if you like."

"Yes please. Oh God! This is a nightmare." Her elbows on the kitchen table, Barbara lowered her head into hands.

"He's very forceful, love. You need to make sure he doesn't get you alone. Ever. We worry about you, and the boys, don't we, Douglas?"

"I know, Mum. He's always been short-tempered but this aggression is new. He's angry that he's not in control and not getting his own way."

"You just take care, love. And we can stay as long as you need, so no need to worry." Douglas smiled, picked up his daughter's hand and gave it a squeeze.

---0---

The solicitor was an old man with half-rimmed spectacles perched on the middle of his nose. His hair was grey and slightly bushy, especially at the edges, and a few faintly ginger whiskers grew down his cheek and jowls. His breath smelt of onions and port and he blew his nose with a large spotted handkerchief which he shoved back into the pocket of his tweed trousers after each session. *He belongs in a Dickens' novel, not in an office in mid-Wales,* thought Barbara.

"So, you and your husband bought the house together but it's only in his name, that's right?"

"Yes. He said it was simpler that way. That it would make the sale go through faster."

"Hmm. Well, that isn't strictly true: it doesn't make any difference with a married couple so I don't know why he'd say that."

"I do. Especially now," said Barbara, shaking her head and pursing her lips.

"But what to do about it now is a little complicated. I think it would be best if you file for divorce and when it gets to the family court, they might decide that the house is part of the settlement."

"So, I can't actually do anything yet? Even though I pay half the mortgage and bills?"

"Not unless your husband agrees and, from what you tell me, that isn't likely."

"Sounds like you've got no choice but to start divorce proceedings, love," said Douglas, leaning forward in his chair. "And deal with the house ownership later."

"Can I change the locks and stop him coming back in?"

"Technically, no. Not unless he's physically violent and threatens you or the children."

"What about if I move out and let him move in?"

"That's not a great move, in the eyes of the law: he'd have possession of the house and your position would be even weaker. Besides, where would you move to?"

"Well, that's the point really... I'm stuck; nothing I can do except let him move back in. But I can file for divorce. Can I do that today?"

"Yes, you can, but there are fees involved I'm afraid, on top of my consultation fee."

"Oh Dad, what a mess." Barbara slumped low in her chair, her head dropped forward and her chin rested on her chest. She sighed heavily.

"It's all right, we can help you out love. We've got a bit tucked away for a rainy day. And this is quite a storm." Her father smiled and rubbed her back.

The solicitor stood up. "I'll start the proceedings. Dai Roberts will receive a letter and you'll get your forms to complete in a day or a two."

"Where will you send his letter? I don't want him reading it in the house. He'll go berserk."

"What about his place of work? The garage?"

"Yes, that's better. At least he'll have his brother with him to ease the blow."

"Yes, that sounds sensible." The solicitor thrust out his hand to Douglas who stood up to take it. "My secretary will send you a bill."

Douglas guided his daughter's elbow gently to ease her out of her chair. "Thank you," she said quietly over her shoulder as they left the office.

The hallway was half panelled in dark wood with paintings of fusty old men hanging in dusty frames lining the wall and up the staircase. The secretary smiled. Barbara suspected news of her visit would be all over town within hours. Dai would find out for sure.

"I need to get back to work, Dad. Thank you for coming with me. I feel so empty inside to think that our relationship is over." She sighed heavily and leaned against her father's shoulder. "I wanted to be like you and Mum; being a divorced parent isn't a place I ever thought I'd visit."

"Sometimes things just don't work out love. It doesn't mean you've failed." He took her shoulders and looked her straight in the face. "We love you and so do your boys." He kissed the top of her head then leaned in and held her tightly in his arms, her cloak enveloping both of them.

"Thanks, Dad. I needed that. So, are you and Mum still okay to pick the boys up from school? I'll be back around five and hopefully we won't have any unwelcome visitors tonight."

"It's all fine love. And your boys are happy with us. Have a good afternoon."

Douglas strode off down the road, his back tall and straight despite his advancing years. Barbara dropped her bag into the basket on her bike chained to the railing, unlocked it then hopped on ready for her afternoon with the ailing and elderly of Barmouth.

---0---

A few days later, in the tiny cupboard of an office at the back of surgery, Barbara and Hazel nursed cups of tea. Their cloaks hung on the back of the door and their bags were under their old wooden school chairs. Empty sandwich boxes sat on the tiny table against the wall.

"How was your morning? Did you go and see Isabella at the cottage?"

"No. Didn't you hear? They've gone."

"Really? That was a bit sudden, wasn't it?"

"Well, it's probably for the best. That cottage, if you can call it that, wasn't the best place for an invalid."

"She was hardly your average invalid by all accounts—very feisty and independent."

"And her husband was sleeping on the settee for two weeks. I wonder if they've sorted things out."

"Oh yeah, he'd been having an affair with her best friend, hadn't he? What an arse! Might be the best thing that she's back at home."

Barbara took a tin from the shelf, pulled it open and took out a Bourbon biscuit. "My favourite; I like scraping the cream out of the middle with my teeth."

"Oh no, that's horrible, you have to eat them whole!" laughed Hazel. "Anyway, Babs, talking about marriage, what are you going to do about Dai coming back? It's tomorrow, isn't it?"

"Yeah, it makes me feel physically sick." She sighed heavily. "Mum and Dad are still there so it's a bit easier, but where does he expect to sleep? Not with me, I hope."

"I expect that'll be his plan. Be prepared for that. He's already tried it on, hasn't he? When he came round and stayed for tea on Monday."

Barbara shuddered at the thought of that encounter. "I know, but what can I do? We haven't got any more space. The boys are already sharing and I'm in Daniel's room so mum and dad can have the double."

Hazel sniffed loudly then offered, "It's not a solution in the long term, but you could come and stay with us for a day or two. I mean my two get on with your two. Tony will be at work on Friday and Saturday so he won't care if we have extra kids in the house. You can either bunk up with me, or sleep on the settee. Your decision."

"Really? That's such a lovely offer. Are you sure? I don't want to impose." Barbara released the breath she'd been holding for the last few days.

"Absolutely. I can't think of you scared in your own home."

Barbara deflated in her chair like a saggy balloon. "It's just so horrible. I never wanted this for my children. I wanted them to have to a happy, stable childhood like I did. How did it end up like this?"

"It hasn't ended, Babs love. This is just a hump in the road. You'll get through it, I'm sure of that. We women are strong and resilient, and you're not on your own."

"Yes, if I keep telling myself that, maybe it'll become true." She sat up straight and puffed out her chest. Suddenly, she

111

remembered, "What am going to do about Mum and Dad? I can't leave them in the house with Dai and his ego."

"Maybe they can have a night away somewhere. Look Babs, let's just get this weekend over with and see where we go from there. It's only a week till half-term then you can take the boys and stay with your parents."

They were interrupted by a tap on the door. Hazel leaned forward in her chair and pulled it open. A head with a red hat poked around the doorjamb. A smile cracked across the broad face.

"Hello, Babs, Hazel. Sorry to interrupt your lunch break, like." The lilting voice filled the tiny room.

"Oh Bryn, how lovely to see you." Barbara's face relaxed; she shone a little.

"Just wanted to say, I heard what Dai told you..." He stopped.

"It's okay, Bryn. I know about all about Dai and Babs," Hazel said. "No secrets between us."

"Ah okay, so anyway, me and Da like, well, we're here if you need us. That's all. Just wanted to let you know that. Da wanted to come and see you too, but the receptionist wouldn't let him in with Dewi."

Barbara's eyes filled up. She sniffed then pulled a hankie out of her pocket. "That's so kind. Everyone's being so kind. Thank you."

Hazel leaned over and held her new friend's hand. "That's because we care about you and Dai isn't behaving like a normal human being."

"Dai has always been stubborn. Doesn't like it when things don't go his way, ever since we were boys like. He's a star when you're on the same side, but cross him or disagree and well, that's not worth thinking about."

"Oh shit, we need to get a move on! Look at the time!" Hazel jumped up and squeezed past Bryn to get her cloak. Bryn

112

backed out of the room so Barbara could do the same. The three of them walked through reception watched by an extremely interested face at the desk.

"Cheerio, Babs, see you tomorrow!" said Hazel as she turned to go into her consulting room.

"Bye, Hazel, and thank you."

Barbara and Bryn pushed the door and stepped out into the brisk afternoon. The sun was low in the darkening sky and the wind whipped around their legs. Owen was by the wall stamping his feet and rubbing his hands together, Dewi sat patiently next to him. He came over when he saw them.

"You'll right there enaid." *Enaid* was a term of endearment, meaning 'soul' or 'life'.

"As well as can be expected, Owen. Thank you for your support, I really need that right now."

"And how's the bachgens?" *The boys.*

"They're fine, they'll be chuffed to bits to see you." She paused and pulled her cloak around her. "By the way, they don't know Dai's moved out. They just think he's working a lot so don't say anything to them, will you?"

"No, of course not. No need to worry them, is there?"

She looked at her watch. "Oh no, I've got to go back up to Mrs Jenkins, and it looks like rain."

"I'll give you a lift," Bryn offered. "You don't want to be riding your bike in this weather. You'll catch your death."

"Oh, could you? That'd be great. I'll be late if I ride; I'm supposed to be there at half two."

"Cheerio, Owen." Barbara and Bryn walked towards the van parked up on the opposite side of the road. As she climbed in, she looked back to see Owen watching them. He nodded slowly and muttered something to Dewi before walking up the road to the beach. Knowing him, he was probably going to let his dog have a little run before he went to collect his grandsons from school.

CHAPTER 15

Owen

Owen was sitting at his kitchen table spreading lime marmalade on his toast, while Dewi watched him from a chewed wicker basket lined with a tartan blanket. A warm orange fire was flickering in the grate taking the chill off the slate floor and draughty window frames. Bryn entered the kitchen.

"Morning, Da." He sat down on the chair closest to the fireplace and poured a cup of tea from a pot with a blue, knitted cosy, then cut two thick slices from the loaf.

"Morning, Bryn. Why you up so early on a Saturday?"

Bryn picked up a brass toasting fork lying on the hearth and put a slice on the end. He held the bread up to the flames.

"Working at the garage. That bloke Tony wants his new car looking at. He bought it in Harlech in the week—says they need two cars now he's working away so much. It's got a few rattles he wants me to look at then give it an MOT."

"Oh him, Clare and Cathy's da. They're picking up Welsh quite fast, like." He took a bite of his toast and chewed slowly. "Dewi likes his dog."

"I hardly know him, but like you say, the whole family seem nice. And Babs gets on all right with his wife—Hazel, is it?" He took his bread from the fork, turned it around and held it towards the flames again. "Anyway, he dropped it off yesterday and Dai asked me to do it; he's busy today apparently."

"He's moving back into the house today. Not sure Babs is happy about that though."

"No, she really isn't. She's really upset, filing for divorce, so she says."

"It's just a feeling I get, Bryn." Owen paused. "But go careful won't you lad?"

"It's fine, Da. It's their business and they'll just have to work it out, however that is."

"But, you need to watch it with Babs. I've seen the way she looks at you."

"I'm just helping her out a bit, that's all, Da." He laughed shortly and took his toast from the fork. "Pass us the butter, will you?"

Owen watched his son spread butter liberally on his toast followed by a drizzle of honey from the jar on the table. Bryn had the look of his mother when he was concentrating, brows knitted and mouth slightly open.

"Your ma used to like honey on her toast." Owen breathed out heavily and dabbed his eyes with a handkerchief pulled from his pocket. "On Wednesday, it'll be three years since she died. Still miss her every day. Taken too early. Should've been me; I'm the old one."

"I know, Da. It's been tough. For all of us, Dai and me. She's left a hole in our lives and an ache, here in my heart." Bryn bumped his fist against his chest.

"We should all do something to remember. Go up to Dinas Oleu and lay flowers or the like. What d'you think?"

Bryn nodded. "Good idea, Da." He put the second slice on the fork, ready to go and took a bite of the other. "What you up to today?"

"I'll take Dewi out, get something for tea later. See who's in town today. Might stop for a pint."

Bryn buttered his toast and stood up. "Right, I'm off, Da. See you later. I shouldn't be too long, maybe we can go and watch the rugby. It's a home game."

"Right you are, son."

Bryn closed the door behind him and Owen collected up the breakfast things and filled a bowl with water to wash up. Dewi

116

watched his progress and gently wagged his tail in his basket. He knew it was almost time for his morning walk.

"Come on then, Dewi, you've been patient enough."

Owen stepped out of his front door; the house he was born in. He turned to walk along the alleyway, passing homes cut into the mountain with wooden front doors painted varying shades of blue. Dewi led him down a set of narrow, higgledy-piggledy steps worn away by centuries of fishermen's boots. Thin shafts of lights landed on the dolerite walls of the homes on either side of the path, their rooftops almost touching above him. As he reached the bottom of the steps onto the High Street, he followed his dog up the road to a set of lights. Around the corner on the Dolgellau Road, Bryn was now in the garage tinkering under a car. They crossed and walked under the railway bridge. Owen looked over the harbour wall; the tide was in and water lapped rhythmically against the seaweed growing on the stones. A few fishing boats bobbed gently on the waves, most of them still out in Cardigan Bay. Ahead of him was the lifeboat shed which he walked past and round to the right where the Irish Sea was alive with foamy waves. Hopefully no lifeboats would be needed today. Dewi ran down the steps onto the sand. Owen pulled his hat down tight over his ears as the wind whipped around his face bringing with it a familiar, briny smell.

Walking along the beach, Owen looked across at his familiar hometown, Abermaw—the place he'd grown up. He knew the history and was teaching Clare and Cathy about it, just like he'd taught his grandsons. He told them about the abundance of sheep and the wool industry, and how the export trade dropped off so there were years when the town limped by on fishing and a few tourists. The railway opening in 1867, combined with the town's proximity to Cader Idris and Snowdonia National Park, meant tourists arrived all year round. As the popularity of the town as a destination increased, more and more guest houses

117

were built along the sea front and up the mountain. The last few years had seen developments mushrooming up all over the place, including the caravan park on the hill outside of the town and the amusement arcade, all of which spread like algae up the road. But it was the wide beach with its acres of sandy opportunities which brought so many families in the summer months. It was autumn now, so the beach was virtually abandoned; Owen and Dewi were the only ones leaving their imprints in the rippled sand.

Leaving the beach, Owen headed back into town up Beach Road, looking both ways at the level crossing. He turned down the road towards the Cooperative, his mind on buying something for dinner.

Suddenly, he heard a low bark followed by girl's voice.

"Look, Mummy! It's Mr Roberts and Dewi. Can we say hello?"

"Course you can, Cathy." She ran up to him as Hazel was dragged along by Charlie.

"Morning, Hazel. Cathy. You're up nice and early. Doing a bit of shopping, are you?"

"Yes, we've come to get something for lunch, and me and Mummy are taking Charlie for a walk." The two dogs were now sniffing around each other, Charlie's lead becoming more twisted with each movement. "George and Danny stayed at our house last night. We all slept in my room: we pulled the mattresses on the floor. It was fun, wasn't it, Mummy? They wanted to stay at our house while we came shopping, so we've got to be quick."

"Oh, did they? I didn't know that." Owen paused and shoved his hands into his pockets. "Me and Dewi here have just been on the beach. Tide's coming in now, mind."

"That's annoying, I can never remember the tide timings. We'll have to walk along the path instead. Go the long way round and pick up Clare on the way back."

"Where is she?"

"She wanted to go to the library to get more books. She takes a while to choose."

"Bit of bookworm, that one," Owen observed. "Not a bad thing like; lots to learn from books."

"She's always been studious; likes the inside life more than this one here," added Hazel.

"Mr Roberts is teaching us stuff about Barmouth, Mummy, like it's actually called Abermaw. And the railway over there opened in Victorian times. The Victorians liked to go on holiday to the seaside and they brought their money and made the Barmouth people rich."

"That's how it works, love," laughed Hazel. "I thought you were teaching them Welsh, Owen."

"Well, a bit history about the town they live in helps too, like. Good to know about your hometown."

"I can speak a bit of Welsh now too. Sut wyt ti—means 'how are you?' doesn't it Mr Roberts?"

"It does, Cathy. And please call me Owen. Mr Roberts is a bit formal, like."

"Okay, Mr Owen. When are you coming to ours again? I want to learn some more." Cathy twisted her hair as she looked up at the pair of adults.

"That's up to your mum, here. On Monday? What d'you think, Hazel?"

"I'm working but I'm sure it'll be fine. Tony'll pick them up from school so I'll let him know you're coming."

"That's sorted then: I'll see you on Monday, Cathy." Cathy clapped and skipped around her mother's legs. Owen lowered his voice as he asked Hazel, "So where's Shirley and Douglas? Surely not with you, too?"

"They're staying in a place in Dolgellau. Thought it best they weren't there when Dai came back."

"That's not going to go down well. I guess I'd better pop round and see him." He scratched Dewi's head.

"Don't tell him about Babs being with us, will you?" Cathy pulled Hazel's arm and she looked down. "Stop it, love. I'm just talking to Owen. It's just for a couple of nights while she gets her head together."

Owen sighed. "I won't say a word, but it's not going to work for long. He'll find out soon enough."

"Yeah, hopefully not immediately though. They're just having a nice time with all the kids together for now."

"Mummy, can we go now?" Cathy asked. "Charlie wants his walk." The dog was pulling harder on the lead towards the squawking seagulls.

"Looks like we're off," laughed Hazel. "Cheerio Owen."

He watched as the little group trooped off over the railway track, across the road, and disappeared along the Promenade. Then he turned and made his way towards his son's house—which he knew would be full of frustration and anger.

CHAPTER 16

Jim

It was a long drive back from West Bromwich. Jim's head was full of his daughter and wife's angry stares and words. He'd been ignoring the heavy knocking sound coming from the engine as he rounded the mountains and climbed the steep hills outside the town. He hoped he'd make it back but the sound was getting louder as he rounded the bend into Bontddu. He knew it needed attention so he drove past the turning that led to his cottage and continued down into Barmouth. The door to the garage was open.

"Oh good, they're still open," he said to his car. "We can get you looked at." He slowed right down, manoeuvred carefully over the forecourt and nosed his way inside. It was dark so he switched on his lights—there seemed to be an obstruction. He stopped the car, pulled up the handbrake and peered carefully through the smeary windscreen.

What have we got here then? he said to himself as he climbed out of the car and stretched his back out. He walked round and bent over the obstruction.

"Bloody hell! You'll right, Bryn?"

He knelt down and touched Bryn's immobile body lightly on the side. The headlights were still on and illuminated the scene. Bryn was face down and a smear of blood was visible across one cheek and looked to be clumping in his hair. Jim picked up his wrist and felt for a pulse—there was a feeble flutter. He jumped and ran to the office where he picked up the receiver and dialled 999, cursing each slow turn of the dial.

"Ambulance, straight away. A man's been attacked. There's blood on his head. He's got a pulse but it's right faint."

Jim gave the address and hung up. He took off his jacket and laid it over Bryn's body. The radio was tuned to the local station and the voice of a Welsh disc jockey echoed around the cavernous space. "Who did this to you, Bryn?" he asked aloud, shaking his head.

He went to the door of the garage to look up and down the street for the ambulance. Only then did he notice that the Transit van, which was usually parked on the drive, was nowhere to be seen. Except for a few cars on the road, the town was quiet, especially for Saturday. Finally, he heard the sound of a siren getting closer and blue lights came into view. The ambulance driver pulled up in front of him. Two medics jumped out.

"Where is he, like?"

"In here, mate. Bit bloody but still with us. Not sure when it happened—he was on the floor when I got here."

Two men got the stretcher out of the back of the vehicle and followed Jim inside.

"Oh, bloody hell! He's in a bit of state, isn't he?" said the first to the second as they laid the stretcher down and knelt by the limp body on the dirty garage floor.

Jim stood against the wall and watched as the first took Bryn's pulse and the second tried to rouse him.

"Looks like someone gave him quite a clonk," said the other.

"Is he going to be all right?" Jim craned his neck to see.

"It's a good thing you found him when you did." The pursed lips and serious face of the first ambulanceman told Jim all he needed to know.

"Right. Let's get him onto the stretcher."

Gently, they rolled Bryn over onto the canvas, cradling his head and neck like a delicate vase. Bryn groaned. They took an end each and carried his almost lifeless body to the ambulance. Carefully, they slid the stretcher into the back. The first medic climbed in the front, while the second stayed with Bryn. Just before slamming the doors shut, he turned.

"Thanks for calling us. You'd better stay here for a bit, mind. There's a police car on its way too."

"Of course. D'you think he'll be all right?"

"I don't really want to say anything at this stage, sorry mate."

Jim watched from the forecourt as the driver negotiated the ambulance out onto the busy main road and disappeared back up the hill towards Dolgellau Hospital. He turned to go back inside. He opened the door of his car to switch off the lights. He didn't need a flat battery as well as a clonking engine.

"Not going anywhere are you, sir?"

He turned to see a pair of young matching police officers blocking the light from the entrance. He stood up and closed the car door. He looked at them: they couldn't be much older than school-leavers.

"No. I was just turning off my headlights. I suppose you want to talk to me about Bryn Roberts?"

"Yes sir, exactly that. So, tell me what you found?" said the one on the left.

"He was on the floor here when I drove in."

"And what time was that, sir?" said the other one, his pencil moving fast across his notebook.

"Well let's see, it's three now so must've been about two thirty."

"See anyone around the place?"

"No, it was completely empty, except for Bryn on the floor. The radio was on and the garage door was open: that's why I drove in."

"And how d'you know the victim?" asked the first. "Mister..?"

"Cartwright," said Jim. "Him and his brother fixed my car a week or two back. He runs this place with his brother, Dai."

"Dai Roberts? I know him. Didn't know he owned this place," said number two, looking up from his notebook and around the garage.

"We'll just take your details, sir, then you can get on. Don't suppose you know where I can find Dai, or any other family members?" asked the first one.

"Well, Dai lives with his missus and kids but I don't know where. His dad, Owen, lives in one of those fisherman's houses up on the rock behind us."

"It's all right, I know where the family live," interjected the second. "We can head up there now."

"Thanks for your help, Mr Cartwright. You may've saved Mr Roberts' life today."

They turned and walked out of the garage into the weak sunlight. Jim went into the office and switched off the radio. He shuffled some papers around looking for the keys to the front door so he could lock up when he left. He found them hanging on a hook next to the door frame. He turned to leave when he noticed the top desk drawer was ajar. An official looking manila envelope was poking out. Jim took the edge of the paper and pulled it out. He read aloud, "Jenkins and Sons Solicitors, 15 High Street, Barmouth." He took the letter out and read it carefully.

Didn't realise things were that bad. Dai won't take this well, he thought, pursing his lips and shaking his head before shoving the letter back where he found it. He then switched off the light and pulled the office door closed behind him.

He got into his car, started the engine and reversed out onto the driveway. He got out and shut the big wooden doors, then turned the key in the lock. Outside, he folded his tall body once again with a sigh into his vehicle, turned left onto the main road, then clonked steadily up the hill towards his cottage. It was beginning to get dark; the October sun not strong enough to compete with the clouds and impending storm. Jim was again engulfed in his own thoughts as he drove up to his home on the hill. He rounded the corner, expecting the familiar sight of his cottage but there in front of him was Dai's orange van. He pulled up next to it and climbed out.

"Anyone here?" A figure appeared in the doorway. "Dai is that you?"

CHAPTER 17

Dai

Dai heard a rhythmic clonk clonk clonk before the Hillman appeared on the patch of earth—it could not be called a driveway—in front of the cottage. He shook his head and stood up to open the door. He would have to take matters into his own hands now.

"Hello, Jim. Wasn't expecting to see you back."

"Well, I do live here, Dai."

"Thought you and the missus had gone back to Birmingham for good, like."

Jim lifted his bag out of the back seat and walked to his front door. "What are you doing here, Dai? Or can I guess? I've just stopped at your garage to find your brother just about alive on the floor."

"That was an accident. Is he all right?"

"Dai, that was no accident. What did he do? Walk into a spanner? And why did you leave him for dead?"

"I panicked."

Dai moved to one side to let Jim into the house then followed him into the kitchen. Jim put his bag down, then took the kettle, filled it with water and placed it on the range. He took some kindling from the basket and lit the fire underneath.

"Look, Dai, I've just driven three and half hours, found a body, and been interviewed by the police. What I need now is the loo and a cup of tea."

Dai had never before heard so many words from Jim in one go. "Right oh."

"Keep an eye on the fire under, add a bit more when that's burning hot." Jim nodded towards the range and exited out the back to the privy.

Dai had a closer look around the room. It was clean and tidy—probably Isabella's influence. A wave of regret washed over him. His thoughts fluttered around his head.

Wives make men whole. Babs holds everything together; keeps us going as a family. God, I've been such a fool with my messing about. And now what am I going to do?

He pulled a few bits of wood from the basket, opened the bottom door and shoved them into the glowing fire, his eyes transfixed by the orange and yellow flickering flames.

"Close the bloody door or the kettle'll never boil," Jim said as he came back in.

"Sorry, Jim, just watching the flames."

"Fire is nature's television." Jim sat down in kitchen and nodded to Dai, who obediently sat. "So, Dai. You'd better tell me what happened."

Something about his tone invited confidence. Dai began, "I love Babs, have done since the day I met her, but everything happened so fast. We met in Glasgow, wrote letters and phoned for a bit, then she moved down here. And it was fun for a while—you know what it's like at the beginning—sex at every opportunity." He paused and smiled; Jim nodded. "But then she fell pregnant and it all changed. Everyone said we had to get married; you know, my Ma and Da, her parents, all going on about making a decent woman of her. Babies born the wrong side of the blanket and all that. We both felt a bit pressured by it all but we went along with it. Got hitched. Council gave us a place, which we bought later on. And it was all right for a while. But then Babs started getting fed up with staying at home and wanted to go back to work—she was a nurse and had been working here before Danny was born."

"I see." The kettle whistled. Jim got up and pulled a couple of cups from the dresser, dropped bags in and poured the water. "No milk. You'll right with it black?"

"No problem. Thank you." Dai took the cup and, wrapping his hands around it, blew across the top creating little ripples. "So, she went back to work for a bit; it was hard juggling Danny and our two jobs. And she was tired—no time for me, like. And..." He paused and sipped. "...I started playing around. Nothing serious, just the odd one-night stand with holiday makers so she wouldn't find out. Discreet, like. But anyway, Danny was about a year and half and she got pregnant again. Had an upset stomach and the pill didn't work. She wasn't best chuffed but got on with it like you do."

"Yep, you do."

"After George, it got even worse. We were like ships in the night; saw each other for about an hour each evening. She was knackered all the time, so went to bed at eight o'clock some nights. I'd just bought the garage with Bryn so I was busy too, and I found my distractions elsewhere—the barmaid at the Pendragon and a few more holiday makers in summer."

"You must've been worn out," said Jim with a wry smile. Dai continued; he was relishing the opportunity to talk about his failed marriage with a kindred spirit, as he saw it.

"So anyway, the most recent dalliance with a woman in the summer has backfired on me, hasn't it? Stupid woman wrote to me and Babs found the letter. She must've been poking around at the garage. That's where me and the woman met, if you get my drift. So, she's chucked me out and got her parents down to help with the kids." He paused. "And now she's bloody well filed for divorce!" The tone and volume of his voice rose to a peak as he finished his sentence. He slammed his mug on the table and tea slopped over the side.

"All very interesting, Dai. But what about Bryn?"

129

His eyes narrowed. "My brother," he spat the word out, "has been round at the house, my house, at all times. God knows what they've been up to. He's always fancied her, from the day she came to live with us. We had Da's room and he moved in with Bryn. Only temporary like; they didn't mind sharing."

"I'm starting to get the picture, Dai. But what happened today?"

"I've been staying at the Pen all week, so I went to the house—*my* house—to move back in; to try and get me and Babs back on track." He stood up and walked around the room, punching one hand against the other as he paced.

"And?"

"Nobody there, was there? All gone—house empty. No Babs, no boys, no Scottish in-laws. So, I went to the garage and Bryn was just finishing up an MOT on that English bloke's car. They were chatting in the office so I went in. I admit I was angry so I shouted, 'Where's my Babs and my kids, Bryn?' or something like that. Anyway, that Tony tried to calm me down. He sat me down in the chair, but I was still seething, like, then he buggered off. Saw a letter in a brown envelope on the desk I did."

"Yes." Jim nodded.

"Addressed to me, looking all official. So I pulled the letter out and read that the bitch has filed for divorce. Wants the kids and half the house. She can't divorce me! And it's my house— did that deliberately; bought the house in my name only."

"So? What happened to Bryn?"

"What? Oh right, Bryn. Well, he started saying that maybe if I'd kept my cock in my trousers this wouldn't have happened. If I'd treated her better she wouldn't have done this. That got my goat so I went for him—just a slap, not a punch or anything. What right has he got to tell me how to run my life? He can't even find a woman to stay with him longer than a few months."

Jim's eyes followed Dai as he paced around the small kitchen. "So?"

"Bryn told me stop this foolishness; said he was going home. So, I said not before you tell me where Babs is. He said he didn't know, which I didn't believe—course he knew, he's been seeing her, hasn't he? He walked out of the office and was crossing the garage. I saw a socket set against the wall and I pulled out the ratchet handle. Rage drove me, I knew he knew where she was. I just hit him, right across the back of his head. Hard." Dai stopped pacing, flopped in the chair and held his head in his hands.

"What happened then, Dai?" Jim's voice was low and his words slow. He took a lighter from his pocket, opened the front of the gas light on the table and lit the wick. The blue flame illuminated the room, throwing two dark shadows on the walls.

"He just crumpled on the floor in front of me. His knees bent and he fell forward, his head hit the ground. I can still hear the thump now. I thought I killed him." He looked up at Jim's face. "I just panicked. I took the ratchet handle, jumped in the van and just drove. I didn't plan to come here, just saw the track and thought I could hide out here for a bit. Till it all died down."

"You know you can't do that, Dai. You'll have to hand yourself in."

"What? I can't do that. Why can't I stay here? It's safe here. Nobody'll find me up here."

"It won't take them long. Someone will've seen your van coming this way or they'll just work it out."

"No way. They'll chuck me in prison. I can't just walk into a police station now, can I?"

"Well actually, you can. And it'll be better for everyone if you do."

"Absolutely bloody not. I'll make a run for it." Dai stood up and walked over to the window. It was dark but the moon was already high in the sky, peeking between the clouds. He could see the outlines of his van and Jim's car. An idea started formulating in his mind. He had visions of being lost in a big city, far away from his hometown and the prying locals. "Right, I know what to do. Get your stuff Jim. We're going."

"Where to, Dai? And why am I coming?"

"You know too much now: I can't leave you here to tell all and sundry my business." He walked towards Jim and bent over him. "Come on, we're going."

"Christ almighty, Dai, you can't just run away. And I'm not going anywhere with you."

Dai tipped the back of Jim's chair to make him stand up, then dragged him by the arm over to the front door. "I think you are."

"No I'm bloody not. I only just got back here."

Jim threw his free arm back and caught Dai under the chin with his elbow. Dai dropped Jim's other arm and rubbed his chin. He took a step back, then with his strength renewed by adrenaline, he grabbed Jim by the arm and twisted it behind his back. He grabbed Jim's bag with his other hand, pushed Jim outside, kicking the door closed behind him with his foot.

"Don't think you can get away from me."

"Dai, you can't do this. There'll be consequences."

Jim twisted his shoulders, trying to free himself from Dai's tight grip. Dai pulled him more tightly. Jim cried out but Dai simply pushed him towards the van. He dropped the bag onto the earth, then with his free hand, opened the door and leant into the front foot well. He pulled out the ratchet handle and waved it towards Jim's head. He dragged Jim to the passenger side and opened the door wide.

"Just get in, Jim, or there will *definitely* be consequences."

"Whoa, Dai. Slow down. I'll get in, but just tell me where we're going." Jim climbed slowly into the van.

Dai slammed the passenger door shut. Then he went round to the side of the house. He returned, pushing the moped. He opened the back doors and lifted it easily into the back, before

132

grabbing Jim's bag and throwing that in as well. "Might need this moped where we're going," he said.

"And where exactly is that, Dai?" Jim exhaled.

"West Bromwich, Jim. West Bromwich." He started the engine and crunched into first gear.

"Could you at least put out the fire and the lamp?"

"No time for that mate." Dai took off the handbrake and grabbed the steering wheel.

Jim looked back at his cottage as they drove away down the track. He could make out a faint halo of light from the fire and gas lamp which became smaller and smaller until it was no longer visible.

CHAPTER 18

Barbara

"I think he's opening his eyes," said Barbara, clutching Owen's hand and squeezing it tightly.

Owen stood up and stroked Bryn's bristly cheek, "You all right there, son?"

Bryn moaned faintly and turned his head slowly to one side. "Where am I?"

"You're in the hospital. There was a bit of accident in your garage."

"How long have I been here?" Bryn placed his hands either side of his body and tried to push himself up. He flopped back and sighed heavily. "What's wrong with me?"

"They brought you in a couple of days ago with nasty bang on the head," explained Barbara.

Bryn lifted his hands to his head and felt around the edges of the bandage until he got to the dressing at the back of his head. "Oh yeah, I can feel that now."

"Bryn, what happened at the garage? Can you remember, son?"

"Dai." Bryn shook his head. "Did Dai do this to me?"

"Nobody's sure. And nobody can find him. Or Jim. They've both vanished," said Barbara.

"What's Jim got to do with anything?"

"He found you and called the ambulance. Good thing he did really, or you might not've made it." Owen squeezed his son's hand. "Anyroad, the police talked to him and told him not to leave town, but now they can't find him."

"Is he not at his cottage?"

135

"Well, that's how we know he's gone. The fire brigade went up there when someone reported seeing a lot of smoke. The whole place is gutted. His car was parked outside but he was nowhere to be found."

"Oh God! He won't be happy about his cottage, that's for sure."

"Not sure anyone's told him yet," explained Owen, "they're too busy trying to find him."

"Any idea where he might've gone?" asked Bryn, his eyes drooping with the effort of speaking.

"Who Dai? Or Jim?" said Barbara.

"Both really. D'you reckon they're together somewhere?"

A nurse in a blue uniform and a starched white cap entered the ward and bustled efficiently over to the bed. "Now then, I see you're awake, Mr Roberts." Her lilting Welsh accent rose up to the high ceilings. "I need to look at the patient now, so would you two mind leaving us for a moment?"

She ushered his visitors out and pulled a lime green curtain around the bed. Barbara breathed out heavily, and Owen put his arm around her shoulders.

"I suppose I should get back to the house. Mum and Dad are picking the boys up from school."

"How are they? Do they miss their da?"

"Yes, they don't really understand where he's gone or why. They enjoyed staying up with Hazel and the girls over the weekend though. Took their mind off things. They loved Charlie." Barbara smiled as she remembered how all the children had played happily with the friendly dog, giggling and joking all weekend. She and Hazel had talked for hours over a bottle of wine after their children had gone to bed.

"What are you going to tell them about Dai?"

"That he's gone away for work or something. Hopefully the police won't come round again. They were there for ages last night, asking all sorts of questions about Dai and where he might be. I have no idea where he is."

"They came up to mine too. They think we're hiding him."

"Do you really think Dai did this to Bryn?"

Owen sighed and dropped his head. "I really hope he didn't. Obviously, I don't want to believe one of my sons would attack his brother."

"But you think he did. Bryn said as much, didn't he?"

"We just need to find him and make him talk to the police." Owen twisted his cap in his hands.

"Maybe it was an accident and he panicked."

"I think you're clutching at straws, Babs, love. It's pretty certain Dai did it; we just need to know why."

The nurse pulled the curtain open to reveal Bryn propped up on his pillow, now wearing a clean set of pyjamas and a freshly shaved face. He smiled weakly as they walked back towards the bed.

"We need to head off now, son. Poor old Dewi's been on his own for hours; he's not used to it. I'll come back later on or tomorrow."

"You're in good hands here, Bryn. These nurses will look after you. I reckon you'll be home in a day or two, once they know there's no lasting effects of the concussion," said Barbara.

Owen bent down and kissed the top of Bryn's head, then Barbara leaned down to hug the top half of his torso. He held her tightly as she breathed in his scent, a mixture of cedarwood and spices. She leaned back and carefully wiped a tiny spot of shaving foam from below his ear.

"Cheerio. See you tomorrow. I'll wait outside for you, Owen," she said and walked away, turning back at the door of the ward to give a little smile and wave. She took in the scene of Bryn and Owen saying their goodbyes, thinking that she'd certainly made a bad decision in the choice of husband. The two men behind her were kind and decent.

Back at the house, a police car was parked outside. Barbara jumped out of Owen's Mini, walked round the car and peered in at the driver's window. Two officers were in the front seats, half-eaten fish and chips wrapped in newspaper on their laps. One of them rolled down the window and the aroma of vinegar and grease drifted out, making her stomach rumble. She'd hardly eaten since breakfast.

"Evening, Mrs Roberts," said the first through a mouthful of chips.

"Evening, officers. Why are you here?"

"We're waiting for your husband to come home. Have you heard from him?" said the second, wiping a greasy smear from his chin.

"No. Not a word."

"You must have some inkling of his whereabouts."

"No, I haven't. I've not seen him for two days—three actually."

Owen appeared beside her. "How can we help you officers?"

"We're just waiting here until Dai reappears. He'll have to come back at some point. Don't suppose you know where your son's hiding out do you, Owen?"

"Nope, not seen him since Friday night at the Pendragon."

"Well, I'm getting cold standing out here, so I'm going inside to see my family. Good evening, gentlemen." Barbara turned to Owen. "Thank you for taking me to see Bryn. It must be so hard for you. D'you want to come in for some dinner at least?"

"Thanks for the offer, Babs, but I need to get back to Dewi. I'd like to spend some time alone. I need to think about my sons. I'll come round tomorrow and bring Dewi to see the boys. Cheerio, officers."

The first officer rolled the window back up and they continued munching on their fish and chips, greasy fingers moving methodically from lap to mouth. The windows gently steamed around them.

Barbara smiled thinly and walked down the front path, taking in the neat hedges, manicured lawn and painted shed containing all the boys' garden toys. Dai was very particular about keeping the place 'respectable' as he called it. 'Everything has its place and everything in its place' was his constant refrain.

As she put her key in the lock, she heard the squeals of her sons as they ran to meet her. The door opened and they flung their arms around her legs before she could even step inside.

"Hello, my lovely boys. Look, Grandpa's out there. He's just going home—wave goodbye." Their little arms raised and they shouted in unison towards Owen climbing back into his car.

"Right, let's get inside. It's cold out here and I'm starving. What's for dinner?"

"Nanny made bangles and mash," said Daniel.

"It's bangers, Danny, not bangles," said George. "Bangles are what ladies wear. And Mummy, I had loads of tomato sauce," he added.

"That's nice, darling." Barbara hung up her coat and changed into her slippers. Shirley appeared in the hall. "Hi Mum."

"Hi love, there's a plate in the kitchen for you."

"Thanks, I could eat a horse. You two, why don't you go into the sitting room with Grandpa? Maybe he'll play Snap or Happy Families with you. Mummy and Nanny want to have a chat."

The boys rushed down the corridor and she and Shirley opened the kitchen door. Shirley picked up a tea towel and removed a covered plate from the oven. "Here you go, love. Get some food inside you."

"Thanks, Mum. I don't know how I'd manage without you at the moment." Barbara shovelled the first few forkfuls down her throat and then slowed to a steadier pace.

"So what's the most recent news? Do they know what happened to Bryn?"

Babs swallowed and paused. "The first word Bryn said was 'Dai', so presumably it was he who hit him."

"What? Dai hit his own brother over the head? Why?" Shirley shook her head.

"That's what they're trying to work out, but Dai has vanished. A witness saw his van heading out of town on the road to Dolgellau yesterday afternoon but nothing since." She took another mouthful, savouring the pork and leek flavours of the sausage. "Where d'you get these ones, Mum? They're delicious."

"That butcher in town. Local farmer, apparently. Anyway, if Dai did do it, he's run away, hasn't he?"

"That's what it looks like. But there's another twist. Jim, you know the bloke in the cottage in Bontddu; his wife Isabella had the accident on the moped."

"Yep, I know who you mean."

"Well, he's also disappeared. And worse still, his cottage's burnt out."

"Oh, good Lord! It just gets more and more complicated."

"And now, two policemen are sitting outside the house in a very obvious police car. What will our neighbours think?" Barbara scraped the last of the peas, potato and sausage onto her fork and finished her meal. "That's so much better, I haven't eaten since breakfast."

"You need to look after yourself, love." Shirley smiled at her daughter. "Look, I'll clear up in here and you go and put your boys to bed. They need some normality in their lives."

"Thanks, Mum." Barbara got up and opened the kitchen door. In the hall, she took a deep breath and blinked back the prickling behind her eyes. Inhaling deeply, she opened the door to the sitting room.

"Hello, love. Danny here's beating us all hands down," said Douglas as he looked up and smiled at his daughter.

"He's cheating, Mummy!" cried Danny.

"No, I'm not, I'm just better at it because I'm older than you," explained George.

"Well, it's time for bed now, anyway, so finish this round and then up the apples and pears for you two."

Barbara sat down on the settee and watched her father and his grandsons play Happy Families. *What cards would we all be?* she wondered. *Mr Roberts the fugitive and Mrs Roberts the accomplice? No,* she told herself. *I'm nothing like an accomplice, I'm simply another one of the pieces in Dai's drama.*

The game finished and Daniel packed the cards neatly away in the box. Barbara hauled herself out of her chair. "Come on then you two, up to bed now; school in the morning."

The boys followed her obediently up the stairs and into the bathroom. As she was tucking them in, Daniel whispered, "When is Daddy coming home?"

"I'm not sure at the moment, love. This job might take him a while. Do you mind him being away?"

"Not really," said Daniel and snuggled under the sheet and blanket, pulling the eiderdown under his chin, his bear under his arm.

"It's nice when it's just us, Mummy," added George. "I love Daddy and I try to be good. But sometimes when he's angry, he shouts at us."

Barbara stroked his head and tucked his little green stuffed dragon in with him. "Well, it's just us for now, and I'm sure Daddy doesn't mean to shout. Settle down now and sleep tight, both of you."

She switched on the night-light between their beds then stood up to leave their bedroom. "Night, Mummy," they said together. She smiled at them then turned off the main light and pulled the door closed behind her. Outside their bedroom door, on the dark landing, she leaned against the wall and slid slowly downwards until her bottom was on the floor. Only then did the silent sobs wrack her body.

CHAPTER 19

Isabella

There was a screech of tyres outside the window of the front room.

"What the hell was that?" said Dai from his position in the corner armchair—Jim's chair.

"Probably nothing. You often hear young lads racing up and down this street, don't you Jim?" said Isabella with a nod to her husband.

"Er, yeah, all the time. They like to show off their new wheels."

Dai's eyes narrowed and he stood up. Slowly he walked over to the curtains, which were pulled shut to keep the warmth in. He pulled them apart slightly and peeked out of the gap. The flash of a blue light reflected off his face. He dropped the edge of the curtain and turned sharply.

"Which one of you called the bloody police? I'll..." He was interrupted by thumping on the front door in the hall and the sound of voices.

"Police, open up!"

Isabella stood up as if to go to the door, but she was not quite as agile since her accident. Dai moved swiftly and grabbed her, one arm around her waist, the other across her throat.

"Don't move, Jim, or I won't be held responsible for my actions." His voice was low and his face menacing.

"Let her go, Dai! She's not done anything to hurt you." Jim went to stand up but Dai tightened his grip on Isabella and he sat heavily on the settee.

"Dai," croaked Isabella. "The police are just outside the door. You can't get away now. Just let me go and hand yourself in, it'll be better for you in the end."

"Be quiet. I need to think."

All thoughts were interrupted by the sound of wood splintering and a metallic ping as the front door hit the hall wall. Isabella tensed as Dai's grip tightened. She caught Jim's eye and raised her eyebrows. Another loud crash startled all three of them as the door burst open and three police officers rushed one after the other into the sitting room accompanied by an icy blast of cold air from outside.

Seeing Dai holding Isabella around the throat from behind, they stopped dead. Isabella relaxed her shoulders slightly as the first one held up his hands and stepped slowly forwards, "Just let her go, Mr Roberts. Let her go and we can talk about this rationally." His voice was calm and, as he approached, Isabella could see his blue eyes shining beneath the rim of his helmet.

"I'll let her go if you let me go."

Dai stepped backwards, almost up against the gas fire, pulling Isabella with him. The flames were heating the backs of her legs, and she was thinking that Dai's must be even hotter. As his eyes darted around the room, all of them frozen in position watching them, the closest police officer's hands moved very slightly towards the pair. She heard Jim clear his throat as he inched forward on the settee. The two other police officers pulled the sitting room door wider. Dai's grip tightened.

Suddenly, Isabella stamped on Dai's foot with all the force she could muster. He squealed and loosened his grip, then stepped backwards into the fire. A few sparks brushed onto the back of his jeans. Her nostrils filled with a faint smell of burning fabric. He hopped from one leg to the other then, realising the potential for danger, loosened his grip on Isabella to bend over to brush them off. She took the opportunity to duck out of his hold and get across the room towards Jim's open arms. Two

144

policemen stepped up to Dai and grabbed both of his arms. One officer said triumphantly, "You're nicked mate."

Dai wriggled and squirmed between them. "You idiot, Isabella!" he spat. The policemen dragged him out of the door towards the front door and the waiting police car.

"Don't go anywhere. We'll need to talk to you about what happened," said the first officer over his shoulder.

"Are you all right Bella?" Jim asked.

"Yes Jim. I'm fine. He was a bit annoyed, wasn't he?"

Jim laughed. "Such an understatement. So typical of you, my love."

"So, what happens now?"

"I suppose we ought to let Nurse Babs know. After all, he's her husband."

"Have you got a number for her?"

"She left it on a bit of paper when you were in Bontddu. I'll have a look in me wallet."

Jim disappeared out into the hallway and Isabella flopped down on the settee. She smiled as she looked at the scorch marks on the hearth and thought about her own quick thinking. "Get me, catching a criminal," she said aloud to the walls.

"Who you talking to, love?"

"Just myself. Can't believe I was brave enough to stamp on him. Hurt my leg a bit though."

"It was worth it. Anyhow, I found her number, shall we give her a ring?"

They pulled the telephone over towards them on the settee and Jim slowly dialled the number. It rang three, four, five times. "Maybe she's not there," whispered Jim. It rang another three times. Isabella took the phone receiver from her husband.

"Hello?" said a breathless voice from across the mountains.

"Hello, Babs. Is that you?"

"Yes, it is. I was just putting the boys to bed."

"Sorry to disturb you so late, but we've got some news dear," said Isabella.

"Oh right."

"Well Jim here—"

"Jim's with you? Well that's a relief. We've all been worrying about him, he just vanished."

"It's fine, love," Jim said. "I'm at home with Bella."

"In West Bromwich?"

"Yes," Isabella confirmed. "Anyway dear, Dai brought Jim with him from Barmouth."

"He kidnapped me, Babs, dragged me into his van waving his spanner at me."

"It wasn't a spanner, Jim: it was a ratchet handle. So anyway, Dai was here for a couple of nights, had us pretty much locked up in the sitting room with the curtains closed. So, when I went to the loo—we've got one downstairs in the hallway—I saw someone at our front door so I grabbed a bit of loo paper and scribbled 'Help us. Call police' on it and shoved it out the letterbox. I had a lipstick in my handbag, my favourite one actually."

"What a clever wife she is," said Jim.

"You really are, Isabella! Sounds like that did the trick," said Barbara. "So, whoever it was phoned the police presumably?"

"Yes, she did."

"She?" said Jim.

"Yes, she. It was definitely Susan, I'd recognise her silhouette anywhere Jim." She raised her eyebrows at her husband. "As you would too."

"I didn't realise it was Susan. What was she doing coming round the house?"

"That's irrelevant right now. So, Babs, Susan called the police and they've just this minute stormed the house and arrested Dai."

146

"What a relief," sighed Babs. "I'll let everyone know. What happens now?"

"We're not really sure. Jim needs to fix the front door though."

"The police asked us to stay here, at least for a day or two. We'll need to give a statement or whatever it's called," said Jim.

"Oh Jim, I've just remembered, we've got some bad news I'm afraid."

"Oh? What?"

Barbara exhaled loudly at the other end of the line. "It seems there was a fire up at your cottage. The firemen went up when someone saw a plume of smoke. The whole place is gutted. That's how we knew you'd vanished. Your car was there, but no sign of you, alive or dead."

Jim exhaled loudly and his chin sunk to his chest, "Oh no." The words whistled slowly from his lips. Bella tapped his knee gently and put her arm around his shoulders.

"I'm so sorry, Jim, we all knew how much you loved that place," said Barbara.

"Thank you for letting us know, Babs dear. Keep in touch, won't you?"

"Of course. And you take care of that leg, Isabella. Cheerio."

"Bye for now." Isabella replaced the handset and pushed the telephone back to its position. She turned to her husband who was still sitting dejectedly on the seat beside her. "Oh Jim dear, maybe we can buy another place, maybe in Barmouth this time."

"But I loved being up in the hills with the woods and fields around me. A little piece of paradise. It was so quiet after this busy town."

"But there was no running water or electricity, love. Not a place for us both to be comfortable."

"I know, Bella, but it was mine and I loved it."

"How do you think the fire started?"

147

"I reckon it was the range, or the lamp. They were both alight when Dai made us leave in such a rush—he wouldn't put them out, or let me do it. And I don't even remember if he shut the front door. One gust of wind, or an animal knocking the lamp might have set it off." He exhaled loudly. "What a shame."

"Well, love, let's have a cup of tea. And I'd like a bath. I haven't changed these clothes since Dai brought you back."

"Sounds like a good idea. I'll take a look at the front door."

He dragged himself up and off the settee, his tall frame filling the space between them. Slowly, he walked towards the hallway and outside to collect some tools. Isabella went to the kitchen and put the kettle on.

She made the tea and took it to Jim on the doorstep. She pulled her cardigan more tightly around her body and shivered a little. "Here you go, dear. It's chilly out here so this should warm you up. I'm going up for a bath, shall I leave you the water?"

"I'm almost done here, so yes please."

---0---

In the bath, Isabella ducked under the surface of the water, holding her breath while her thoughts were whizzing around like cars on a bumper car track. She pulled herself upright, "Susan!" she said aloud, as the water slopped up the side of the bath and trickled over the edge. "Why did Susan come round? That bloody woman!"

She examined her body under the bubbles: her small breasts were still rounded and quite pert, not falling under her armpits quite yet. Her stomach wasn't as flat as it once was, before the children, but she only had a very faint stretch mark down one side. Her legs were slim, and the bruise on her hip had almost completely faded now. *I'm not looking too awful for a woman in her fifties. Why did Jim need Susan? Maybe he likes more of a handful? Maybe he was bored with slim...*

She filled a jug with warm water and poured it over her head to rinse off the last of the shampoo—and the comparisons with her best friend. Her clenched jaw an outward sign it hadn't worked. *What the bloody hell did she want, anyway? Coming round here where she's definitely not wanted.* Isabella stood up and placed one hand on the side of the avocado green bath, tentatively lifted first one leg, then the other, and placed them on the mat. She wrapped a towel around her head and another around her slender body.

"Bathroom's free!" she called down the stairs on her way to their bedroom.

"Thanks, love." His heavy steps reverberated across the landing as he stomped up towards her and the waiting bath.

As she dressed and blow-dried her hair, Jim was shaving and bathing. *I wonder if he'll say anything about it?* she thought as she curled the brush around her locks. *We still haven't discussed what we're going to do next—Dai interrupted all that.*

She looked at her reflection in the long wardrobe mirror as she pulled on clean knickers and a bra, then a slip, her dress and finally a cardigan. She decided not to bother with tights. Now Jim had seen to the door, the house was warming up.

Stuffing her dirty clothes into the washing basket, she looked at their two single beds. *When had that happened? Two years ago, maybe.*

The photos of their children in their last year of school sat proudly on the dressing table in matching gilt frames. *Where in the world is Freddie now? And Irene. Good thing she was away with Gerald this weekend. So good she's settling down now; maybe there'll be a wedding next year. Something to look forward to. Where does that leave me and Jim? No children at home—maybe we need a new start. Away from all this unpleasantness. Away from temptation.*

149

Her reverie was disturbed by a loud sloshing followed by gurgling as the water drained away down the plughole, and with it, the memories of their unusual weekend. She heard the rhythm of her husband rubbing the towel across his back then chest, then the change in tone as he moved down each leg, and then between them. She blushed slightly as she remembered how intimate they'd once been.

Is that a thing of the past? I haven't felt the urge for years. That's the trouble with the change—takes all the fun away. Unless you're Susan, that is? She clearly hasn't lost her desire for a piece of it, and my piece at that!

Jim appeared in the doorway, his chest bare and firm despite his advancing years. She realised he was handsome and strong, still the same man. He looked at her staring at him.

"What's up, Bella?"

"I'm just remembering our first time. Before our wedding night, we got carried away, didn't we?"

"Yes, we did." Jim smiled. He dropped his towel and walked over to her, wrapped his arms around her and bent down to kiss her tenderly: first on the lips, then on her neck and round to her throat and behind her ear. Her body tingled and she didn't want to push him away. Slowly, she relaxed into his caresses.

Encouraged, he lifted her onto the single bed and waited for her reaction. He carefully undid all the buttons she had so diligently done up on her cardigan. His attention switched to her hands as he kissed each finger, focussing on her wedding band. His hands strayed to her knees, where he began stroking her legs from her ankles to her thighs; her dress ruching up as he got further. Isabella closed her eyes and breathed in gently, and exhaled more quickly as his hand reached the edge of her knickers. She allowed him to remove them slowly and run firstly his fingers and then his mouth around her. A gasp escaped as his tongue gently explored places she'd forgotten she even had.

---0---

Later, lying squeezed together on the pink counterpane, Isabella asked, "Why did we stop doing that, Jim?"

"I don't know, Bella, love. Wish we hadn't though."

"Well, let's remember this." She turned and kissed his cheek. "Right, we'd better have something to eat. It must be nearly ten o'clock."

Jim leant over to his bedside cabinet to look at his little alarm clock. "Nine thirty. Let's just have a sandwich then."

"We've got a bit of ham, I think. You like that with a bit of piccalilli."

"Sounds lovely. Just like you."

Isabella bustled around the bedroom, hanging her dress back in the wardrobe, folding her cardigan ready for the drawer and finding a nightie. Jim lay on the bed in his naked glory and observed her every movement. When she was ready, he jumped up and pulled on his pyjamas, dressing gown and slippers, then took her in his arms.

"Look at us, we're like teenagers again."

"Yes, but with a world of trials and tribulations behind us."

"We're going to be all right now, me and you. Aren't we?"

"It's a starting point, Jim." She smiled and nodded. "Let's see how things go. I've still got plenty to think about."

CHAPTER 20

Owen

The local sergeant showed Owen into a room where his son was sitting at table with his head in his hands. A tall constable stood in the corner, watching everything.

"You've got ten minutes. Don't normally allow it, but since it's you, Owen..." He closed the door and left the three of them. Owen heard his footsteps plodding away down the corridor.

Owen walked towards the table. Dai stood up. The policeman glared at him. He sat down again and held out his hands. "I'm so sorry, Da. It all just got out of hand. One minute I was happily married and the next I'm sitting in a police cell and I'm a criminal."

"What were you thinking, kidnapping Jim?" Owen shook his head and looked around the stark room with peeling white walls.

"I dunno, Da. I wasn't myself. I just panicked."

"You're lucky he isn't pressing charges. It's just the attack on Bryn they're looking at now."

Dai held his head in his hands, his elbows propped on the small table in front of him. He looked up, his chin wobbling as he said, "I know, I know, Da. I'm so ashamed of myself. I saw red—thought he'd been with Babs. Saw the rest of my life flash before me: weekend dad, living in a small flat. And Bryn smiling in my house with my life."

"You've made some bad decisions which have led you here. Bryn had nothing to do with them, did he? He was just helping Babs and your boys at a difficult time."

"How is he anyway?"

"Who, Bryn? He's out of hospital, a few stitches and a large bump on the back of his head still."

"And Babs and the boys?"

"They've gone to Scotland for a little holiday with her mum and da. It's half-term, apparently."

"Oh right."

"You know she wants a divorce, don't you?"

"Yes, the letter came to the garage: that was another thing that set me off. Saw the bloody brown envelope again and it made everything wash over me. I've been such a bloody idiot."

"Well, we'll have to see what happens now. I don't think Bryn is going to press charges either so the police'll have nothing to hold you here for."

"What's he thinking of doing then?"

"He's coming here to talk to you, then he'll decide what to do. He just needs to get his thoughts straight, Dai. It's been a bit of shock for him and all. It's not every day your brother hits you over the head. With a ratchet handle, wasn't it?"

"Don't remind me, Da. Every time I lie down and close my eyes, I can see it all happening in slow motion, over and over again. It's a nightmare." He dropped his chin to his chest and sniffed.

"It's not been easy for anyone, Dai." Owen's lips were tight and his eyes unblinking. His mind full of his two sons at war and his heart full of sadness. What would their mother have thought?

"I'm so sorry, Da. I never meant things to get so out of hand." He lifted his chin slightly and a small sob escaped.

"We're here now and we'll just have to see what happens next. But you'll have to change your ways, Dai. You can't use violence when things don't go your way." Owen's jaw was set, hard and unmoving. Sympathy for this stranger in front of him would be slow to grow.

"Time to go now, Mr Roberts." The policeman in the corner broke his silence and stepped towards them both.

Owen stood up. "Right son, you have a good think about what you're going to say to your brother when he comes to see you."

"Yeah, I will. And Da..." He stood up and reached out to his father. "I love you."

"I love you too, son, but sometimes it's not enough just to say it. We need to see it, too."

Owen walked slowly down the steps of Barmouth Police Station. He looked around at the empty sky and the trees losing their leaves. He caught sight of Dewi, tied up by the railings, wagging his tail and seemingly smiling at his master and friend.

"Hello Dewi, old boy. See, I wasn't that long, was I?" His fingers unclipped the lead and he stroked Dewi's furry back. "Right, where to now, eh? Think I need a walk to blow away these troubles."

He pulled his hat out of his pocket and over his ears, slipped on his gloves, stood his collar up, then strode purposefully down the road towards the beach. As he walked, a few locals looked at him and then away quickly. Long term friendships were stretched by these current circumstances. Owen knew the gossip about his family would be filling the air like cumulonimbus for a few weeks yet, until the next crisis took over. He didn't much care for that aspect of small-town life.

He looked out to sea and thought about his close friends from his fishing days. As the waves broke on the sand, he remembered all those nights and days out on a small boat in all weathers and conditions, and how it cemented trust and loyalty. He smiled at the thought of their conversations on the boat, especially old Gareth and his philosophising. What was the name of that German bloke he used to go on about, was it Nitka? No, Nietzsche. These thoughts were interrupted by Dewi barking excitedly. He looked up: there was Charlie running headlong towards them both.

"Hello, old boy!" He ruffled the labrador's ears as Tony approached. Clare and Cathy, wrapped up in hats and scarves, jumped and skipped around him. The dogs ran off across the beach, chasing seagulls and seaweed. The small group walked together along the sand in the lea of the sea wall.

"Good to see you, Owen. Heard about Dai. Must be a relief to know where he is."

"That it is, Tony. How are you two lovely girls?"

"I'm all right, Mr Roberts. Owen, I mean," said Clare.

"Su'mae, Mr Owen. That means 'how are things?' Daddy," said Cathy. "It's a bit windy, isn't it?"

"Very well, Cathy. And yes, it certainly is windy. Blows away the cobwebs, like."

"Sut dach chi?" said Clare slowly, chewing the unfamiliar Welsh sounds. "That means 'how are you?'"

"I'm fine, thank you. Sut wyt ti?"

"Iawn, diolch," replied Clare, a broad smile lighting up her face. "I said 'thank you' in Welsh."

"They're coming on all right, aren't they? Good to hear them speaking Welsh a bit now," said Tony. "Thank you so much for all you've done, Owen. And if there's anything we can do for you, please let us know, won't you?"

"Thank you, Tony, I'll let you know." Dewi ran over and dropped a clump of bladder wrack on his owner's feet. "Diolch yn fawr iawn! What am I supposed to do with that?" He threw his head back and laughed aloud as he kicked the seaweed back onto the sand and watched the dogs barking and frolicking.

"That means 'thank you very much,' Daddy," Clare translated.

"Thank you, Clare," said her father putting his arm around her shoulders. "Right you two, time to go. Mummy's probably finished work now, so we could go and meet her. We want to spend some time together as a family," Tony said to Owen. "We're off to the pictures in Dolgellau this afternoon."

"Oh, that'll be lovely. What you going to see?"

"They're showing the second Herbie film again, because it's half-term."

"Herbie? Never heard of that one."

"It's about a car that's like a person," said Cathy. "Daddy had a car like that before he crashed it."

Owen turned his head to the side and looked at Tony, "Did you?"

"Yeah, stupid thing really. Too fast round a bend, skidded and rolled it right over."

"Sounds serious. You're okay, obviously."

"Yeah, lucky the girls weren't in the car with me."

They stopped at the bottom of the steps and Tony bent down to put Charlie on the lead. The girls jumped up, each one holding hands. "We'll be off now, Owen. Take care and let us know if we can do anything, won't you?" Tony put his hand on Owen's shoulder and smiled at him.

"Thank you, very kind. Enjoy the pictures, girls." They waved down at him. "Bye for now, Tony."

He watched as the family made their way up the road towards the Doctor's surgery, then he turned and walked back along the beach, Dewi by his side with his tongue lolling out of the side of his mouth. As the wind whipped around his ears, he wondered if the people living far away across the Atlantic Ocean in America and further south, in the warm and sultry Caribbean, had the same worries and family concerns that he had. The seagulls cawed, repeating the words and thoughts from those living across the bay—in Ireland and far beyond. He shrugged and continued his path.

Before long, he was back at Ty Crwn, the Round House as the tourists called it—an old jail. *Lucky Dai wasn't put in there!*

He smiled wryly as he and Dewi continued on towards the garage.

He pushed the big door open and called out, "Bryn?"

"Hi Da. I'm in here." A familiar, but disembodied, voice reached his ears. Dewi ran towards the office and looked back at his owner. Owen followed him into the dim garage space and looked at the tool cupboards around the edges and up on the wall. The smell of oil and grease filled his nostrils.

"Sut wyt ti, Bryn?"

"I'm fine. Just finishing off a bit of paperwork here." He looked up from a blue, oil-stained notebook. "You'll right, Da?"

"Yeah, just seen Tony and the girls on the beach. Went for a walk to clear my head. I saw Dai this morning."

Bryn jerked his head up. "And how is he? Murderous bastard."

"No need for that, Bryn. He's actually quite remorseful."

"He would be, wouldn't he? He doesn't want to end up banged up in prison." Bryn slammed his pen down and shut his book with a bang.

"Look, Bryn, son. He'll only go to prison if you press charges—"

"Why shouldn't I? He tried to do me in—hit me over the head for God's sake."

"Just listen to me. He wants to put things right. Wants to apologise. Just give him a chance."

"Oh Da, you're a fool to believe him. He'll never change. He's always had a temper and he treats other people like shit. Look at what he's done to Babs and the boys, and now to me. I don't trust him and never will again."

"He's your brother, Bryn. Just go and talk to him and then make your decision. This has frightened him and he'll learn from it. I promise you."

"How can you make that promise? Only he can do that." Bryn stood up and climbed out of his blue overalls then hung

158

them on the back of the door. He looked at his father whose shoulders were slumped and his head hung low, his chin almost touching his chest. "Okay Da, I'll go and talk to him." He sighed. "And let's see how things go from there."

"Thank you, son. Means a lot to me, and maybe you and he can have a reasonable conversation."

Together they walked to the doors. "Fancy a bite to eat, Da? Must be almost lunchtime."

"Sounds good to me. I've got some lamb soup leftover. Let's get a loaf and have it at home."

Bryn nodded and together they walked up the narrow footpath and steps to the cottage, Dewi leading the way.

CHAPTER 21

Jim

Jim climbed off the moped, stretched out his long limbs and pulled the goggles over the top of the helmet. *How the bloody hell did Bella do that journey on this little thing?* He looked at the number on the front door and checked a piece of paper from his pocket, then undid the elastic cables from the back of the moped, threw his bag over his shoulder and walked down the path to the Sea Breeze Bed and Breakfast.

"Afternoon, Mr Cartwright. Good journey?" asked the landlady as he came inside.

"I've had more comfortable journeys," he said, nodding his head to the direction of the moped parked on the road.

"All that way on that little thing?"

"Yes, so I could kill for a loo and a cup of tea."

"Oh yes, come on in out of the cold; the loo is just down the hall on the left." She laughed.

"Ta." Jim dropped his bag and helmet on the floor and dashed inside. The landlady closed the front door and waited at the bottom of the stairs with a key on a lighthouse keyring swinging in her hand. When Jim reappeared, she led him up to a room on the first floor overlooking the bay.

"You're lucky; no way you'd get a room along this road in summer. We're full to bursting then, like." She opened the door to reveal a large double bed to the right and a wardrobe to the left. Straight ahead of them a huge bay window with heavy brocade curtains dominated the space.

"It's only for a day or two, just got some things to tie up in town." Jim followed her in and dropped his bag on the bed.

She turned to look at him, "Are you that bloke that found Bryn Roberts?"

"I am indeed." He nodded slowly.

"Well, good thing you did. He's a good bloke, well-respected in the town. Not like that brother of his—bit of a Casanova that one. Feel sorry for their da, I do. Must be heart-breaking to have that split your family apart. Bad enough when Owen's wife died, he was broken then." She shook her head as if to dislodge her memories from the depths of her mind.

"I can't comment on the family. But thank you for the room. I'll just get my stuff sorted then." He moved towards the door and tried to gently usher her with his arms open.

"So, I'll do breakfast from eight till nine. Sausage, bacon and all the works all right with you, Mr Cartwright?"

"Yes, yes, that's perfect. Thank you." He closed the door and leaned against it, pausing to admire the magnificent view over Cardigan Bay: the sea grey, the white caps on the waves hinting at the strength below. Swiftly, he unpacked his pyjamas, washbag and clean clothes, and found space on the dressing table and in the drawers.

A knock on the door interrupted him. He sighed and opened the door. "I brought you a cup of tea. I added sugar. Most men take sugar, don't they, like?"

"Yes, thank you, that's very kind. I'll drink this and then I need to pop out." He took the mug from her and firmly closed the door. Sitting on the chair in the bay window, he stretched out and took a sip—thankfully one sugar was just enough to make it palatable.

---0---

Jim stepped out into the cold air and walked down the sea front towards the arcade. There, he turned left and walked along the High Street and stopped outside Walter Jones Estate Agents.

162

For a few moments, he studied the cards in the window and then opened the door; a bell rang as he entered.

"Can I help you sir?" A young man asked. He looked as if he had only just started shaving and wore his suit uncomfortably. There was spot of blood on the collar of his white shirt and his black lace-up brogues were a little scuffed.

"I'm looking to buy a house."

"Well, you're in the right place. Come and sit down and tell me what you're after." The lad's chirpy manner reminded Jim of Freddie.

Twenty minutes later, Jim had appointments to view three properties: two in Barmouth and one in Bontddu. The first viewing was at five o'clock; it was lucky the owners were home. He looked at his watch, it was just four. He turned his head to see the sign outside the Pendragon swinging. He'd pop in there later for a quick pint but for now he headed in the opposite direction. The door of the garage was open and the sound of music floated towards him, and a voice singing, "I'm gonna make you a star!" from under a burgundy Ford Anglia.

"You hit that top note well there."

"Oh what?" The voice and the body connected as Bryn slid out and stood up. "Well, hello there Jim. Good to see you. And thank you for saving my life, more to the point."

"It were lucky I stopped and found you, weren't it? Good to see you on your feet... well, your back. Just thought I'd pop in, see how you're doing."

"I'm fine, actually. Fully recovered and back to work, as you can see."

"So what's up with this beauty then?"

"Hole in the exhaust, blowing smoke. Shouldn't take too much longer. And what are you doing back in Barmouth then?"

"Me and Bella have decided to sell up and move here for good. And I need to collect my car. Is it still up at the cottage?"

"Yes. Sorry to hear about your cottage. That brother of mine leaves a trail of destruction wherever he goes."

"It wasn't his fault, not entirely anyhow. And it's pushed me and Bella back together and that can't be bad."

"Where is she? Not with you this time?"

"She needed to get things ready in the house in West Bromwich, and she had to work her notice period. No point her leaving until we have somewhere to move to. Costs a lot to move house, so we're learning." Jim felt uncharacteristically talkative, animated about this new stage in their lives.

"Okay, that'll be a change for you both then." Bryn wiped his hands on his overalls. "So, the good news is: your car is still at the cottage. The bad news is: big end's gone."

"Is that what the clonking was then? Thought it sounded serious. You can fix it though, can't you?"

"It's a long shot but we'll need to get it here somehow. I'm not sure I'll be able to get it down that track, especially after the rain. Maybe we can borrow a tractor, though? I'll ask around tomorrow."

"Thanks Bryn, much appreciated. Can I come up there with you? I want to have a last look at the cottage and see if it's worth selling. The estate agent didn't think so, but he was hardly more than a kid, so what would he know?"

"Probably more than you think, actually, Jim. Nobody round here will want to buy a place up there. The only people fool enough to live there are holidaymakers like you." He thumped Jim on the arm. "But you never know, you might find another gullible bloke like you, entranced by the beautiful scenery and the peace of the Welsh mountains." He put the final words in inverted commas with his hands and guffawed.

"Very funny. So shall we say, ten o'clock tomorrow morning to go up there?"

"Yeah, no problem. Where are you staying?"

"The Sea Breeze on the front."

"Oh that Mrs Davies, doesn't half talk, doesn't she? Heart of gold, mind."

"Yeah, I noticed that." Jim looked at his watch. "Right, I'd best be off. I'm going to see a house up on Gibraltar Lane. Looks nice in the photo."

"That's not far from us. No parking though, so maybe it's a good thing your car's buggered, or might be at least."

Jim screwed up his face, "I hope not. Anyroad, Bryn, glad you're back on form. Say hello to your dad for me and I'll see you here at ten tomorrow."

"Bye, Jim. See you tomorrow."

---0---

The following morning dawned bright and clear. The roads were slippery with the previous night's rain and Jim tiptoed around big puddles spanning the pavement. His stomach was full of fried food and he burped with every step.

"Morning, Jim," called Bryn from inside the garage. "Just wait there." He drove the van onto the road outside and Jim climbed inside. Bryn started off in the direction of Bontddu and the burnt-out cottage.

"When did you get the van back? The police took it from ours the day after they arrested Dai."

"They brought it back when they brought Dai. Said there was no need to keep it. Glad they did, I need it to do the job."

"Isn't it Dai's though?"

Bryn exhaled heavily. "Dai said I could keep it—well, I still need to pay the rest of the loan payments—to make up for nearly bashing my brains out. He's looking at his options at the moment but I don't think he's going to stay around here."

"Oh right. He didn't go to court, then?"

"I didn't press charges. In the end, he's my brother and this is a family matter so we've dealt with it in the family."

165

"Me neither. Didn't want all that bother."

"Sounds the most sensible thing to do."

There was a silence for a while then, as they went round the steep bend leaving Barmouth, Bryn asked, "How was the house yesterday?"

"Not right for us. A bit small and you're right about the parking. There was no space outside at all. Bella wouldn't want that. She likes and a bit of garden for her flowers."

"That's the problem with those old fishermen's cottages. Like ours. But Da was a fisherman so that's why we live in one."

"I've another one later today and one in Bontddu."

"We can have a look at while we're here if you like."

"That'd be great. If it's not too much bother. Just to have a look from the outside. Young fella at Walter Jones needs to make an appointment."

"Can't you look at it without the owners? They must have a key."

"I'll ask again." He went quiet and looked out of the window at the surroundings which were soon to become his home. As they rounded the bend and crossed a bridge over the mountain stream, a row of houses appeared on the left.

"Look, there's a sign! That must be it. Can you pull over, Bryn?"

Bryn pulled into the layby in front of a bright red phone box and post box. To the left, behind the houses, tall trees projected from the mountain rock. To the right, across the road, were more trees and beyond them, the estuary. Jim jumped out and slammed the door behind him. Leaves crunched under his feet as walked to the bottom of the steps where he took a deep breath and looked the house up and down. The windows winked in the sunlight and the door smiled invitingly, encouraging him in. His stomach turned over and he was drawn almost involuntarily up the steps. Ahead of him danced his family: his wife, daughter, son and future grandchildren. All of them waving at him from the windows of the tall, white property in front of him.

Bryn leaned out of the passenger window. "You'll right, Jim? You look a bit peculiar, like."

"I'm fine. I think I've found it. I've bloody well found it." He turned round and started to walk back to the van.

"Oh, right." Bryn raised his eyebrows and shook his head. "Ready to go now?"

"Yep. Thanks."

Silence prevailed for the remainder of the journey. Bryn revved the engine as he negotiated his way up the bumpy track and parked in front of the shack. They climbed out and stood side-by-side, taking in the damage. Jim shrugged and exhaled as he took in the charred remnants of his cottage. The door was wide open and the blackened kitchen curtains flapped through the cracked window glass.

Bryn broke the silence. "Bit of a mess, isn't it?"

"Yep, it certainly is."

"What you going to do with it now?"

"I dunno. Nobody in their right mind would want it now, would they?"

"What about that pair up the track a bit?"

"The teachers? Nah, they've done their place up now. Think they like the privacy."

"What about the insurance?"

"Never got any. Didn't think I'd ever need it." Jim sighed heavily and sunk his hands deep into his jacket pockets.

"You'll just have to let nature take it back."

"Yep." He turned to his little car. "Best get this sorted out now then."

CHAPTER 22

Dai

Dai turned the envelope over in his hands. He was sitting on the edge of the lumpy bed in his room at the Pendragon. His dark hair, in need of a wash, flopped forward and he sighed heavily. Slowly, he extracted the letter from the envelope and read again the scratchy words telling him his marriage would soon be over. He shook his head and sighed deeply. A gentle knock on the door interrupted his thoughts.

"Come in, it's open."

A blonde head appeared around the doorframe. "Oh, hi Bethan."

"What you got there, Dai?"

"Divorce papers. She wants a divorce. And maintenance and half the house."

"What are you going to do?" She stepped into the room and sat down next to him.

"Got no choice really, have I?"

"Well, you could always fight it."

"After what I've done? Not a chance. I'm lucky she's letting me have half the house—most women would go for the lot."

"But you've got to have somewhere to live and something to live on."

"Yep, I can't stay here for much longer. I need get my own place and find a permanent job. I've got a couple of irons in the fire."

"What about the garage? I thought that was yours?"

"No that's half Bryn's and I've said he can have the business. He doesn't want me around after what I did." His face was dispassionate and his tone flat.

"Well, you did that in anger, it wasn't all your fault." She put her arm around his shoulders. He turned to face her. He tried out a smile, pleased that at least one person wasn't against him. She looked him in the eyes and continued, "A crime of passion, isn't that what they call it?"

He laughed wryly. "Yeah, I suppose it was. But I'm lucky Bryn didn't have me thrown in jail, so it's the least I could do."

"What's your plan now then?" She shuffled her bottom closer to him, their legs now touching. He put his hand on her thigh, her warmth a welcome change after his experiences of the previous weeks.

"I'll sign these papers, then look for a better job. Maybe somewhere else, away from the scene of the crime so to speak. I'll need somewhere to live where the boys can come and visit."

"And how are your boys? Have you seen them since you've been back?"

"Yeah, I went round with Da yesterday. Daniel was his usual self and George was a bit tearful. Lucky Da brought Dewi, that cheered them up a bit."

"It must be so hard for you, Dai. Losing your home, your job, and your family." She gently rubbed her hand up and down his leg, her long pink fingernails lingering at the top of his thigh. His body hardly responded, a whimper of a strain in his groin which quickly passed. He turned his head towards hers and she caressed his stubbly cheek.

"It really is, Bethan. I'm a broken man." His words were interrupted by her tongue exploring his mouth. He broke away. "What are you doing with me? I haven't got anything to offer you."

"I've always wanted you, Dai, ever since we were kids at school. I was gutted when you married Babs." Her chest heaved as she inhaled and her eyes widened, holding her breath, anxious for a response.

170

"I never knew that. Well, looks like now's your chance. Nobody else wants me." He studied her face with its flawless complexion, and full pink lips. Her eyes were shining and expectant. She looked the same way she had as a teenager and made him feel like he was back there too.

"We could run away together," she said. "Somewhere new, start our lives again." Her smile was fixed in place with a mixture of encouragement and plea. Her hand started its progress towards the growing bulge in his trousers.

"Are you sure, Bethan? What about your husband and family?"

"My marriage was over before it began. My heart was never in it: I just said yes to please my mam and da. It was always you I wanted, Dai."

Dai leaned in, inhaled her perfume, and pushed her blonde hair back behind her ears. He kissed her tenderly at first but with a growing hunger. She responded eagerly. His libido jumped to attention. He pushed her back on the bed, the white counterpane ruching as he pulled her legs up and her trousers down. She wriggled as she lifted her backside, then her bellbottoms landed with a gentle thump on the carpet.

---0---

The following morning, Dai walked down the High Street with a bounce in his step. He thought about the lovely Bethan and their lovemaking the previous night. His confidence was restored by the idea of starting a new life with her.

The manila envelope under his arm did not detract from his good humour. The heavy door gave under his push and he entered the dark reception hall, smiling broadly at the secretary sat behind her wide, wooden desk.

"Morning, love. Just need to drop this off for Mr Jenkins."

"Thank you, Mr Roberts. We can get things moving now. You'll soon be a free agent again." A whisper of a smile crossed her lips.

"I suppose that's one way of looking at it," he agreed. "Well, must get on. Things to do, people to see."

"Cheerio." She waved the envelope. "I'll make sure Mr Jenkins gets this straight away."

"Ta. See you around." Dai smiled and walked out, a slight swagger in his gait.

He stepped outside and took a deep breath, looking up and down the road a couple of times then turned left. He pulled his hat down as the wind gusted, bringing with it the salty smell of seaweed and fish. The slate steps up to his father's house were worn from years of fishermen's boots. He took each one carefully, knowing which were loose and which were still solid. Arriving at the familiar front door, he paused. He remembered his father's face in the police station and his harsh words. As he breathed in and out slowly, he felt like a child again.

The lilting tones of his father's voice, heavy footsteps and the scrape of dog claws on the flagstones drifted outside. He steadied himself before rapping the knocker.

"Who d'you think that might be, Dewi?" The door creaked open. "Oh, it's you Dai."

"Well, that's not much of a greeting, Da. Aren't you pleased to see me?"

"Of course I am. Come on in—the kettle's just boiled." He ushered in his son and pushed the door closed. Dai sat down in a kitchen chair usually reserved for Bryn. Owen slowly made another cup of tea and placed it on the table across the table from his own. "So what brings you here, Dai?"

"Just wanted to let you know what my plans are, Da. Thought you might want to know."

"Ah, okay." Owen nodded slowly and stroked Dewi's head and ears.

172

"So, I've just dropped off the forms at the solicitor. I've agreed to give Babs half the house and I'll start paying the maintenance as soon as I get a permanent job."

"That's the right thing to do. Does Babs know yet?"

"Not yet, but I'll go and see her next."

"Good. She needs some reassurance. She's been worried sick about what you might do."

"Yeah, I suppose she has. But she's no need to fret anymore. I know I've made mistakes."

"That's an understatement if ever I heard one." He took a sip of his tea and placed the cup carefully on the old oak table.

"So, the bigger news is, I've decided to move away from Barmouth. Too many people know my business here and they'll judge me every time they see me. I want to put it behind me and start again somewhere else."

"Oh right." Owen's words were slow and deliberate. "What about your boys?"

"I'll see them as often as I can; holidays and such."

"They'll miss their da. Not good for young sons to grow up without a father."

"I know, but I need to put myself first."

"No change there." Owen paused and Dai wrinkled his forehead. "Where are you thinking of going then?"

"I've sent off an application for a job on the oil rigs in the North Sea. They pay good money and once you're trained up the pay goes up even more. Plus, you get plenty of holiday."

"Oil rigs? That means you'll need to be in Scotland."

"Yep, Aberdeen probably. Sort of works with Babs' parents living up there. Danny and George can come up to see me and visit their grandparents at the same time."

"It's still quite a distance between Glasgow and Aberdeen though."

"I'm sure we'll work it out, Da."

173

Owen sighed. "Well it's your life, Dai. You do what think is best. And you're right, people round here won't forget what you've done, not for a long time."

"I know, but I'll be back to see you. It's not forever."

"How long before you know if you've got a job? You'll need to get things sorted round here, won't you?"

"About a week, two at the most."

"What about your police record?"

"I haven't got a record. Bryn and Jim didn't press charges, did they?"

"And references, don't they need those? Bit difficult when you work for yourself. And you can hardly ask Bryn now, can you?"

"The bank manager is one and the chap I'm working for at the garage over in Harlech. It's just temporary while I wait to hear about the new job. I need to earn something to live on for now. It's all under control, Da, and it's my problem anyway."

"Yes, I know that son. I'm happy for you, but only if you're sure this is the right path to take."

"I'm sure." Dai gulped the last of his tea and stood up to leave. "I'll be off, need to catch Babs on her break now."

Owen stood up and stretched his back. Dewi got up and brushed against his owner's leg. Owen reached down and put his hand on his dog's head, mutual reassurance flowing both ways. Awkwardly, Dai leaned in to embrace his father. Their elbows knocked as Owen lifted his arms to return the gesture.

"Bye Da. Maybe we can catch up for a pint in a couple of days."

"I'd like that." Owen nodded, his blue eyes clouding with sentiment.

Dai turned to wave at his father standing in the doorway and walked down the cobbled path to the steps, shrugging his coat around him. His next stop was the surgery, a more modern building; single storey with a pebbledash frontage and metal windows, typical of buildings thrown up so quickly in the sixties. He pushed open the glass front door and nodded at the receptionist. She was on the phone and indicated with her head that he could go through to the tiny staffroom where Babs would be. He knocked gently on the door and it swung open. As ever, an involuntary tightening in his stomach gripped him when he caught sight of his soon-to-be ex-wife.

"Babs. Good to see you."

"Dai, I wasn't expecting you."

"Just come to tell you that I've returned the divorce papers to the solicitor."

"Oh right." She waited.

"You can have half the house, and the maintenance you asked for. Might take a while for that to start: I need to get a few wage packets under my belt first. Need to pay for my lodgings at the Pendragon for one thing."

She breathed out slowly, "Okay. And what about you?"

"Don't worry about me. I'm sorted for now. I'll keep you updated."

"Thanks." She smiled, her lips tight. "The boys miss you. When can you come and see them?"

"I'll collect them from school today if you like. Take them to the swing park and maybe get a drink in the café."

"I'm sure they'd love that, and I'd really appreciate it too. Organising childcare is really hard since mum and dad went back."

"I'm sure it is, but I can help today. I took a day off to sort a few things out. Need to collect the last of my stuff from the house at some point."

"Do you want to pop in when you drop the boys back then? I'll get home for about four thirty."

"That's a good idea."

"Thank you, Dai." She reached out to put her arm on his coat sleeve. "For everything."

"Well, it's the least I can do, isn't it?" She nodded. "Bye Babs, have a good afternoon."

"Cheerio, Dai."

---0---

The sea air was bracing, all hints of summer well and truly forgotten in the cold November wind. Dai's hat was pulled low and his hands were plunged deep in his pockets as he fought his way along the beach path. He'd stopped off in the pub for lunch and some afternoon delight with Bethan and was now on his way to school to collect his sons. So much had changed in a month, and he felt exhilarated by the prospect of a new life. He was grinning to himself, caught up in his own thoughts as he entered the playground.

"Hello, Dai, wasn't expecting to see you here." A black dog thrust its cold, wet nose into his crotch.

"Oi! Get away!" He pushed Charlie's head away. "Oh, hi Tony. Just collecting the boys—helping Babs out, you know."

"Oh right." Tony wrinkled his forehead and tilted his head to one side.

"And here they are now." With a squawk, a gaggle of children ran into the playground and matched up with their responsible adults.

"Daddy!" George ran towards Dai and flung his arms around his legs. He was followed by a more composed Danny, accompanied by Clare and Cathy either side of him like escorts. As they came level with their respective fathers, they peeled off, leaving Danny alone in front of Dai.

"Hello Dad. Good to see you." His eldest son had matured considerably in the last month, growing into his new position as man of the house. Dai half-expected him to hold out his hand.

176

"Hello Danny. George, can you let go so we can actually walk please?" George dropped his arms and moved round to grab his father's hand. Danny fell into step next to them but made no attempt to hold his father's hand as together they walked to the swing park, the curious eyes of Tony and his daughters on their backs.

CHAPTER 23

Barbara

Barbara watched from the kitchen doorway as Dai slowly unpeeled George's arms from around his neck and placed him gently on the floor. Daniel kissed his father's cheek, then Dai picked up his suitcase and a canvas holdall.

"Be brave for Mummy. I'll see you at the weekend; we can do something nice together. Go to the pictures or something."

"All right, Daddy. We'll be good, like you said," said George.

"Bye, Daddy. See you on Saturday," added Daniel.

They waited on the doorstep as their father left the house and walked down the front path. He turned and waved, then shrugged the holdall onto his shoulder, heading off towards town. The boys ran inside and back into the sitting room and the television.

Barbara closed the front door and leant heavily against it. The sound of Dai's footsteps echoing in her ears. She exhaled then sniffed back some involuntary tears. A vaguely nauseous sensation grew in the pit of her stomach, another physical reminder that her marriage was over. This new chapter would be difficult; being a single mother with two young boys was uncharted territory. She stood up straight and went to join her children. Plonking herself onto the settee, George climbed onto her lap and put his thumb in his mouth. Daniel sat himself next to her and pulled his legs up underneath his body. She put her arm around him and he leaned his head towards her shoulder.

"We're going to be all right boys, don't you worry."

"It's fine Mummy, we'll look after you," said Daniel, his big eyes full of love and concern.

Barbara stroked his head and pulled him closer. George laid his head on her other shoulder. "I love you Mummy," he said moving his thumb to one side.

"And I love you two very much. So, what's this programme about, then?"

---0---

Barbara and Hazel were on their break in the staff cupboard. "I don't know how I'm going to make ends meet. My wages only just cover the mortgage and bills and Dai's given me no maintenance yet. He said he'd give me enough to support the children, but it's been a month since he moved out and so far I've had diddly squat. And Christmas is just round the corner. What am I going to do?"

"Oh God, Babs, I don't know what to suggest. What did he say when you asked him for money?"

"He said he hasn't got a permanent job yet and he had to pay in advance for his rent. But I know for a fact that he's found a place with that Bethan from the pub so they've got two wages coming in."

"Can you ask Owen to talk to him?"

"I could, but he's got enough to worry about as it is. I don't want to add more problems."

"Look, Babs, I obviously don't know him as well as you do, but I'm sure he wouldn't want you and the boys to go short. Just talk to him; he is the boys' grandfather after all."

"I suppose I'll have to. Dai's not stopped being a controlling arse, has he? Now he's just doing it with money. Wish he'd just bugger off." Barbara took a gulp of her tea.

"What about the solicitor? I thought maintenance was a court order. Surely, he has to pay it?"

"I thought that too, but somehow he's wriggled out of it."

180

"Well, here's your plan: first, next time he comes round, demand some cash immediately. Say it's for food for his children. If that works, great, but you'll also need the assurance that he'll start paying you regularly. You'll need him to set up a standing order for the amount agreed in the divorce."

"You're right; I'll just have to be strong. I just really don't like having anything to do with him, Hazel. It's bad enough when he picks up and drops off the boys."

"I don't envy you, Babs, but it's got to be done. When is he due round next? You have to talk to him then. And in the meantime, just mention it to Owen. That might be the prick of conscience he needs."

"You're as sensible as ever. I'm so glad I have you to tell me what to do."

"All part of the service. Talking of which." Hazel glanced at her watch. "We need to get a move on."

They gathered up the detritus of their lunch, straightened their uniforms and left the cupboard. Hazel headed to the reception desk as Barbara pulled on her cardigan and cloak around her shoulders and went outside to her bike. She disliked the winter. Despite sheepskin gloves, thick socks and knee-length boots, her fingers and toes never really warmed up. She deeply regretted not taking driving lessons so she could drive when the weather turned so cold.

Cycling along the High Street, she caught sight of Owen up ahead with Dewi trotting along beside him. He stopped at the crossroads and turned left into the garage, pulling the door closed behind him. Barbara changed direction on her bike and pulled up on the forecourt. She climbed off and leaned her bike against the wall. The familiar voices of her father and brother-in-law chatting drifted out.

"Look Da, I've always loved her, more than Dai ever did. I could look after her and the boys so much better than he did."

"She's still your brother's wife, Bryn. The divorce hasn't come through; it's all a bit quick, and not really appropriate. Not yet at least."

"But she'll need a man about the house. And why not me? I'm already part of their family, and the boys know me. Better than some stranger coming in."

She pushed the door open with a squeak. The voices fell silent. "Talking about me, were you?" Her annoyance rose with her tone. "I'm sure I can make my own decisions."

"We didn't see you there, Babs, love," said Owen turning to her.

"Clearly. Look, I appreciate your concern Bryn, but I'm perfectly capable of deciding who I live with and who my boys live with."

"Well, now it's out in the open." He smiled and shrugged. "What do you think?"

"About which bit, Bryn? You love my boys, your nephews? You want to look after me? I might meet some stranger? Which part of my life do I get a say in?"

"I'm so sorry, Babs. I didn't mean to offend you. I just want to make things easier." Bryn stepped from one foot to the other and continued to wring an oily rag in his hands. His face twisted like a schoolboy caught misbehaving by a teacher. Barbara watched his discomfort dispassionately as her own indignation grew to the size of a beachball.

"Well, you bloody well have offended me! I can make my own decisions about the person I want to live with. And right at this moment, it's neither of you menfolk!" She lifted her head high, turned on her heel and strode out of the garage.

Her legs pumped as she pedalled her bike up the hill to Mrs Jenkins, muttering under breath, "Bloody cheek of it. Bloody men. Think we women can't manage without them to look after us." Her words disappeared on the wind behind her and any

182

others remained in her head as all her breath was exhausted on the effort of forward propulsion.

She leant her bike in the bush and, puffing and panting, took her bag to the front door. She hammered the last of her indignation into the wooden panel. The sound of Cerberus' yapping and claws scraping up the wooden hallway were accompanied by his mistress' voice and stick.

"Okay sweetheart, it's only Nurse Barbara. She's right on time." The door squeaked open. "Come in, it's blooming freezing out there. I've got a nice cup of tea in the pot."

"Afternoon, Mrs Jenkins. Get down Cerberus, you'll ladder my tights."

Barbara followed her and the dancing dog down the corridor to the back sitting room. The last rays of sunshine lit up the wallpaper giving the room a warm glow. Barbara unclipped her cloak and swung it onto the back of a well-worn, leather Chesterfield. Mrs Jenkins sat down in her wing-back chair and rested her shins on a footstool. She poured a cup of tea from a pot on a side table, added a drop of milk, stirred with a silver spoon and handed it to Barbara.

"Here you go, dear. You look like you need this."

"Thank you. It's always an effort getting up that hill, but good exercise so I shouldn't complain too much. Anyway, let's have a look at your leg now." Barbara rubbed her hands together and examined the offending leg.

"I don't mean that, dear. You've got a face like thunder. What's wrong?"

"Nothing really. Just men being men, thinking they can rule your lives and that you can't look after yourself and you can't live without them." Barbara continued pressing and prodding around the wound which was well on the way to healing now.

"That doesn't sound like nothing, does it? Tell me what's happened. I've lived a life without too much input from men interfering. In my experience, they always try, but you can let them in just on your terms."

"Hmm. It took ages for that wound to heal but it looks fine now." She looked up at Mrs Jenkins' face rather than her leg.

"That face tells me you need to talk about it. Drink your tea and tell me more."

Barbara took a slurp and put the bone china cup back on its saucer. "So, you know that waste-of-space of a husband of mine and me are getting divorced."

Her patient nodded slowly and tapped her lap for her little dog to jump up. "Well, he hasn't paid me any maintenance yet, and I know he can because he's got a job and he's sharing the rent with some bimbo from the pub. Well, that's half the problem. Then, I've just overheard my brother-in-law telling my father-in-law that he wants to move in and look after me. The bloody cheek of it!"

Mrs Jenkins let the information settle while she stroked the black furry mound on her lap. "And why would that be such a bad thing?"

Babs huffed. "He's my husband's brother, that's one of the unwritten rules, isn't it? Don't sleep with your husband's relations!"

"That's just biblical nonsense. You can't help who you fall in love with. Or who falls in love with you."

"Well, I don't want to be talked about like a chattel." Barbara put her hands on her hips. "Besides, I can manage without him. Why do men always think we need them to take charge and solve every problem?"

"In this case, it might not be such a bad solution. Look dear, you can allow them to think they're in charge when in fact it's *you* making the decision."

"How does that work? Bryn, that's the brother, said I need looking after."

"Babs my dear, you're clearly an independent woman but at the moment you're struggling because you're doing everything. And your soon-to-be ex-husband isn't paying what he should. Get him to cough up and financially you'll be back on your feet. And how are you going to make that happen? Enlist some help." She nodded emphatically.

"From whom?"

"His father for one. But sounds like you might be able to use Bryn, too. He's desperate to get into your good books."

"Are you suggesting I start seeing Bryn?" Barbara's eyes narrowed.

"Do you like him? In that way?" She raised her eyebrows.

"I've never really given it more than a passing thought, but yes, he's a good-looking man. And actually much nicer than his brother—kinder, more compassionate. But I've never spent time with him on his own so I don't know what he's really, like."

"He sounds perfect. Well, why not ask him out for a drink, somewhere out of town? You're in charge this way and you can make the decision, not him."

"I just wanted a bit of time to myself, with no men around to cook and clean up after."

"That, my dear, is a luxury few women can afford. Not if they want their career, their children, and their sanity."

"It is a bit of a juggling act at the moment. In fact, I need to get on to go and collect the boys now." Barbara jumped up and picked up her cloak, throwing it around her shoulders.

"Well, think about Bryn's offer and don't dismiss it too quickly. And get that waste-of-space of a husband to pay his share."

"I will. I'll see him tomorrow when he collects the boys."

Mrs Jenkins and Barbara walked up the corridor with Cerberus running around their ankles.

"And my last piece of advice: have your wages paid into your own bank account. Fiscal independence cannot be overrated."

Barbara laughed and shook her head. "You're so right. I don't want to be caught out like this again. Thank you, Mrs Jenkins."

"It's Gwendoline, just call me Gwendoline." She looked at the bike as Barbara climbed onto the saddle. "You seriously need to pass your driving test. I'll teach you."

"Will you? That'd be great. I've got to go, I'll be late again. Cheerio."

The front door slammed shut and Barbara turned the bike onto the road. As she freewheeled down the hill, her cloak billowed out behind her and her face was set against the cold. Her mood was lighter as she thought about Bryn and what he might look like with his clothes off. She smiled at the image and mentally thanked Mrs Jenkins—Gwendoline—for the suggestion.

CHAPTER 24

Isabella

"Have you got everything?" Isabella was standing by the front door with her handbag and coat slung around her shoulders. Jim was leaning over the top of the car pulling a rope and two bungee cords over a collection of suitcases. His nose was blue and a little dewdrop was about to drip. He sniffed it back in hard then attached the hook on the cord to the roof rack.

The sound of clattering down the stairs announced Irene's arrival. She stood next to her mother in the open hallway and shrugged her shoulders into her coat.

"I'm here and ready to go." She picked up her handbag and stepped outside. "Oh, it's cold today, hope it doesn't snow on the way." She rubbed her hands together and stamped her feet.

"It's not forecast and if we get on the road now, we'll be there before it's dark. Your dad knows the way; he's done it a few times now. I'll get a couple of blankets though, just in case." Isabella went back inside the house.

"You ready, love? Already said goodbye to Gerald?"

"Yes, Dad. I saw him last night. I'm only going to be gone a couple of nights. I'm sure he'll manage without me." She laughed. "It'll be nice to see where you and Mum'll be living."

"It'll be good to have a new start after everything that's happened."

The front door slammed shut and Isabella appeared next to her daughter. "Are we ready then?"

In response, Jim held the back door open so Irene could climb in, then he folded himself in. Isabella sat her backside in the passenger seat and pulled her legs forward with a slight wince. The healing process was never going to be complete and she still suffered with certain movements. At her feet was a Thermos flask and on the back seat next to Irene was a wicker basket with a selection of sandwiches wrapped in greaseproof paper, three packets of Walkers crisps and three Granny Smith apples. At the bottom, Isabella had secreted a Battenberg cake and a Tupperware box of homemade jam tarts.

"Right, let's be off then," said Jim.

"Cheerio, house," added Isabella.

"You'll be back here a lot though, Mum. It's not goodbye forever."

Jim pulled out and their journey out of Birmingham, across Shropshire and into the Welsh hills of Snowdonia National Park, began.

---0---

Four hours later, Jim pulled up outside the white, three-storey house in Bontddu. He switched off the engine and opened his door.

"Let us out of here, Dad. My backside's been numb since Welshpool!" Jim negotiated his way out, stretched his back and pulled the driver's seat forward. Irene emerged like a snail from its shell and pulled her shoulders back.

"Can you give me a hand please, Jim?" Isabella called from the passenger seat. "My legs are stiff as anything."

Together, they stood and looked up the house which was now their home. "It's all right, Dad. You chose a good-looking place. I like the shutters."

Jim put his arm around his wife's shoulder. "What d'you think, Bella?"

"It's lovely, Jim." She nodded. "Let's get inside and have a look around."

He picked up her bag and guided her up the steps, Irene following behind. The key turned smoothly in the lock and he swung the door open. He stepped inside, flicked the light switch, and held the door wide open.

"Welcome to our new home, Bella." He helped her over the threshold and into the corridor. Irene followed and pulled the door behind her.

Bella looked around at the narrow entrance hall and glanced up the stairway to her right. The peeling wallpaper was reminiscent of William Morris with unspecified yellow flowers and pale green leaves on a dark blue background. Wooden floorboards were covered with a moth-eaten hall runner which at some point in its life may have had a Turkish feel about it—again in shades of navy blue. Someone had painted the skirting boards and spindles in a sickly hue of pale yellow, presumably to match the flowers on the wallpaper. The same patterns repeated up the stairs. Her eyebrows arched and her mouth pursed, Irene cleared her throat to speak but thought better of it. Jim led them towards a dirty cream door with two smeared glass panels in the top half. He put his hand on the metal handle and pushed it open with a flourish.

"And here's the kitchen." He swung his arm out and invited them in. They walked slowly into the L-shaped room and again inspected the area. To the right was a tall melamine larder unit in pale green with sliding glass doors at the top and drawers and cupboards below. Another unit of a similar style was against the back wall. To the left, around the corner, was a yellow, drop-leaf dining table with six matching chunky chairs. The room was dominated by a large window which looked out onto a wall of rock and there was a door to the garden down a passage on the right.

"Well, it's big," said Irene.

"And it has running water," added Bella, nodding towards a Belfast sink under the window. "And electricity." She ran her hand over the top of a fridge and inspected the grime on her fingers.

"Better than the cottage for definite. And it has an inside loo and bath. Wait till you see upstairs. The view from the sitting room is magnificent." Jim smiled broadly. "Come and have a look."

Jim put an arm around his wife and his daughter standing in the bay of the window in the upstairs sitting room. "Would you just look at that? It's what sold the house for me."

The height of the house gave them a panoramic view across the top of the trees opposite and right across the estuary towards Cader Idris in the distance. To their left, as the sun set, it cast a pinkish glow which reflected off the sea.

"Beautiful, isn't it love?" He pulled them in more tightly. "You don't get views like this in West Bromwich." He exhaled allowing a grin to split his face.

"Yes, dear. It's beautiful." Bella shifted herself and looked around the room, her eyes taking in a three-piece suite with mustard and brown stripes and a long low, teak cabinet with short, tapered legs. "Good thing they left the furniture; saves us buying more for here."

"And it means we'll have something to sit on," said Irene.

"See, it's all working out perfect, love." Jim turned to look at Bella, trying to draw her into his enthusiasm. "Let's take a look at the rest of the place then." He showed them a double bedroom and a bathroom, the other rooms on that storey, then up the stairs to two further bedrooms. "And there's plenty of space when the kids come to visit. And any grandkiddies when the time comes." He grinned at Irene.

"Bit soon to be thinking of that, Dad! Gerald hasn't even proposed yet."

"He needs to get a move on before someone else snaps you up, love!" Jim guffawed.

Bella started walking down the stairs and called back. "Come on you two, we better get the bags in and some tea on or we'll be eating at midnight."

Irene and her mother climbed out of the car by the harbour, watched by Bryn, who was taking a break with a cup of tea. As Isabella turned, balancing on her stick, she caught sight of him and raised her free hand, smiling in greeting. He nodded and smiled back.

"Who's that, Mum?"

"That's Bryn Roberts. The one your dad saved after his brother whacked him over the head."

"Oh right. He looks all right now though. What happened to the brother?"

"He seems to have got off scot-free. Nobody pressed charges, so he'll carry on as if nothing happened. Come on, let's walk around harbour—nice to see the sea when you come from a city."

As they passed Ty Crwn and round the corner to the Promenade, the wind picked up and the spray from an enormous wave crashing over the railings splashed them from head to toe. Irene jumped to the right and shook her arms and head.

"I'm soaked through, Mum!" Irene was indignant that nature had played such a trick on her.

"You'll survive, love, it's just a bit of water! Can't stop that." She laughed and carefully crossed the road to avoid further splashing. "We can stop at the Milk Bar for a cuppa and you'll dry out."

The front window of the café was steamy, indicative of the warmth inside. Bella pushed the door open and stepped inside followed by Irene who immediately took possession of a small table by the wall. On an adjacent table was a group comprising two mothers deep in conversation while four children played a game of *Happy Families*. One of the boys was surreptitiously feeding pieces of toasted teacake to a black dog sitting under the table, licking his lips.

Bella walked back with a tray holding a teapot, two cups and two slices of Victoria Sponge. She placed it carefully on the table then hung her stick, which was slung over her arm, on the back of her chair. "Wasn't sure what you'd want but I know you like cake, love."

"Isabella, is that you? I thought I recognised you with your limp but wasn't sure. How are you?" The Scottish accent cut through the chatter from the other table.

"Oh hello, Babs. I'm fine now, thanks—almost completely back to normal—just need a stick for balance. This is Irene, my daughter. Irene, this is Babs, the nurse who looked after me when I was at the cottage."

"Nice to meet you, Irene," said Barbara extending her hand across the table. "This is my friend, and colleague, Hazel, and her children." Hazel gave a little wave and turned her attention to the children were arguing over their game. "What do you think of Barmouth so far?"

"It's a nice town. Probably better in the summer, I'd think." Irene indicated to her wet coat. "Not so soggy!"

"Irene got caught by a wave," Isabella said.

"Bit of a hazard when you live by the sea, I'm afraid," laughed Barbara. "Well, you enjoy the rest of your stay. How long are you here?"

"Just for the weekend. Dad brought us to see the new house."

"Oh right. I'll have to come up and see it when you're settled."

"Yes, that'll be super, Babs. Irene's going back tomorrow afternoon on the train. Jim and I are staying so I'd love a bit of company while he's doing some decorating."

A squawk from one of the boys drew Barbara back to her group. "Sorry, need to get back to this lot. Speak soon, Isabella. Nice to meet you, Irene."

192

"You know a lot of people, Mum. You were only here a few weeks and you've got friends already."

"It all happened by chance, love. Mainly due to my accident. And everyone is really friendly. I need some friends now, anyway, don't I?" Her face darkened and she took a sip of tea.

Irene reached across the table and placed her hand on her mother's. "I'm sorry, Mum."

"Oh God! It's not your fault Irene. You had no choice but to tell me. Don't you worry, it's probably all turned out for the best now."

"Why did she do it? What friend would behave like that? She must've known you'd find out."

"Don't blame it all on her, love. It isn't always the woman's doing. Men are half to blame when it comes to infidelity."

"How can you be so understanding?" Irene stuffed a forkful of cake into her mouth.

"You learn a lot about people and their demons when you've been on the planet a while. Susan had her reasons, as did your father. I have enough room in my heart to forgive him but it's easier for me if I don't see her. Too painful to imagine them together, so I won't. That's why being here, in a different town, a new country, will help." She took another sip and leant back as much as her chair would allow.

"Are you sure, Mum? Everything is new here." The sound of Welsh conversation drifted towards them. "Even the language."

"I know that, love, but this is my choice and I want to work it out with your dad. I'll be fine here. It feels right."

Irene finished the last of her cake and took a slurp of tea. She looked across the table at her mother, her eyes a little watery. Isabella turned her head on the side. "Oh, Irene. You'll be fine too. I'll come back whenever you need me to. Remember, you're a grown woman now, with a job and friends as well as a potential fiancé of your own. You'll enjoy the independence, just like Freddie has embraced his."

"I know, but it feels so final. I'm not ready for you to leave. Isn't it supposed to be the other way round?"

"Well, you know me, never been one to do the conventional thing!" Isabella held her daughter's hand and squeezed lightly. "Look, love, if it all gets too much, there's plenty of space at Bontddu. You can always come here."

"Thanks, Mum." Irene sniffed then looked up at the clock on the wall. "Anyway, shouldn't we go and get the shopping? Dad's coming back to pick us up in an hour."

They stood up and pulled their coats around them just as the group next to them were doing the same. As one, they left the café and headed up the High Street to the various destinations. Isabella took a deep breath and planted her stick on the pavement. This was her hometown now and she was determined to make her mark.

CHAPTER 25

Owen

Owen turned the envelope over in his hand. The postmark was from Aberdeen and his own address was scrawled across the front. He sat down at the table with his tea and rubbed the ears of his faithful friend.

"Dai's always had awful handwriting, hasn't he, Dewi? Mrs Llewellyn used to make him practise at break times—obviously made no difference though." Dewi nodded and growled quietly in agreement. "I suppose I'd better find out how he's getting on." He slid his letter knife under the flap, sliced open the envelope and extracted one page of lined foolscap. He read aloud:

Dear Da

Finished my training and the first week on the rigs. You'll be pleased to hear we're safe, the training was very thorough, taught us about the dangers and how to be aware of them. Glad you taught us to swim for one thing! There's a lot of sea around us.

We have to work long hours, usually start at 6am and finish at 6pm when we're actually on the rig. It's hard work, glad I'm fit but my muscles are getting bigger by the day, and dirty as a coal miner, as you can imagine working with oil. Nice blokes though, from all over but mostly Scots. Made a few friends already. They give us all our food and we sleep in bunks in a dorm so it's easy to save your money, there's nothing to spend it on.

"I hope he's paying Babs properly now." Owen shook his head and stroked Dewi's.

We work two weeks on, two weeks off, which means I'll have time to see the boys when they come up. We've found a little place in Aberdeen, just a flat for me and Bethan...

He lowered the letter and exhaled, "Oh Dewi, that son of mine. Poor woman doesn't know what she's letting herself in for." He continued reading.

...and a spare bedroom. She's made it nice and homely and she's found herself a job in the local pub, only part time. She's doing a secretarial course so she can get a job in the oil rig offices.

I've written to Danny and George to explain how I work now and not to worry if I don't reply straight away. I want them to come up after Christmas, maybe they can come back with Shirley and Douglas and me and Bethan can bring them home again. I can see you then too. Just need Babs to agree. Maybe you could have a word with her?

Anyway Da, need to sign off now. Love to you and Dewi. And Bryn of course.

Owen carefully folded the letter and slid it back into the envelope, then lay it on the table, leaning back in his chair to absorb the contents. He shook his head and stroked his chin then stood upright, shrugged on his coat, and unhooked the lead from the back of the door.

"Come on, Dewi. Let's go out for a walk."

Together, they ambled down the steps and at the bottom turned left towards the garage. A train was rumbling over the track on the bridge above the harbour on its way towards Dolgellau and beyond to Birmingham. The train which every summer transported thousands of holiday makers from the industrial metropolis to the clean air of the seaside. On this particular windy Wednesday in late November, it was half empty.

Owen pushed open the door of the garage and Dewi ran inside, then Owen stepped over the wooden threshold. It was dim and dingy inside and a sporty Triumph Spitfire took up most of the central space. The bonnet was up but no sign of Bryn tinkering with the engine. He looked to the left and spotted a bike leaning against the wall, a medical bag in the basket. Owen walked towards the light shining from the office at the back. As he got closer he distinguished faint sounds, one male and one definitely female. He recognised from many years back the sounds of lovemaking. He shook his head and tutted under his breath.

"Come on Dewi, doesn't look like now's a good time..." he whispered. He turned to leave the garage as quietly as he'd arrived, Dewi trotting obediently behind him.

---0---

Bryn was whistling as he opened the front door. He peeled off his gloves and hat and shoved them in his donkey jacket pockets then hung it on the peg.

"Bit parky out there today, brass monkeys and all that." He turned around to greet his father who was in his chair puffing on his pipe. "Everything all right, Da?"

"I've had quite a day. Letter from Dai on the table. Read it if you like."

"It's okay, just give me the gist." Bryn sat down and pushed the envelope away.

"He's settled in all right up there it seems. Taken that Bethan from the pub with him and got a place in Aberdeen."

"Bethan? I thought she was married."

"If she was, she's not no more."

"Blimey, he does create a drama wherever he goes."

"He's not the only one, Bryn."

"What do you mean, Da?" Bryn's jaw hardened and he stared his father in the face.

197

"I popped into the garage to see you around lunchtime today. Wanted a chat about the letter." Bryn's chin dropped to his chest. "So, I saw Babs' bicycle inside and heard noises I shouldn't have heard."

"Oh Da, I'm sorry. You shouldn't have to find out like that."

"What are you thinking, Bryn? Your brother's wife?"

"They're divorced, Da, and she needs some company. I'll do the right thing. This isn't just a bit of fun: I love her and I hope she loves me."

"They're not divorced yet; the paperwork hasn't come through." Owen's voice was level and his face set.

"But it will soon. And meanwhile, he's shacked up with a married bird in Aberdeen, for goodness' sake! It's just not the same thing at all." Bryn's voice raised with each word until he was almost shouting.

"You need to talk to Dai. You don't want someone finding out and telling him. He's a jealous man and, as you already know, he's dangerous when he's angry. And he's planning on coming back here after Christmas."

"You're right, Da." Bryn's voice had returned to his usual timbre. "I'll write to him and explain. I'll do it now, in fact. Hopefully with him being so far away, he'll have time to get used to the idea before he gets back here."

"You'd best clear it with Babs first. He'll take it out on her, too."

"I'm sorry, Da. This is all you need at your age. We shouldn't still be causing you grief; we should be settled and happy so you can be too."

"Well, what I've learnt after three score years and ten, is that life isn't like that. It's full of heartache and pain along with the good stuff. All I want, all I've ever wanted, is for my two lads to be happy. So, if you're sure about Babs, then make it work. For all of you, Danny and George included."

"Thanks, Da, I definitely will. Anyway, I best go and see her now—let her know what's happening."

"What about your dinner? I've done us a lamb hot pot. Why don't you have that and then go? Give her time to put the boys to bed."

"Good idea."

Owen went over to the dresser, picked up two bowls, took two spoons out of one drawer and two mats out of the other. He laid them carefully on the table. He put on his oven gloves, decorated with Welsh dragons, and removed the two-tone brown casserole dish from the range. Bryn placed the metal trivet on the table and Owen put the dish on top and took a ladle with a brown, wooden handle from the utensil set on the wall.

"How hungry are you, son?"

"Fair to middling."

Owen sat down and scooped two generous portions into each bowl. "You can always have seconds. Plenty here."

Bryn blew on a spoonful, put the spoon in his mouth, chewed rapidly and swallowed. "This is delicious, Da. You'll have to show me how to cook. If I'm going to be a step-da, I want to do it properly, like."

"Don't get ahead of yourself son. You don't know if that's what she wants yet. It's a big step for Babs."

"I know, but I'm happy and excited for the first time in years. This could be the family I've always wanted. She might even want to have more children, with me." He shovelled in another mouthful.

"Slow down, Bryn. With your food, and your plans. You'll give yourself heartburn, in more ways than one."

Bryn grinned and put in another mouthful in slow motion. "You're right. I need to take it slowly. We've only been seeing each other, secretly of course, for two weeks. But I'm sure it's right for us."

"Two weeks isn't long enough to know really."

"That's rich, Da. You and Mam were only courting a few weeks before you popped the question."

"True, but we knew each other from school and I'd always liked her, just from afar, till I was brave enough to ask her out."

"So, much the same as me and Babs, then. I've known her ten years." Bryn wiped a piece of bread around the bowl to sop up the remaining gravy then dropped his spoon and rubbed his trim stomach. "I enjoyed that."

"I suppose your situation isn't that different in terms of time, but in terms of family complication, you win hands down." Owen looked down at Dewi who was waiting expectantly for the bowl to lick. "In a minute, Dewi, I'm still eating. Not a glutton like Bryn here."

"Right, I'll just do this washing up and then I'll be off to have that conversation."

"Let me finish off first!"

Owen took the last mouthful and placed his bowl on the floor. Dewi slurped and pushed the bowl around. Bryn collected the crockery and took it to the sink. The fire burnt in the grate as Dewi flopped down in front of it on a rag rug. Owen leaned back and filled his pipe, his eyes settling on a photo of his wedding day which had pride of place of the dresser. He sighed and smiled.

"Right, Da. I'll be off." Bryn interrupted his father's reverie as he opened the door to a blast of chilly air.

"Cheerio, son. Hope it goes well." Owen smiled at Bryn as his son left the warmth of the cottage kitchen.

CHAPTER 26

Jim

"What about this, Bella?" Jim held up a can of vivid orange paint.

"You must be joking! That's completely the wrong shade. We need something a bit more subtle for a bedroom." She moved along the aisle and found a can of mustard yellow. "This might work if we can find wallpaper to go with it."

"Okay dear, whatever you want." He picked up two cans and placed them in a trolley and they made their way to the wallpaper section.

"Ooh, this is lovely," cooed Bella, pulling out a roll of primrose and sage green circles and flowers with oversized petals.

Jim sighed deeply. "Yep, it goes well with the mustard."

She dropped an armful of rolls in the trolley. "How many will you need?"

"Not that many. I ain't doing the whole room. It'll be a right pain to match up with not one straight wall in the house."

"What will you do then?" Her face fell as she put back all but one roll.

"I'll just paper the back wall behind the bed and paint the others."

"But then you won't see the lovely pattern."

"You'll see it, love." He put three rolls in the trolley.

"Really? Well, I suppose you know best."

"I have decorated a few rooms in my time, Bella. Trust me." She sniffed and asked, "Have we got everything we need?"

"I just need some more sandpaper and white spirit and that's it." They gathered up the last of their shopping and headed to the till.

"Back again, Mr Cartwright? You must be almost finished now." The owner in his brown housecoat checked the labels and carefully entered the price of each item into the till before placing it to one side.

"Yep, that I am."

"This is the last room and then he's finished—for now at least," added Isabella. "There are a couple of spare bedrooms at the top which he'll do after Christmas. But he's been working all hours to make it ours, haven't you, love?" She smiled at him. "And it needed a lot of attention, didn't it, dear?" Jim nodded in agreement.

"At least it's not summer. You wouldn't want to be stuck in the house with a paintbrush then."

"True," said Jim pulling out his wallet from his back pocket.

"That'll be £8.27 please."

"Here you go." Jim handed over a ten-pound note.

With their change and their goods, Jim and Isabella walked out to the car and loaded them into the boot. Isabella pulled her belt around her coat tightly and put a hat on. Slipping her hands into her gloves, she said, "Remember I said I've got an interview at the shoe shop then I'm going to meet Babs and Hazel for a cuppa. They've both got an hour for lunch today; doesn't happen very often."

"All right, love. I'll go home and crack on with the bedroom. Have a nice time."

"I'll get the bus back so no need to worry about collecting me." She gave him a peck on the cheek and walked briskly in the direction of the surgery.

Jim climbed into his car and headed in the opposite direction, down the High Street, past the garage. He grimaced as he remembered Bryn in a pool of blood. He drove carefully out of

202

the town, up the hill and around the grey rock jutting out into the road. It was a clear, crisp day and the white, winter light shimmered across the surface of the sea to his right. He smiled, thinking about the contrast to the Midlands and the good choice they'd made to leave it all behind.

As he approached Bontddu and their new home, Jim wondered about what had happened to Dai. Owen had told him that his son had moved away, working on the oil rigs or something. It was tough when your son left home, especially when they were so far away. It was months since he and Isabella had seen Freddie and he missed him, like an ache in the centre of his being. He took the bag out of the boot the car, reflecting on how parents became irrelevant to young lads. He tried to recall how he'd been with his mam and dad as a man in his early twenties. Had he been dismissive and careless with their feelings? He hoped not.

Once in the house, he admired his handiwork in the hall, stairs and landing. It was now much brighter, with primrose yellow walls and pictures of birds—Bella's choice—hanging on the walls. The paintwork was a crisp white and he looked closely to see if he'd gone over the edges anywhere. He dropped the bag on the floor and went to the kitchen to make himself a cup of tea. He looked around: it was a massive improvement and he nodded and smiled proudly to himself.

The kettle whistled and he poured the water in the pot and found a couple of Garibaldis in the biscuit barrel. Sitting at the dining room table, he contemplated how much had changed since the summer. A slight flush of shame crossed his face when he thought about Susan, followed by a naughty grin at the memory of her peachy bottom and full breasts. He pushed away the vision. He couldn't afford to let desire take charge again; that just caused everyone pain and hurt. He was lucky Bella had taken him back and he didn't want to risk losing her now. He finished the crunchy raisin biscuit and took a slurp of tea. *Right,* he thought. *Onwards and upwards. Sitting around like this isn't going to get the baby washed.*

He picked up his transistor radio from the table, finished his tea and took the bag upstairs to the empty bedroom which was ready for the final push. There, he pulled on his blue working overalls, spattered with paint from every room he'd ever decorated. He tuned to Radio 4, put up the pasting table and got stuck into the job at hand, whistling away to the first tune of Desert Island Discs.

A couple of hours later, he was interrupted by an insistent knocking. He turned down the radio and realised it was someone at the front door. He put down his paint brush, wiped his hands on his overalls and clomped down the stairs. As he reached the bottom, he heard the clattering of the letterbox and echo of boots going down the steps. He yanked the front door open and shouted, "Hello! Can I help you?"

A dark blond head turned around. "Oh you do live here then, Dad!"

"Freddie! What on earth?" Jim held his arms wide as his son turned and came back up the steps. Their embrace was long and hard, each man enjoying the comfort of the other. "I've missed you." Jim kissed the top of Freddie's head.

"Oi, no need to get all soppy on me, Dad. I could kill for a cuppa though. Get that kettle on and show me your new place." Freddie stepped inside and dropped his kitbag on the floor at the bottom of the stairs.

"I've done the downstairs and I've been doing the main bedroom today, I'm nearly finished; just the last of the skirting to do." Jim ushered his son into the kitchen where he sat at the table while his father bustled around getting a pot of tea ready. "Are you hungry? I can make you a sandwich."

"Yes please, I'm ravenous. That journey seemed to go on forever—one train after another and then the bus up here."

"Mum'll be over the moon to see you. She was only saying yesterday she hoped you'd be home in time for Christmas."

"And as if by magic, here I am! Where is Mum?"

"Still in town. She went for a job first. She's probably gossiping with her new friends now." He cut four slices from a white loaf and buttered them thickly, then found some ham in the fridge and held it up. Freddie nodded vigorously.

"So, Mum's getting a job. That was quick."

"You know her, she don't hang about."

"That's true enough." He laughed then asked, "Can I have some mustard too please?" Freddie took in his surroundings. "You've made a good job of this, Dad. Shame about the view though, it's just a load of rock."

"Yeah, but it's fantastic from upstairs." He put two plates on the table followed by two mugs of steaming tea, then sat himself down with a sigh next his son. "Eat this and tell me all about your job. Where've you been and what's it like on board a ship?" Jim's grin split his face in two and he struggled to take a bite of his doorstep sandwich.

"So, there's about two hundred of us on board, from the Commander right down to the lackies like us. We've all got our jobs and we're on a sort of rota system in teams so there's always one on duty. My team's great; we're from all over. Lads from London, the Midlands like me, and even a couple from Wales." He paused as took a bite of his lunch.

"So what's your job?"

"You know I finished my training as an apprentice?"

Jim nodded.

"So now I'm a proper engineer. I'm often down in the engine room, checking things are running smoothly. But when we get into port and need to do a full assessment, that's when I'm busiest. There's so much machinery that can stop functioning properly, you wouldn't believe it."

"You must get some time off though?"

"Oh yeah. This tour we were in Hong Kong and Singapore. Amazing places; so different from home—just people everywhere and the smells and the noise. It was great." Freddie leaned back in his chair savouring the memory. "And it's so hot, like the minute you walk outside, your body's just drenched in sweat. Not nice really, but we all stank so we didn't notice."

"I'm glad you're enjoying it, Freddie. And you look very healthy, very tanned."

They heard a key in the door and the faint squeaking of the hinges as it was pushed open followed by footsteps on the newly laid floor tiles.

"Whose bag is this?" came the voice down the corridor.

The kitchen door swung open. "It's mine, Mum," Freddie said.

CHAPTER 27

Dai

Dai jumped off the train and pulled a holdall over his shoulder. After him stepped Bethan with a suitcase. She glanced first left then right, as if checking the path was clear. Seeing it was safe, they set off hand-in-hand up the platform to the exit. Bethan fell behind as she struggled to carry her case and hold his hand at the same time.

"Hurry up, will you?"

"I'm trying, Dai, but this case is heavy."

"Well, you shouldn't have brought so much stuff with you then." He paused and turned to face her. "Just give it here." She handed it over, her face crumpling. "Oh, don't bloody well cry again woman."

She sniffed, then fished in her handbag for a hanky and blew her nose. "My dad said he'd be waiting in the car park but we're late, so he might be in the pub."

Dai looked around the car park for a blue Austin Maxi. "The car's over there but he's not in it. Do you want to wait here or come into the pub with me?"

"I'll come with you. It's a bit dark out here on my own." She half-ran after him, teetering on her too-high heels, trying to keep up.

He pulled open the door of the Pendragon and stepped inside, pushing a drooping string of tinsel out of his face. They both stood with their backs to the doorway and the faint strains of *Lonely This Christmas* by Mud filled the air. Bethan scanned the faces of the four customers: in the corner, next to a spangly Christmas tree, an older gentleman nursed a pint of bitter; at the bar, where a string of paper bells was hanging, was a younger man in workwear swilling down the last of his lager; a couple sat at a table near the window decorated with fake snow. She recognised them immediately and almost ran over to them, attempting to fling her arms around her mother's neck, "Mum, Dad! I'm so pleased to see you. I've missed you so much."

"Hello, dear," said her mother, unpeeling her daughter's arms. "You made it then." She looked over at Dai, her face hard.

Bethan stepped back, her face crumpling and the tears brimming in her eyes reflecting in the streetlight from outside. "The train from Birmingham was delayed." Her voice dropped with her chin.

"Hello, Dai. Good of you to bring our daughter home," said her father gruffly.

"Evening, Mr Evans, Mrs Evans. It's been a long journey so excuse me while I get a drink. Bethan?"

"Not for me, Dai, but I do need the toilet." She disappeared out the back and up the stairs.

"Dai, I'm sure Bethan told you, but you can't stay at ours. Our neighbours do like to gossip and it was bad enough her running out like that," Mrs Evans explained with a straight back and determined face.

"What? She didn't say a bloody word. Where the hell am I supposed to stay?"

"Not really our problem, Dai," added Mr Evans, standing up next to his wife.

Dai looked around and up at the ceiling. The other customers stared at him then turned back to their drinks. The new barmaid pulled another pint. Bethan appeared in the bar and acknowledged the stoney faces. "You told him, then?"

"Yes, love. Now let's get home, shall we? We've got a lot to discuss," said her mother briskly.

Mr Evans picked up the suitcase and asked, "This everything, love?"

"Yes, Da." Her parents headed towards the door; she turned to her partner. "Sorry Dai, I'll come and see you tomorrow, shall I?" She leaned towards him but he turned his cheek away.

"Don't fucking bother. Looks like I'm going to have to stay here again, doesn't it?" He shook his head and pointed to the doorway. "Your lift's waiting."

Bethan walked slowly away. As she got to the doorway, she turned and mouthed, "Sorry, Dai."

Dai stepped towards the bar and the barmaid looked up. "Looks like you might be needing somewhere to stay."

"No shit, Sherlock. So have you got a room, then?"

---0---

Dai scowled over his pint, debating what to do next. He needed to see Babs and the boys, but also his father. He sighed at the inevitability of bumping into his brother. His thoughts were interrupted by a group entering the pub. He looked up to see the Harlech darts team and realised that meant Bryn would be there too. That made up his mind for him. He gulped down the rest of his lager, hopped down from his bar stool and pulled on his coat. He pushed the door open just as a familiar figure appeared at the other side pulling the handle. They met face to shoulder, Dai's cheek grazing the rough wool of his brother's donkey jacket. They pulled apart and Bryn's startled eyebrows raised.

Bryn stepped inside, followed by another two men, and the door swung closed behind them. He nodded sideways at them and they went to take their usual table. "Dai, what're you doing back?" Bryn said.

"I'm allowed to visit my hometown, aren't I?"

"No need to get so defensive, Dai. Look, Da's on his way; he's just walking Dewi. Why don't you stay and have a drink with him? I'm sure he'd love to see you. I'm playing darts tonight. Last game of the year."

"Thanks for the offer, but I need to go and see the boys really."

Bryn looked up at the clock on the wall. "It's eight o'clock, Dai. They'll be in bed or at least getting ready for it."

"I suppose it is a bit late." He turned and walked back to the bar, followed by his brother. "I'll just wait here for Da then."

"So how's it been then, on the rigs? Living in Scotland?"

"It's fine. I've got a new life now, just back here to see Babs and the boys, is all."

"And Da?"

"Of course, Da," he snapped then looked over to the door as an old man and his dog entered. "And here he is now." He took off his coat as the barmaid placed two pints on the mat. She returned to the bar and started to pull a third pint of bitter.

"Hello, son. Good to see you, albeit a bit unexpected. I thought you were coming down after Christmas." He pulled his son into an embrace. "It's good to see you." He held Dai at arm's length and studied his face. "You're looking thinner. They feeding you enough on them rigs?"

"Yes, Da. It's just hard physical work."

"I'll just go and join the lads," Bryn said. "I'll leave you two to catch up."

"Okay Bryn, good luck," said Owen, then faced his other son. "So why the change of plan?"

"Bethan wanted to spend Christmas with her parents and sisters. Said it was a bit sad just us two on our own in the flat with a turkey. I was off anyway."

"She's got a point, I suppose." He looked around and took a sip of his Banks' bitter. "So where is she, then?"

Dai sighed and led his father to a table the opposite side of the pub to the darts players. "Her parents don't want me in the house. Say it brings shame on them. They haven't forgiven her for leaving, especially with me."

"Oh right, I can understand that. Can't you have a word, explain that you're a changed man?"

"They didn't give me the opportunity."

"Ah well. They're traditional folk; don't like scandal. Did you know that was the plan?"

"Nope. Not a scooby. They told me as soon as we saw them. Bethan was too chicken to tell me herself, like."

"Ah. That's awkward. S'pose you'll need somewhere to stay. We could squeeze you in at mine, but you'll have to sleep on the settee."

"Thanks, but I think it'll be best if I stay here, Da. What with the situation between me and Bryn."

"You're probably right." He took a gulp of his beer. "So anyhow, what about the job?"

"It's all right. Lots of machinery to work on and I'm learning a lot about oil! Best thing is that it pays well."

Owen stroked Dewi's head and took another sip of beer. "So have you started paying Babs, then?"

"Yes, of course."

"Only, she asked me to have a word. She was really struggling to begin with. I had to lend her some money."

"Da, I've been paying regularly since I got my first proper pay packet. Quite a lot in fact, she should be all right." Dai's indignation reflected in the beer slopped on the table.

"Well, that's good then, it was just the first month, she had no money for food shopping after all the bills, so I gave her £20."

Dai whipped his wallet out of back pocket and pulled out a crisp twenty-pound note and thrust it towards his father. "Can't have you out of pocket, Da. They're my kids and my responsibility."

"That's not why I told you, Dai. Just wanted to be sure, that's all."

211

"It's fine now, so no need to fret." He sipped his pint. "What are you doing for Christmas Day, Da? Doesn't look like I'll be invited to Beth's family."

"We're planning on spending it with Babs and the boys." Owen wriggled uncomfortably in his seat and stroked Dewi's head again.

"Ah right, well that might be difficult. Looks like it's me on my own and a seaside walk then."

"You know I wouldn't want that, Dai. Christmas isn't a time to be on your own. Besides, the boys will want to see you. Let's talk to Babs and see what she thinks."

"Thanks, Da." He dropped his chin and sighed. "I've made a right bloody mess of things, haven't I?"

"That you have, son. But if you're really sorry for it, then I'm sure you can sort things out. Babs might be trickier, mind. You've definitely got some work to do there." He looked over at Bryn who was concentrating hard on aiming his dart at the board. "You need to have good chat with your brother, too. He's got a kind soul, but don't take his forgiveness for granted."

"Yeah, I know." Dai went up to the bar and returned with two packets of crisps. He dropped the cheese and onion next to his pint and handed the salt and vinegar to his father. "Your favourite."

"Thanks son." He smiled as they turned their attention to the match.

---0---

Dai rolled over on his lumpy mattress. Seagulls were squawking outside his window and the dawn light shone through the flimsy, pink curtains. He groaned as he swung his legs out of the single bed and stretched his arms outwards to welcome the new day. He gathered up his wash bag and clean clothes and headed out of the door and down the corridor to the shared bathroom. He stood close to the lavatory bowl and cleaned his teeth to his own steady stream. The hot water took a few moments to come through in the shower cubicle and he spent those moments inspecting his face in the mirror above the sink. "Not too bad considering I'm heading towards forty," he said aloud to his reflection. In the shower, he whistled the tune of Slade's *Merry Christmas Everybody* as he soaped and shaved, banging his razor against the shower wall and leaving a black stain of whiskers.

Dressed and breakfasted, he headed out towards his old home, hoping to take his sons to school for their last day before the Christmas holidays. He turned right out of the pub and walked briskly down towards the Promenade and along the road. The tide was in, and the sea came right up to the wall, with the occasional wave splashing over onto the pavement. He nodded a greeting to the few dog walkers and workers on their way to the shops in town. They'd be busy the next few days; the last week of Christmas swelling the coffers despite the financial state of the nation. Arriving at his old front door, he knocked and rattled the letterbox. He heard the sound of feet stomping up the hall and the door flew open.

"Hello boys! Surprised to see me?"

"Daddy!" shouted George.

"Daddy, we weren't expecting you!" added Daniel.

"I came early so I can take you to school."

"Mummy, Daddy's here. He's going to take us to school."

"Can I come in then?" Dai stepped inside, closed the door behind him and went into the kitchen. "I'll just wait here while you get your stuff together."

He sat down on the kitchen chair and looked around: a few new pictures on the fridge door, different curtains too. His eyes settled on two wine glasses on the draining board. He drew his brows together and his eyes narrowed. There were a series of thumps from above and the sound of whispered voices followed by noisy steps on the stairs. He scraped his chair back and stood up, pushed open the door to the hallway to find Daniel and George waiting with their coats and satchels.

"Is Mummy upstairs?"

"Yes, I'm here." He watched the familiar form of his ex-wife descend, her uniform crisp and tidy as ever. He sighed heavily as he admired her. "This is unexpected, Dai. But the boys are pleased, aren't you?" Their heads nodded vigorously in agreement. "Are you both ready to go then? Have you got the presents for your teachers?"

"Yep, got mine here." George held up a badly wrapped parcel.

"Me too," added Daniel.

"Right, off you go then." She kissed the tops of their heads and looked up at her ex-husband. "I'll see you after work. We need to have a chat, Dai."

The door slammed behind them and the boys ran excitedly down the path and out of the gate where they caught up with Clare, Cathy, Tony and Charlie. Instinctively, Dai looked both ways up the road. He squinted as he noticed the back of an orange Transit van parked around the corner. It looked suspiciously like the one he'd signed over to Bryn. Sharply, he looked back at the house. Through the net curtains of the upstairs window, he made out the shape of two people. One was most definitely Babs. Behind her was the blond head of his brother.

214

CHAPTER 28

Barbara

"Phew, that was close. I was sure the boys would see you and blab to Dai. I want to tell him, just not like that."

"Whenever it happens, it isn't going to be easy, Babs. He's got quite the temper on him as we both know."

"I know. Anyway, much as I'd like to go back to bed with you, I need to get to work." She laughed as he kissed the back of her neck beneath her bun.

"Me too. We'd better get a move on before he comes back and finds the van. I only parked it round the corner."

"It was a bit of risk coming here when you knew he was back in town." They were in the hallway pulling on their coats and winter boots. "Good thing he didn't find your coat or your shoes." Babs' stomach turned over at the thought of Dai's reaction. She was dreading the conversation later. "Maybe you could talk to him first, or we could do it together."

"I'll try and find him this morning and at least give him some warning." Bryn took her in his arms and kissed her deeply. She pulled away and looked in the mirror at the red smudge around her mouth. She took a gold tube from her make up bag on the shelf by the front door.

"I'll have to re-do my lippie now!" She laughed, wiped her chin and then re-applied the lipstick carefully.

Bryn opened the front door and stepped outside, "Cheerio, love of my life." He sauntered down the path. Babs wrapped her cloak around her, tied the tapes across her cardigan and pulled on her hat and gloves. Then she picked up a small bag and followed him out. Her bike was leaning on the fence so she climbed on and cycled in the direction of the surgery, looking forward to her last day of work before the holiday started.

---0---

It was a chilly morning. The December wind blew across the Irish Sea and froze the tips of her fingers despite her sheepskin gloves. Her cloak fluttered around her and she wished she had a car, and wished she had taken up Mrs Jenkins' offer to teach her to drive. Bryn had given her a few lessons but she found it difficult in the van, so progress was slow. She'd managed to move off and change into second gear in the empty car park but so far she hadn't been on the road or driven any faster than ten miles an hour. She laughed as she remembered her own fear of the moving metal machine. She was still grinning when she walked into the surgery.

"What are you so happy about this fine morning?" asked Daphne the receptionist, with a smile.

"Just thinking about my first driving lesson. Can't wait to drive, especially when it's Baltic like today!" She placed the bag on the desk. "Merry Christmas."

"Oh thank you, Babs, you're really kind." Daphne put it under the desk with her handbag and winter boots. "It doesn't help that you're still wearing a cloak; it doesn't even do up properly across your front. Most nurses nowadays have modern coats and wear trousers. I don't know why you and Hazel insist on your old-fashioned capes."

"We like a bit of tradition; reminds us of our training. But that said, it might be time for a nice warm anorak and a pair of thick trousers."

"What's that about an anorak?" Hazel appeared in the reception hall, a piece of tinsel encircling her starched white cap.

216

"Oh hi, Hazel. Just saying it's too cold to wear my cloak, especially on my bike. Nice hat."

"You know what, I was having the same conversation with Tony this morning. Maybe it could be our New Year's resolution. Ditch the cloak!"

"We could get matching duffle coats, like Paddington Bear! Looking forward to warmer boobs in 1975. So, what's on your agenda today? Got many appointments?"

"Just Mrs Jones and her new baby, plus whoever comes in. I'll get the paperwork up to date and sort out the office. What about you?"

"Just the usual, except Mrs Jenkins. She's gone to Nice to stay with her sister. Lucky bugger, what I wouldn't do for a bit of sunshine. I'll be off then. See you at lunch?"

"Yes, definitely. I'll have the kettle on ready." Hazel disappeared down the corridor to her treatment room.

Barbara picked up her medical bag from behind the desk. "Cheerio, Daphne," she called as she left the building and started off on her rounds.

It was already busy in the town with people out early doing their Christmas shopping before the rush which would inevitably come later on that day. The town was cheerful, with lights dangling between the buildings and a decorated spruce in almost every shop window. She smiled as she remembered the evening the lights were switched on by the Mayor. She and Bryn had brought the boys into town, just like many other families. They'd met Hazel, Tony and the girls and they'd all been on the fairground rides and stalls. She recalled that everyone had really enjoyed themselves, especially Bryn.

Babs loved this time of year. She loved buying presents for others, in particular for her boys, much more than receiving them. This year, though, she'd had to be a little less extravagant: only one big present each plus a few little things for their stockings. The toy shop on Beach Road was a mine of gifts for children of all ages; she particularly liked the wooden floors and high ceilings and the smell of children's excitement. For George, she'd bought a toy he'd been going on about since seeing an advertisement on television. Daniel wanted *The Guinness Book of World Records*, again. He wanted the same book every year so why force the issue? She had almost everything she wanted, she just needed one last special present. She smiled as she thought about it.

As she stopped at her second patient, old Mr Evans, Bethan's grandfather, her thoughts returned to the present and immediate issue of Dai. She hoped Bryn would have time to talk him. She shook her head slightly, propped her bike up against the railing and lifted her bag out of the basket to begin her way up the slate steps to his house. She knocked on the front door, wondering what sort of mood her patient would be in. He could be a bit grumpy, which was hardly surprising with that leg ulcer of his; it must be so painful. She heard his heavy steps and the clonk of his stick as he approached the door and pulled it open.

"Come in, Nurse. Bloody freezing out there."

"Morning, Mr Evans." Barbara stepped inside and followed him to the living room.

"So I hear that ex-husband of yours is back in town." He carefully sat himself down in his armchair by a gas fire, lifted his bad leg onto a footstool and pulled his woollen cardigan around his shoulders. His eyes narrowed as he looked at Barbara.

"Yes, he is. But never mind about that, let's have a look at this leg of yours." She untied her cloak and put it on the back of the other chair, and knelt on the faded, worn carpet.

"Can't believe our Bethan." He shook his head and pursed his lips. "Leaving her own husband for yours. What's the world coming to that two people can't make a go of it? Finishing their marriages without a thought for their families. Me and my

Gladys were married fifty years, and we never once even considered separating."

"Well. That's quite an achievement, Mr Evans. You must really miss her." She gently pulled up his trouser leg and removed the dressing with a pair of metal tweezers.

"I do. I miss her every day. But glad she didn't have to witness the shame and scandal Bethan created with that Dai fellow. Gladys loved Bethan so much; our first grandchild." He winced as Barbara cleaned the ulcer and dabbed it with TCP.

"Yes, it must've been a shock to you all. But she's home for Christmas now, isn't she?" Barbara took a clean dressing from her bag and ripped open the paper wrapper.

"Yes, she is, but that Dai isn't welcome. Goodness what was going on up there in Scotland. Bethan was in tears on the phone every week to her mother."

"Oh right." Barbara sniffed and shook her head before gently placing the new gauze square over the ulcer. She unrolled the tape and ripped it with her teeth.

"Good riddance to him! I know he's your husband and all that, but he's upset our girl. Hopefully she'll make it up with Rhodri now she's back for good."

Barbara stuck the tape on the gauze and pulled down his trouser leg. "Right. You're all done, Mr Evans." She packed her things back in her bag and stood up. He tried to push himself up out of his chair. "You stay there, I'll let myself out." She pulled on her cloak and walked to the sitting room door. She looked back at him. "Happy Christmas, hope you all have a lovely day. I'll see you next week."

She closed the front door behind her and exhaled loudly. "Bloody hell, Dai." She shook her head and walked down the steps again. Looking over at her bike, she saw the figure of a man in black donkey jacket and woollen hat leaning against the front wheel. He looked up at her.

"Thought I recognised the bike—guessed it was yours."

"Dai. I wasn't expecting to see you."

"Time for a chat, Babs?"

"I've got another couple of calls to make. But you could walk with me."

"Okay then." He pushed the bike as Babs walked alongside him on the narrow pavement.

"My next call is up by the church. We can talk on the way." They walked slowly on the narrow pavement, the bike forming a barrier between them.

"So, Babs. How are you? Get my money all right?"

"Yes thanks, Dai. Took you a while but thanks. Will it come automatically every month now? That would help me budget."

"Yes. That's not really what I want to talk about though."

"Oh right." Babs' stomach clenched and she swallowed hard. The memory of the close shave that morning jumped into her head.

"I saw my old van parked around the corner from the house this morning. So obviously that got me thinking. Why would my van, which I signed over to Bryn, be parked there so early in the morning? So after I dropped the boys off, I took a little walk down to the garage to see if my brother was there." Babs sniffed hard and pulled her cloak around her. "He'd just turned up, had a bit of lipstick on his neck, not like Bryn at all. I can't remember the last time he had a girlfriend. Same shade as the one you're wearing." He stopped and pointed at her mouth. Babs curled her lips inward.

"What do you want me to say, Dai? You're the one who had numerous affairs with who knows how many women over the years. And then you left Barmouth with Bethan."

"Yes, I admit to all that." His tone was clear and even, his eyes hard. "But Babs, I didn't jump into bed with your sister, did I?" His pitch and volume was beginning to attract stares from passers-by.

Her cheeks flushed, and she could feel the bile rising from the depths of her stomach. She was afraid of Dai. Her fear made her words tumble out. "It just happened, Dai. He was helping me out with the kids. It was really hard on my own, getting them to school and back and running the home. I couldn't manage and he was there and it just happened."

"Do you hear that everyone?" Dai shouted. "Incest. With my brother. It just happened!" He raised his arms theatrically. A few people stopped to look at him, others put their heads down and walked past briskly.

"Keep your voice down, Dai. Everyone's staring."

"And so they should, Babs, you slut!" He grabbed the bike.

"Give me my bike! I'm not standing here being insulted by you of all people! I've got work to do." Her tone shifted, her voice becoming icy. She looked him in the eye. Through tight lips she hissed, "Just listen to yourself, you bloody hypocrite. And don't you dare hurt Bryn again or I'll be the one to put you in prison."

Dai shoved the handlebars towards her glaring face. "You haven't heard the end of this, Babs." He stormed away, head down, feet pounding the pavement.

Barbara stood firm, her insides turning to jelly, nausea rising up through her oesophagus. Her heart was pounding and her breathing too fast. Inside her uniform, a trickle of sweat was running between her breasts. She took a few deep inhalations and exhalations until her breath finally came evenly. She blinked back tears, not of sadness but of anger. *What gives him the right to speak to me like that after the way he's behaved!*

She turned her bike around and climbed onto the saddle. One foot on the pedal, she pushed away, moving off quickly, adrenaline powering her legs as they pumped up and down. Fears about Dai and his wrath spun around her head. She tried to blink back the image of the brothers fighting. The words she should have said to him taunted her, along with frustration that it was now too late—she'd missed her opportunity.

She reached the corner of the street where her next patient lived. At the junction, she turned onto the road. Her concentration elsewhere, she didn't look, so she didn't see the Hillman Minx coming towards her. She braked hard. It was too late. She skidded and hit the front wheel. Slowly, she went rolling over the bonnet and landed in a heap on the road.

Jim jumped out of the car and hurried to her side. Freddie jumped out of the other side. Jim knelt down next her and cradled her head in his arms. A trickle of blood was running down her forehead. "Are you all right, Nurse?"

A crowd had gathered around the pair. "You ran right into her, mate."

"Weren't you looking where you were going?"

"It wasn't his fault actually. He had right of way, she should've stopped." Freddie stood between them and the pair on the ground. "Look, why doesn't one of you go and call an ambulance?" He tried to usher them away as he picked up the bike and held it shieldlike between them.

There was moan from the heap on the tarmac. "She's coming round," said a woman in the crowd urgently.

"It's okay, I'm all right." Barbara tried to lift herself up. "Ouch, my bloody head hurts."

"I'm so sorry, Nurse. I couldn't stop quick enough."

"Jim, just call me Babs. You know me well enough now. And help me up." Jim held her elbow as she pulled herself into a standing position and brushed down her dress and cloak. "Nothing to see, everyone. I'm fine, no need to worry." The crowd reluctantly dispersed, the drama seemingly over.

"Are you sure you're all right, Nurse?" asked Freddie approaching, carrying her bike with its buckled front wheel and bent spokes. The medical bag now shoved back into the basket.

"Yep, think I've laddered my tights, though." She picked at a hole in the black nylon and watched the rip crawl up her leg. "You must be Jim's son. Isabella told me you'd come back for Christmas. Nice to meet you." She held out her hand, sheepskin glove intact but scuffed with the black tarmac.

"You can't get back on your bike now," Jim said. "Can I give you a lift somewhere? Freddie, you'll take Babs' bike back to the surgery, won't you? It's just down the road back into town, you'll see the signs."

"That'd be great, Jim. Bryn can pick it up in the van later." She turned to Freddie. "If you get lost, just pop in the shop and ask your mum for directions."

"Rightie ho!" Freddie handed Barbara her bag then hoisted the bike onto his shoulder and headed off down the road.

"Where to, Babs?"

---0---

"You really need to go home. Don't worry about your afternoon patients; I'll go and sort them out." Hazel handed Barbara two aspirin.

Barbara swallowed them with her tea. "Well, I'm not feeling too great to be fair. Would you mind? I'll just finish my tea and head off."

"Not at all, what are friends for? You've had a hell of a morning. Dai sounded furious. How's that going to play out?"

"I dread to think. I hope he hasn't clonked Bryn again. That'd be the worst. I really like Bryn. I've not felt this way about someone for years, if ever."

"Ah that's lovely, I'm so pleased you've found a good one after Dai."

"Me too." Barbara's smile spread across her face and her eyes lit up.

223

"Look, I'll ask Tony to pop in and check on him if you like. He's got the day off so he can go down the garage after collecting the girls. Who's picking yours up today?"

"Owen said he'd do it. They finish early, don't they?"

"Yeah, two o'clock, I think. Gives you time to get home and changed and have a rest before they arrive. Just go now. And don't worry, everything's under control."

Barbara pulled on her cloak, hat and gloves and walked into reception, limping slightly on her right leg. "Have a good Christmas, Daphne."

"And you, Babs. And look after yourself." Daphne gave a knowing nod. Gossip had travelled on the wind through the town and landed on her desk before Barbara had even arrived back at the surgery in Jim's car.

Outside, Barbara looked at her bike with its bent front wheel leaning up against the surgery wall, unusable. She took a deep breath and started to walk ever so slowly along the road, across the railway line and down onto Marine Parade. As she approached home, she spotted an orange van parked outside. Anxiety and relief swelled inside her and a small sob escaped. By the time Bryn had her in his arms, her face was wet with snot and tears.

CHAPTER 29

Isabella

Isabella checked the receipts, emptied the till into money bags, and put them in a canvas sack ready for banking. She'd have to leave it in the safe until Monday morning with the bank being shut on a Saturday. It had been a long week and she was looking forward to getting home and ready for Irene and Gerald who were arriving on Monday afternoon. She pulled on her coat and tied a floral scarf under her chin, then straightened a couple of boxes on her way to the front door. Switching off the lights, she took one final look around and went outside. She was just locking up when she heard the beep from Jim's car parked over the road.

"Hi Mum. Good day?" Freddie leant over to give his mother a kiss on the cheek before pulling off.

"Hello love. It wasn't busy at all. It seems people don't really buy shoes for Christmas. Where's your dad?"

"He was just finishing off the spare room ready for Irene. I don't think he was expecting to do any more rooms just yet."

"No, he wasn't, but I want it nice for you two. Your room's okay, isn't it?"

"Yeah, it's fine, Mum. It's bloody luxury after sharing a bunk room with twenty blokes for six months!"

They stopped at the lights outside the garage to see Bryn locking up. "Give him a pip, love." Bryn turned his head and waved cheerily as Isabella grinned at him through the window.

Pulling up outside the house, they could see the light shining from the dormer window on the second floor. "Looks like Dad's still at it." Freddie switched off the engine and they climbed the steps up to the house.

"Better put the kettle on then."

---0---

Isabella stood on the platform stamping her feet and blowing on her hands. The train was due in five minutes and she wanted to be there to welcome her daughter and Gerald. Jim had sensibly stayed in the car, and Freddie was in the pub with his new friends.

She turned her head to the right as she heard the horn cut through the cold air. She smiled and clapped her hands. The two-carriage train pulled in, a few passengers stepped out, slamming the doors shut behind them.

"Mum!"

"Irene, you're here." She flung her arms around her daughter, then looked around. "Where's Gerald?"

"Oh, he's here: he's got the suitcases and presents."

Isabella turned around to see a tall, slim man with a sandy moustache and glasses struggling up the platform laden with baggage. "Shall we give him hand, love?"

"Oh, yes, I was so excited, I just left him. How rude of me!" She ran towards him. "Here, let me take that bag."

"Nice to see you again, Mrs Cartwright. And thank you having me for Christmas."

"It's our pleasure, Gerald."

Together they walked back to the car park where Jim had got out of his car.

"How do, Gerald. Nice to see you again, it's been a while." He took the suitcase and placed it in the boot then opened the back door so the women could get into the back.

"It certainly has, Mr Cartwright, and it's good to see where you live now." Gerald sat comfortably in the front seat. "Oh, Mrs Cartwright, I should've let you sit here, I'd forgotten about your poorly leg."

"It's fine, Gerald, love, I'm happy here with Irene."

"Yep, don't worry, love, your legs would be round your neck back here," Irene laughed, ruffling the hair on the top of his head.

"Right, are we fit? Can we get home now?"

In the kitchen of the house in Bontddu, Isabella bustled about getting the kettle on and slicing up the fruit cake she'd made the evening before. Jim showed Irene and Gerald up to the freshly decorated bedrooms and left them to unpack.

"You have put Gerald in with Freddie, haven't you?" asked Isabella as her husband returned to the kitchen.

"Yes dear, that's what we agreed."

"Well, they're not married so it wouldn't be seemly to put them in together."

"They wouldn't be the first couple to share a bed out of wedlock, dear. As I recall, we didn't wait till our wedding night." He grinned and kissed her cheek.

Isabella flushed and gently pushed him away. "Well, not under my roof, that's all I say."

They heard the sound of footsteps on the stairs and the low hum of voices in the hallway. The couple walked into the kitchen hand in hand and sat at the table.

"You've made a good job here, Mr Cartwright. The house looks really nice."

"It's his job so he should be good. But you're right, Jim's transformed the place."

"And how's the business going, Dad? Have you got any customers here yet?"

"A few. Takes a while to build a customer base. I doubt I'll be as successful as back in Bromwich. Not so many people for one thing."

"What happened to your business there?"

Isabella placed the pot of tea and four slices of cake on the table. "He sold it. That and my parents' shop paid for this place."

"It looks like that's worked out well for everyone." Gerald took a bite of cake. "Oh, this is delicious," he said with full mouth.

"What are we doing for the rest of the day, Mum? I need to get something from the shops."

"Thought you might like to go back into town and have a look around. We need to pick up Freddie before tea anyway."

"It's a bit of trek for Jim, backwards and forwards twice in one day."

"It's not unusual— " started Isabella.

"Certainly not for Tom Jones," finished Irene with an air drum roll.

"Ha bloody ha. But your mum's right, I often go in twice a day. Thank goodness my car's reliable now. Thanks to Bryn Roberts down the garage."

"Drink up and get your stuff together and you can go then. I'll stay here and get things ready for tea tonight. While you're in town, could you pick up the turkey from the butcher's. He said to come any time after two today."

When the others had left, she picked up the dirty crockery, carried it over to the sink, and turned on the hot water tap. Looking out at the grey rock and then farther up to the cloudy sky, her thoughts went back to the cottage. How primitive that kitchen had been. And the outside privy, and the damp. She was glad it had burnt down; she'd certainly not be in this house if it hadn't. What a long way they'd come since October. She placed a cup in the dish drainer and thought about Susan. She'd been a catalyst really, the reason they were here, in Bontddu, with a new life and new home. Maybe she should write and thank her, or at least send a Christmas card. It was a bit late, though. Might not get there in time. She wiped her hands on the towel hanging on the oven door and opened a drawer in the unit to extract a box of cards and pen. She sat down at the table and took a deep breath and started to write.

Dear Susan

Best wishes for Christmas and the new year. Hope 1975 is a better year for you.

She paused and wondered about how to end it. Not Bella, that was too friendly. Make it formal and definitely not from Jim.

From Isabella.

On the other side, she wrote:

Don't think this is forgiveness. But I do want to thank you for making our marriage better and for pushing us into making some big decisions about our future. We love it here in Wales.

That'll do. Short and sweet, she thought as she popped the card into an envelope and found the last first-class stamp in her purse. Looking at the nativity scene, she wondered if Susan was worth four and half pence. The answer was in the affirmative so she licked it and stuck it on, then slipped on her shoes and walked briskly to the post box by the bridge. The next collection was at six thirty so it might arrive by tomorrow; if not, it'd be after Christmas. She took a deep breath, imagining Susan's expression as she recognised the handwriting. *Do I feel sorry for her? Not yet—she can suffer a bit longer.* She shook her head. Sleeping with your best friend's husband broke a primal rule.

She went back inside and upstairs to the sitting room. She walked to the big bay window and looked out at the estuary and the lowering sun above a band of pale grey nimbus. The tide was out so the train bridge crossed a wide expanse of wet sand where a few sea birds were wading and searching for sand worms, others swooping and diving on the thermals. *It really is a beautiful place. Jim chose well.* She sat down on the settee and picked up the Women's Weekly magazine and a pen to complete the crossword she'd started last week.

Back in the kitchen later on, Isabella cocked an ear to the rattling of the key in the front door, then wiped her hands on her apron. The steak and kidney pudding was bubbling in a pan on the cooker and the prepared carrots and potatoes were in saucepans of water. An apple and blackberry crumble waited proudly on the kitchen table. It had been a productive afternoon, and she'd finished the crossword.

"Oi, Freddie, stand up straight and get out of my way." She heard Irene's laughing tone from the hallway and opened the kitchen door to investigate.

"I'm fine, just fine. Where's my new friend? What's his name?" slurred Freddie, pulling unsuccessfully at the left sleeve of his bomber jacket.

"His name's Dai and he's right behind you," replied Irene, helping him remove his coat.

Isabella's heart sank. "Dai? What's he doing here?"

"Freddie wouldn't leave the pub without him, Mum."

Isabella looked over the heads of her children and around the tall outline of Gerald. She caught the eye of Dai, clearly a bit the worse for wear. He smiled and nodded. Jim was behind him. He pulled the door shut and shrugged his shoulders as he caught his wife's eye. She shook her head, her stomach churned with fears of the bad influence her son had hooked up with. She placed her hand on the wall to steady herself at the memory of Dai's hands on her throat. She backed away from the group assembled in the hall.

"I've got some things to finish up in the kitchen." She turned and went back into the safety of her own space.

"You lot, go upstairs to the sitting room. I need to talk to Mum." Jim pushed his way through them towards his wife.

"What the hell, Jim! He kidnapped you and took us hostage and you bring him into our home. What were you thinking?"

"I didn't realise Freddie and he had made friends. They've been on the pop all afternoon. We just nipped in for quick pint before coming home."

"I can't have him here, you know that."

"Apparently, he's having a bit of hard time at the moment. The girlfriend he took to Scotland has dumped him. Gone back to her husband, so he says."

"Oh Jim, we can't go taking in every waif and stray. Especially not one who did that to us."

"Come on, love, he's got nowhere to go. He's on his own, staying in the pub."

She shook her head. "I'd really rather not, Jim. I just don't trust him."

"Just for this evening, Bella. The chap needs a bit of family time."

"Well, he can go to Owen's then, he should take responsibility. Dai's his son after all."

The door opened slowly and Dai's dark head appeared in the gap. "Hello, Isabella. I'm really sorry, this is all a bit awkward. I did say to Freddie it wasn't a good idea, but he insisted."

"It really isn't a good idea."

"Can I use your phone and I'll ring Da, see if he can pick me up?"

Jim stood up, "No it's fine, Dai. Maybe it's time to forgive." He looked pointedly at his scowling wife. "It's that time of year for good will to all men after all."

Isabella sighed, defeated. "Oh all right then. I'll need to peel another couple of spuds though. You two, leave me in peace."

They left the room. Pursing her lips, she stood up and banged her chair under, got another potato from the cupboard and slammed it on the table, then picked up the peeler from the draining board. Almost as an afterthought, she pulled a glass and a bottle of sherry from the cabinet. Tipping her head back, she took a big slug and squeezed her eyes shut as it hit the spot.

"If you can't beat them, join them!" she said aloud to the potato. She picked up the peeler as she poured herself another generous glassful.

CHAPTER 30

Owen

Owen and Dewi tramped up the steps towards Pen Y Craig. The house loomed over the valley below, the windows like eyes looking out to sea, checking for fishermen in their trawlers. The mountain behind formed a protective shield from the whistling wind. Owen opened the gate and walked up to the kitchen door which served as the main entrance. A small face appeared at the steamy glass top panel and Dewi growled softly in response to Charlie's bark.

"Hello, Mr Owen," said Cathy, smiling from ear to ear. She tried to stroke Dewi who was more interested in greeting his canine companion. She followed them around the kitchen, part of the pack.

"Hello Cathy, Merry Christmas." Owen stepped inside and closed the door.

"Hello Owen, lovely to see you. Fancy a cuppa?" Hazel entered the room, her tall frame filling the doorway. She picked up the kettle and held it under the running tap.

"Yes please. Just taken Dewi up the Panorama Walk—bit windy on the beach."

"The weather's certainly a bit strange, isn't it? Much too warm for this time of year."

"When it's mild, it's wet, mind. Air's coming from the Caribbean across the Atlantic Ocean, picking up moisture on its way. When it hits the mountains of Wales, it falls on us."

"That's a lovely thought. Our rain, all the way from Barbados!"

Hazel handed him a cup of tea and indicated with her head to follow her through to the sitting room. They walked past a wooden open-stepped staircase leading upstairs. They sat down on brown corduroy armchairs either side of a matching settee which formed a circle around the television and scattering of sheepskin rugs. He put his tea on a side table taking in a large slate fireplace dominating the room. The fire was laid ready but it hadn't been cold enough to light it for over a week. A door and a window were to the left. Both had thick, red velvet curtains on wooden poles—at that moment, drawn open. Owen stood up again and went over to the look out.

"You've got a nice view of the sea from here, haven't you?"

"Yes, that's one of the reasons we rented this one and not one in town. It's nice to be up higher. Those steps are hard work with the weekly shopping though."

"Keep you fit, Hazel, that's for sure. Look at me, I'm still a sprightly seventy-three-year-old!"

At that moment, Clare ran down the stairs, her slippers flapping on each step.

"I thought I heard you, Mr Owen. Mummy, where's the present we bought?"

"I put it on your bed, didn't I?"

"It's not there now." Her face was crestfallen. "Where's it gone?"

"I put it under the tree," said Cathy skipping into the room, the two dogs on her heels.

Clare ran over and looked through the presents until she found what she was looking for. "Here you are! Nadolig Llawen."

"And a Merry Christmas to you, too." Owen dabbed his eyes with a handkerchief as he accepted the package. "Shall I open it now?"

"Whenever you like," said Clare.

"I'll open it now while you're here." He sat down again and pulled the paper off to reveal a pair of sheepskin slippers. "Oh, these are perfect! My others are just about worn through at the sole. Diolch." His smile was broad and genuine.

Cathy plonked herself on his lap and put her arms around his neck, then leaned back, her words coming slowly and falteringly, "Diolch am fod yn athrawes i ni. You're the best Welsh teacher ever. Better than Mrs Llewellyn." She slid back down onto the floor next to the dogs.

"But you two are the best learners." He thrust his hand into a bag, and pulled out a small gift. "This one's for you." He handed one to Clare and went back into the bag. "And this one's for you."

"Can we open them now, Mummy?"

"Of course, it's Christmas tomorrow so a day early won't hurt."

The girls sat on the floor and ripped open the presents.

"Look at this, Mummy." Cathy held aloft a red, pottery Welsh dragon. "I'm going to put this on the shelf next to my bed."

"They're supposed to represent power. It was a symbol of our Welsh King, Cadwaladr, a thousand years ago."

"Thank you, Mr Owen, this is lovely." Clare turned over a doll in traditional women's Welsh costume. A tall, black stovepipe hat with white lace around the edges, a red shawl over a white blouse, a long red and white striped skirt and black boots. "I can add it to my collection."

"When I was a lad, we had many an occasion when everyone dressed up in the traditional costumes. I still have my wife's hanging in the wardrobe; the hat's in a box under our bed."

They made their way back to the kitchen, leaving the girls to take their gifts to their bedroom. "This is so generous of you, Owen. You didn't need to buy the girls anything."

"But I wanted to. Anyway, I need to get on. I've got some mediating to do between my sons and daughter-in-law so we can have a peaceful Christmas."

"I don't envy you that. Sounds like quite a delicate situation from what Babs has said. Finish your tea first."

---0---

The conversation had gone better than Owen had hoped. Babs agreed that it was important the boys saw their father on Christmas Day. The more difficult part had been persuading her that despite all that Dai had done, he didn't deserve to spend the day alone while the rest his family were together. Now all he needed to do was break the news to his sons.

He pushed open the door to the garage just as Bryn slammed the bonnet down on a green Ford Escort and wiped his hands on an old tea towel. He jumped as Dewi ran around his legs.

"You'll right, Da? Wasn't expecting to see you till later."

"Yes son. You almost finished? Thought we might go for a pint."

Bryn looked at him, his eyebrows knitted together and his head on one side. "Why? What've you got to say to me?"

"Just get yourself ready and we'll walk down together."

"Er, okay then." He disappeared into the back office where he stripped off his overalls, took a big dollop of Swarfega from the tin and rubbed his hands together at the sink. He rinsed it all off and dried his hands on a grubby, pink towel. Then he pulled a comb through his hair and reappeared with his coat and hat on, ready to go.

They walked side by side along the High Street. "How's that apprentice coming along?"

"He's good, he's a fast learner. Goes to college once a week too, so he'll be properly qualified in a year."

"Good, you need someone to work with—too much business for just you."

"Da, what do you need to talk about?"

"Let's just wait till we're sitting down with a drink, Bryn." They arrived at the pub and pushed open the door. *Step Into Christmas* was blaring on the juke box and a rowdy bunch of youngsters were taking up the main bar area. "What do fancy? My round."

"Just a pint of Banks, please. I'll find a quiet table."

Owen walked over with a pint in each hand, put them carefully on the table, and sat himself on the wing back chair opposite Bryn. "So, I've been to see Babs this morning. She's much better after her accident." He took a slurp of his pint. "Though I'm sure you know that anyway."

Bryn nodded. "And?"

"Well, we got talking about Christmas and how it's important that families spend it together."

"Er, yes. And?"

"It can't be nice for one of the family to be on his own, stuck in a small room, away from his own children."

"What are you driving at, Da?"

"Well, she agrees we should all spend Christmas Day together."

Bryn leaned back, his eyes narrowing. "All of us?" Realisation struck like a stone. "You mean Dai as well, don't you?"

Owen nodded slowly. "I know he's been an utter idiot, but he's my son too and I can't see him shut out of a family occasion like this."

"For goodness' sake, Da. He's got you round his little finger." He shook his head. "What if he kicks off again? Danny and George shouldn't have to see that."

"I'll make sure he doesn't. Maybe you and Babs could be a bit discreet though. Your relationship is a definite sore point for him."

"You can say that again. The boys don't know yet so that's easy enough. Look, I'm not comfortable with it, but I get it.

237

Let's call a truce. You just need to make it clear to him that no nasty comments or snide remarks are welcome."

"That I will." Owen nodded and absently stroked Dewi's head. "He got back this morning at about seven, hammering on the door. Couldn't get back into the pub, left the key or something."

"Where'd he been?"

"Up at Bontddu apparently."

"With the Cartwrights? Bet Isabella wasn't happy about that."

"I'm sure she wasn't but he's going to stay at mine till he goes back. I think he needs family around, and I'm all he's got."

"Not in my room, I hope." Bryn sat up straight in his chair and scowled.

"Oh, for crying out loud Bryn, most nights you're at Babs' and it's only for a few more days. He's back up to Aberdeen on Saturday."

He slumped. "I suppose you're right." He took a mouthful of beer. "It wasn't meant to work out like this, Da. It's been hard for you, the last few months. Let's hope things get better next year."

"Amen to that."

Owen walked back up to his cottage, Dewi at his heels. He pushed open the door of his cottage, then hung up his coat on the hook. Dai was leaning forward in his chair, examining his bare feet. He looked up his father, his eyes red and his face stubbly.

Owen put the kettle on the range and took down the pot and two cups. He sat down in the chair opposite Dai. "Not feeling any better then?"

"Not really, I've got such a headache." His voice was gravelly and he dropped his chin to his chest. "I shouldn't have started on the rum. That Freddie can't half drink."

"That's the Navy for you. Never drink with a drinker."

238

"That walk back didn't do my feet any good either, I've got blisters all over."

"Ah well, just have to put up with it till they heal." The kettle whistled and Owen got up to pour the boiling water in the pot. He covered it with a knitted cosy and got a milk bottle from the fridge. "So anyway, I've got some good news for you."

Dai lifted his head, his black hair flopped over his eyes. "Yeah?"

"I've just been round to see Babs to talk about tomorrow." He put a strainer over the first mug, then the other and poured the tea followed by a splash of milk. He handed one to Dai.

"Thanks, Da. What about it? Doesn't look like I'll be having my best day ever."

"Stop feeling sorry for yourself. She said we can all go have dinner at hers so you get to see Danny and George."

Dai's eyes widened and his demeanour immediately lifted. "What? She said that? After what I said to her?"

"Yep. She admitted it'd be a bit awkward like, but for the sake of the littl'uns that's what she decided."

"She's not wrong there, awkward is an understatement. Presumably, Bryn's going too."

"Of course he is. And her parents. We'll just have to be civilised and act normally. Well as normal as we can be given the circumstances."

"Thanks so much for talking to her, Da. I suppose I'd better get the boys' presents wrapped. Got any paper?" He leapt up. The maudlin hangover disappeared into the ether; the space now filling with Christmas cheer.

CHAPTER 31

Barbara

Christmas Day dawned bright and sunny in Barmouth with a mild breeze from the south. Barbara was awoken by two boys pushing open her bedroom door, dragging multi-coloured striped pillowcases full of presents. She sat up in bed and smiled broadly.

"Merry Christmas, my gorgeous boys."

"Look what Father Christmas left, Mummy!" George climbed up and planted a kiss on her face. She held him closely, inhaling the scent of baby shampoo.

"We've got such a lot of presents, Mummy." Danny sat down on her other side. She put her arm around and pulled him close.

"I know, you're really lucky boys. You can open one each now and save the rest until Daddy arrives. He won't want to miss it. Which one do you want?"

The boys felt through their pillowcases and extracted a present each. Just then, Shirley entered the room with two cups of tea. "Merry Christmas, love. Morning, you two. What has Father Christmas brought you?" She sat on the end of the bed and handed the cup of tea carefully to Babs.

"Look at all these, Nanny." George held his wide open. "How does he know what we want, Nanny? And how does he know where to bring them?"

"It's all magic, love. Let's see what you've got then."

Danny carefully unwrapped a heavy rectangular gift. "It's *The Guinness Book of Records*!" He flicked through the pages and stopped, "Look at him!" He held the pages wide and everyone peered at the pictures. Danny read aloud, "The tallest

man who ever lived was Robert Wadlow from Alton, Illinois."
He sounded out each letter in the state name. "He was eight foot
and two inches tall. How tall is that, Mummy?"

"At least up to the ceiling, I reckon."

Douglas entered the room. "Well, I'm five foot eight inches
and you're about three foot, so he's almost as tall as us two stuck
on top of each other."

"That's enormous!" gasped George. "I'm going to open this
one." He ripped the paper off a square box and grinned with
delight as he saw the picture on the front. "It's a *Rock 'Em Sock
'Em Robot*. How did he know I wanted that?" His eyes reduced
to slits as he looked at each of the others sat on the bed. "Who
told him?"

"Well, you have been going on and on about it since
October, George!" laughed his mother. "Let's get up and have
some breakfast. You can open the rest of your presents when
Daddy and Gramps arrive."

"Is Bryn coming too?" asked Danny.

"Yes, love. It'll be the whole family together," replied
Barbara, ruffling his hair.

"Good. I like it when everyone's here," Danny answered and
wandered off to their shared bedroom to find some clothes.

Shirley was peeling potatoes at the sink while the boys were
finishing off their Weetabix at the kitchen table. Danny had his
new book next to him and was flicking through the pages,
reading out random facts. The doorbell rang. George jumped up
and ran to the front door, wiping the milk dripping down his
chin with the back of his hand. He pulled it open.

"Merry Christmas, Georgie boy!" Dai lifted him up and
swung him round. He squealed with joy. "Where's Danny?" He
put his youngest son back down.

"I'm here." Danny's serious face broke into a smile when he
saw his father, grandfather and uncle— as well as Dewi—
waiting on the doorstep. "Are you coming in?"

"Of course we are," said Owen. "We've come for Christmas, and we've got presents." He held up a Woolworth's bag bursting with packages and parcels.

Barbara came down the stairs wearing an orange and brown crossover top over a pair of tight bellbottoms. Her hair was piled on her head and her lips shone. Dai and Bryn both stared, transfixed and immobile. One regretting who he'd lost, the other amazed by who he'd gained. Owen pushed past and took off his coat. "Get out of the way, you two."

"Merry Christmas, Owen." Barbara leaned in and kissed him on the cheek. "And to you, Dai and Bryn." She gave each a light peck on the cheek in turn, leaving behind a slight lipstick smudge. It galvanized them into action and they quickly removed their coats and followed her into the sitting with Dewi and the boys around their legs.

"Who wants a cup of tea?" called Shirley from the kitchen. "Babs, come and give me hand to carry them in."

The boys were on the floor, surrounded by a diminishing mound of presents and an increasing pile of wrapping paper and toys. The male adults sat on various armchairs, the settee and the pouffe, while the two women prepared the turkey and vegetables for lunch. "Blooming typical, isn't it?" Barbara complained as she inspected the turkey giblets. "The women in the kitchen while the blokes sit on their backsides."

"It's just the way of things, love," Shirley replied as she stripped the peel off a potato with a deft flick of her wrist. "You must be used to it by now."

"I tell you what," Barbara declared, shaking the giblets to emphasise her point. "I'm not bringing my sons up to be like it." She rammed the giblets into the turkey with a little too much force. "They're going to help around the house and learn to cook."

"You do that," Shirley said, nodding. "Big changes to society have to start somewhere so why not make it happen in your own home?" She put the last peeled potato in the pan. "Anyway, I think that's all we can do in here for now." She wiped her hands on a towel. "Let's go and join them."

Barbara washed her own hands. "And when the boys have opened all the parcels," she said as she towelled dry, "we can go for a walk on the beach." She made a small smile. "It'll do the boys good to get a bit of fresh air."

CHAPTER 32

Isabella

Up the hill in Bontddu, the Cartwright family was eating breakfast of scrambled egg and fried bacon with big cups of tea. A pan of potatoes was on top of the cooker and a bag of brussel sprouts was on the draining board. The turkey was stuffed and already in the oven.

Their chatter and joking was interrupted by Gerald standing up and clearing his throat. "I've got something to say."

"Oh, this sounds important."

"Be quiet, Freddie. Let the man speak," Jim said gruffly.

"I'm honoured you've welcomed me into your family and invited me to spend Christmas with you all here in your lovely new house in Bonterdew."

"It's Bont Thee," corrected Isabella. "Easy mistake. This Welsh spelling catches everyone out."

"Bont Thee. Anyway, I've known Irene for a year now and I really can't imagine not having her in my life. In order to keep her by my side, I've decided—"

Isabella breathed in sharply and "Oh my goodness" escaped her lips.

"Irene, would you..." He dropped to one knee. His voice quavered as he finished the sentence, "...do me the honour of being my wife?" He pulled a ring case out of his pocket and opened it up. A small white solitaire stone glittered in the kitchen light.

"Oh Gerald, you mad fool. Yes, yes, of course I bloody will." She pulled him to his feet and flung her arms around him so violently that his glasses wobbled on his nose.

"Well, that definitely calls for a celebration!" Freddie exclaimed. "Have we got any bubbles?"

"No we haven't, Freddie, it's not really our thing."

"I bought a bottle in town yesterday in the hope Irene would say yes. I'll go and get it." Gerald strode out of the kitchen and rummaged in a bag by the front door. "Ta da!" He waved a bottle of Pomagne. "Couldn't afford the real stuff!" He grinned.

"It's the thought that counts," laughed Jim, grinning from ear to ear as he placed a glass in front of everyone.

"What a lovely Christmas surprise!" Isabella added. Gerald popped the cork and poured.

"Let's raise a toast to Gerald and Irene," said Freddie lifting his glass high.

"Cheers!" They clinked glasses and sat down.

"Opening our presents will be a bit of let-down after all this, won't it?" said Irene, admiring her ring and twisting on her finger.

"No it won't, love. But why don't we go for a walk on the beach? Otherwise we'll be stuck inside all day. I've done pretty much everything for lunch so we've got time. We can open presents after lunch before the Queen's Speech."

"Good idea, Mum." Irene smiled broadly at her mother and glanced down at her ring finger yet again.

CHAPTER 33

Barbara

The tide was far out, leaving behind it worm holes and driftwood. Dewi chased the seagulls on the wide sandy expanse. Daniel and George chased each other with clumps of seaweed. Bryn and Owen walked ahead of Dai and Barbara.

"Thank you, Babs."

"It didn't seem right, you not seeing the boys on Christmas Day."

"I really appreciate it. And I'm sorry. I've caused all this mess anyway and I truly regret it."

Babs looked at him, her eyes squinting. "Don't even think about it, Dai."

"I don't mean anything. I'm just sorry I made your life a misery. I hope you and Bryn will be happy, that's all."

"So do I. And I hope you find some peace, Dai. You need to have a good long think about what you want to do with your life now."

He hung his head. "I realise that now. I've been behaving like a teenager despite being married to you and being a father."

"Time to grow up." Barbara smiled as Danny threw a piece of seaweed at her. "I'll get you, you little tyke!" She ran after him with the seaweed trailing in her hand.

Another dog appeared on the beach and ran over to Dewi. Down the steps came a family of four wrapped up warm. Hazel wore a new duffle coat and a bobble hat. She walked towards Babs and waved.

"Merry Christmas, Babs my love."

"Merry Christmas, Hazel. Nice coat."

"Yeah, Tony bought it for me in Shrewsbury." She did a little twirl. "So, how's it been so far?"

"All right, actually. Much easier with lots of us in the house. Dai even apologised and wished me and Bryn well."

"Did he?" Hazel raised her eyebrows. "Well, I never thought that would happen."

"How's it been at yours with Tony's mother, the old dragon?"

"She's such hard work. I still have to call her Mrs Saddler, even after all these years. She blames me for corrupting her son." She sighed and shook her head. "But at least she's doing the cooking so we can get out and walk Charlie. And give the girls a run."

"Christmas can be fraught sometimes. All that excitement and extra people in the house and stuck indoors all day. That's why we've come out."

"Isn't that the Cartwrights over there?" Hazel peered down the beach. In the distance, five figures were getting bigger.

"I think it might be. I'd recognise Isabella's wonky gait anywhere."

They linked arms and walked more briskly towards the group walking towards them.

"Morning, Isabella. Merry Christmas."

"It's amazing, Gerald proposed to Irene at the breakfast." She clapped her hands in glee.

"Oh, how lovely."

Hazel and Barbara turned to look at the couple who were gazing out to sea; Gerald standing behind Irene, his chin resting on her head. Their future ahead of them. Dai and Freddie shook hands and turned to walk together, deep in conversation. Owen and Jim walked side by side, commenting on the unusually mild weather. Tony and Bryn chatted amiably about cars. Dewi and

Charlie jumped and barked spraying sand at each other. Sheila and Douglas held hands and looked contentedly, first at their daughter with her new friends, then at their grandchildren, playing happily. Shirley squeezed her husband's hand.

"It's going to be all right, isn't it, love?"

"That it is, dear. That it is."

SIX MONTHS LATER

Dai

"So, you're definitely fit and able, Mr Roberts. You can start whenever you've worked your notice period. A month, isn't it?" The recruitment officer put his pen down and looked at Dai from under the brim of his peaked cap.

"That's fantastic news, that is. You've really made my day. I'd been worrying about this medical for days." Dai smiled at him across the desk.

"There was no need for that, you're as fit as a fiddle; probably in better shape than some of our younger recruits." He stood up, the seams up the front of his black trousers ironed to a stiff point and his white shirt spotless. Dai had taken up enough of his valuable time.

"All that lifting and shoving on the rigs. You soon build up the muscles." Dai also stood and pulled on his Harrington jacket.

"Okay, then. We'll see you here on Monday 16th June and you'll start your training once you've taken your oath and sorted out the necessary admin." He thrust his neat hand into Dai's calloused palm and shook vigorously as he pushed the door wide with his shiny black shoe.

The journey to Barmouth was uneventful. On the train, Dai read a discarded newspaper, full of doom and gloom: inflation rising, recession looming, Margaret Thatcher, leader of the Conservatives, calling for fiscal management. The front page was dominated by a report of a coach crash. He read slowly and deliberately, it happened at Dibbles Bridge, near Hebden, North Yorkshire. The brakes failed and the coach went over the bridge, killing the driver and thirty-one female pensioners on board, the highest ever toll in a UK road accident. Dai shook his head. *Who checked the blooming brakes? Shouldn't've been allowed on the road. Those poor families.*

He turned instead to the back page for the sports. Leeds United were beaten 2–0 by Bayern Munich of West Germany in the European Cup final in Paris, France. Peter Lorimer had a goal for Leeds disallowed and this sparked a riot by angry supporters, who invaded the pitch and tore seats away from the stands. Dai wasn't that interested, it wasn't his team. In fact, he didn't support any team in particular—rugby was more his sport.

As the train went over the bridge across the estuary, Dai looked out and breathed in. He was looking forward to seeing his boys and decided to pick them up from school and surprise them. They'd like that.

---0---

Later that evening, after putting Danny and George to bed, Dai walked up the slate steps to his father's. Owen pulled the door open.

"Dai, what a surprise! I wasn't expecting to see you. Why aren't you in Scotland?" Owen pulled Dai into the cottage and sat him down in chair while he put the kettle on.

"I've got some news and I wanted to tell you in person."

"Oh? And what might that be?" Owen's eyebrows drew closely together and his eyes flashed.

"Nothing bad, Da! I'm joining the Navy as a marine engineer mechanic. I start in the middle of June."

"The Navy? When did you decide that?" Owen got up and made the tea.

"I've been thinking about it since Christmas."

"Doesn't that mean you'll be away? Even more than you are already?" He put down the two cups and slumped in his chair, stroking Dewi's head.

"I've got two month's training in Plymouth and then I'll be drafted to a ship. I'll be away anything from a few weeks to six months. It'll be hard but you'll all get used to it." He took a sip of tea. "Looks like everyone's managing without me anyway. I hear Bryn's moved in with Babs."

"Yes, he has." Owen's head dropped then he lifted it up again. "Look, if this is what you want, then I really hope it works out for you. All I've ever hoped for is that my sons are happy. You know that."

"I do, Da. I'm excited to be starting a new, challenging job, meeting new people and travelling the world."

Owen smiled and stroked Dewi's head.

Two weeks later, Dai whistled as he strode towards the Navy Office with a straight back and arms swinging. He nodded: Freddie was right, this was definitely going to be the life for him.

Susan

Susan picked her light, cotton summer dress off her sticky back and breasts and stared at the wide, still water around her. There was nothing to see for miles. The horizon was a flat graphite line which the sun would not cross for another three empty hours. A sudden gust of wind blew her loose, blonde hair across her face and the salt carried within it stung her eyes. She leant forward and dabbed them with a handkerchief.

"Everything all right, love?" A fellow passenger appeared beside her on deck, presumably doing the same as her, escaping the heat of the cabin and crowded communal areas.

"Yeah, fine. Just a bit of salt in my eyes." She turned briefly, then leaned against the railings once again. He joined her, their bare elbows almost touching. She noticed his tanned ankles between the turn up of his cream chinos and his brown, leather deck shoes.

"Looking forward to getting there?"

"Yeah, definitely. I can't wait to get off this boat."

"I think you'll find it's a ship!" He laughed, the sound starting in his stomach and shaking his body. He gently nudged her, and she laughed too.

"The old ones are the best." She grinned at him and took in his light blue, short-sleeved shirt. "I'm Susan, what's your name?"

"I'm Walter. Pleased to meet you, Susan." He held out his hand and she accepted his energetic handshake with a small laugh.

"So, what scheme are you on?"

"No scheme, just family. My son's already there; he arrived two years ago. He's met a nice young lady called Ann. They're getting married. He asked me to come out for the wedding and see what I think. Maybe I'll stay." He tried to catch her eye as he added, "I'm a widower, see."

"Oh right." Susan studied his eyes: they were mostly brown but the bright sun picked out speckles of green. "Nothing for me at home now, so I sold up. I'm on the Nest Egg scheme because I've got enough to buy my house if I want to stay."

"Oh right. Is that how it works then?" Susan nodded as he continued. "Have you got a job to go to?"

"I'll see if there's any work when I get there and settled. I've been a secretary for years, but I reckon I'm a bit old now. There's probably loads of young women looking for jobs, so

254

why would they choose me?" She rested her elbow on the railing and half-turned towards him.

He mirrored her position, his eyes studying her form and face. "Don't underestimate your worth, dear. I'm sure you've got plenty of skills those young whippersnappers haven't."

"Thank you for your kind words. Do you work?" She estimated judging by his grey hair and wrinkled face that he was slightly older than her, but still in good shape and, she noted with satisfaction, attractive.

"I'm a university lecturer so they might want my skills." He puffed out his chest, lifted his shoulders and held his hands out, palms up.

"What do you..." She turned her head on the side and screwed up her nose, "...lecture?"

Walter laughed. "Civil engineering. Designing roads, bridges, that sort of stuff. Not very exciting, really."

"I bet that's exactly the sort of skills they need over there."

"Maybe, but I'm not sure if I want to work. I might just enjoy the sunshine." He mimed surfing and swimming. "Have you got any family out there?"

"My sister, but I don't want to impose on her and her husband for too long." She flicked her hair out of face.

"Where are you heading to when we dock?" A hint of hope in his voice.

"I'm staying in Brisbane. You?"

His optimism flowed as he gushed, "Me too. My son lives in one of the suburbs. Works as a teacher, same as Ann."

"Oh, clever then: like father like son." She smiled broadly and tilted her head in his direction.

"Yes, I suppose so. Anyway, Susan, it's been lovely to meet you and have a chat. There aren't many older, single people like us onboard." He turned and gently took her hand. "So, would you do me the honour of having dinner with me later?"

"Yes." She smiled. "I'd love that, Walter."

"Super, shall we say six thirty for cocktails in the Ballroom Bar?" He took her hand and placed a gentle kiss on the back.

"That sounds just perfect." Susan watched his straight back and confident gait as he walked away. When he reached the door, he turned back to wave and smile. Her stomach gave a little jump.

Susan exhaled and looked at her watch: half past three. Plenty of time to soak her feet and wash her sweaty body. *How am I going to manage in the tropical climate?* she thought as she made her way to her cabin thinking about the dinner invitation with a mixture of trepidation and excitement. *This could be a new beginning. Maybe my bad luck is behind me.* She gave a little skip and a giggle escaped as she landed on the linoleum outside her poky cabin.

THE END

AUTHOR'S NOTE

When I first met my husband, we realised that as children we had both spent time on the same beach in Barmouth, probably during the summer of 1974. It was such a wonderful coincidence that we decided to spend a few days together and take a trip down our respective memory lanes. We walked around the town, along the beach and up to the house on the rock where I had once lived with my family (now a holiday home). Then we took a drive out to the place his grandparents had owned and John showed me the places he'd played as a child. With these memories fresh in my mind, the idea for a story crystallised. I wrote *The Barmouth Affairs* shortly after that first visit.

The characters of Jim and Isabella are loosely based on John's grandparents who came from West Bromwich. The affair with the best friend, named Susan in the book, was real and Jim did run away to his cottage in the hills. He 'hid' there for a few weeks before his wife started to write to him and eventually went to see him. Nobody in the family can remember what happened to the cottage after they bought the Bontddu place. Perhaps, nature took it back, perhaps it's still there.

Isabella's accident actually occurred at a point on the road from Dolgellau to Barmouth which their family always referred to as 'Millie's Folly'. Millie, John's grandmother's actual name, broke her leg and was in hospital for six weeks. With a lot of forgiveness and understanding, their marriage prevailed, they bought the house in Bontddu and 'Susan' was never mentioned again.

Babs is an entirely fictional character, although my mother was the district nurse in Barmouth for the year we lived there. The story of the old lady who ordered her 'combinations' from

Harrods is one that sticks with me from childhood. Owen is based on an old fisherman who taught me some words of Welsh when I was struggling, like Cathy, at school. All other characters are fictional, as is the name of the pub in the town. However, the descriptions of Barmouth are hopefully accurate and show the beauty of the land and seascapes.

Finally, there is a brief reference to 'the teachers up the hill'. They were real and one of them wrote a beautiful account of the time spent doing up their cottage. The book is called *Four Fields, Five Gates* by Anne L Hill; John's grandfather—Jim—is mentioned when he helped them with some repairs. The book was published in 1954 and is still available on Amazon.

BOOK CLUB QUESTIONS

1. Why do you think Isabella followed Jim to Barmouth?

2. What was the attraction of the cottage for Jim? What did he like about being there?

3. The English weren't immediately welcome in Wales in the 1970s. How is this shown in the story? Can you empathise with the Welsh in any way?

4. Who do you think holds the story together?

5. Bryn and Dai are very different characters. Do you know siblings who are also very different?

6. Babs and Hazel form a very close bond. Why are friendships so important to women?

7. Was Isabella right to forgive Jim?

8. Was Babs right to start a relationship with Bryn?

9. Nursing has changed significantly since the seventies. Can you give examples of how?

10. Did the happy ending work for you? How would you end the story?

ABOUT THE AUTHOR

Vanessa M. Tanner lives in Devizes, Wiltshire with her husband, John and her cat, Willow.

She has two grown-up sons who live and work in London. She recently retired after twenty years of teaching English, both in England and overseas, gathering stories along the way.

Now she devotes her time to her community as a member of the Town Council and local sustainability groups. In her free time, she enjoys writing, gardening and visiting her family and friends scattered all over the UK.

This is her first novel and she is currently working on another book, provisionally called *Streams*. Watch this space!

winteranddrew.com

Printed in Great Britain
by Amazon

53282271R00148